Reckoning

The Last Woman Memorial caused something to shift inside her.

By Mark Bertrand PhD

Copyright © 2025 Mark Bertrand

This is a book of fiction. Names, characters, places, and incidents either are the product of the author's imagination or are used fictiously. Any resemblance to actual historical events, real people, or real places is entirely coincidental.

First edition: September 10, 2025
Publisher: https://markbertrand.com
ISBN: 979-8-9931043-0-0 paperback
ISBN: 979-8-9931043-1-7 ebook

Chapter One: Literary Agent Vacation

The sun dipped low over the crystalline waters of Mallorca, casting a golden hue across the exclusive beach bar where Lydia Daniels sat with her husband, Mark. It was their first day of vacation. The air was filled with the scent of the salty sea and tropical blooms. Lydia, her slim exposed belly concealing her three-month pregnancy, perused the drink menu with a gleam in her eye. The soft murmur of bar chatter surrounded them, interspersed with the clinking of glasses and the occasional sound of cutlery bouncing and hopping like joyful kangaroos after falling to the stone floor. The palms swayed in the summer breeze, mimicking the rhythmic crash of waves just a few hundred feet away.

"I'll have a tequila soda," she said. Anticipation coloring her voice. Her fingers toyed with the black coaster boasting the bold gold logo of the hotel.

Mark's face tightened. "Lydia, remember, you're pregnant. Maybe you should request a virgin Mai Tai?"

A momentary hesitation in the bartender's rapid and dexterous mixology display passed after she observed Lydia's expression following Mark's suggestion.

A flood of irritation surged through Lydia. She slammed the menu onto the table; the sound drawing the attention of nearby patrons. "Are you fucking serious, Mark? Are you really going to start this vacation by policing me?" Her voice rose, sharp and cutting through the ambient music.

Mark's cheeks flushed. "Lydia, I'm just looking out for us and the baby."

"Looking out for us? By treating me like a child?" Lydia's anger escalated. "This isn't some draconian town in Texas where women are property of the state and you are not the sheriff. I am sick of you act-ing like you know what's best for me! I am capable of making my own decisions!"

"Lydia, please lower your voice," Mark said. While his own temper was flaring but held in check. He was aware of the growing number of observers in the bar.

"Lower my voice? How about you stop treating me like your personal project? I'm pregnant, not an invalint!" Lydia's tirade grew louder. "I'm tired of men like you, always thinking they know better. Always trying to control women!"

A burly man at the bar turned on his barstool, clearly annoyed. "Hey, lady, why don't you calm down? You're ruining everyone's evening."

Lydia's gaze snapped over to him. "Why don't you shut your mouth and mind your own business? Maybe if you spent more time thinking with your brain instead of your dick, the world wouldn't be such a mess!" She looked away, "Typical man. Pretending to defend the bar patrons. Self serving hypocrite."

The man's face reddened. Others murmured their disapproval, some standing to leave. The bartender motioned to the manager, who approached with a nervous smile.

"Ma'am, I'm going to have to ask you to calm down or leave," the manager said. His voice wavering slightly.

Lydia stood up demonstrative, her face a mask of rage. "Or what? You'll throw out the pregnant woman? Go ahead, make the headlines! 'Beach Bar Kicks Out Pregnant Woman for Speaking Her Mind!'"

Mark stood up as well, trying to guide Lydia away gently. "Lydia, let's go. We don't need this."

She wrenched her arm away from him. "Oh, now you're the reasonable one? Resorting to manhandle the weaker sex. Treating the poor dear woman as if she is having a mental lapse. Well, newsflash, we're done taking your shit!"

Mark's face was pale, his eyes a mix of frustration and helplessness. "Lydia, please."

"Fine! We're leaving. Enjoy your drinks, everyone. Enjoy your little slice of paradise."

"My apologies everyone," the manager announces, in a clear rational tone that ends with a spark of holiday joy. His smile was an attempt at beating back the outburst. "There's a full moon rising in twenty minutes. Everyone gets a drink in the house. We've set up tables and chairs on the sand. Let's head to the shoreline to watch."

The bar rush was instant, and dozens of cheerful patrons placed drink orders. Others went to the beach to grab a table and chairs before they were gone.

Having said that, Lydia stormed out, leaving Mark to hastily apologize and follow her. The patrons watched in silence, the atmosphere thick with discomfort and the remnants of Lydia's explosive outburst lingering in the air.

"Why can't I stop?" Lydia mumbled to herself as she pushed past the last couple near the exit. Low-voltage lighting lit the path back to the hotel. The sweet smell of the Mexican-flame blossoms, a stark contrast to her bitter mood. The gentle scented breeze was no match for the tempest raging inside her.

By the time Lydia reached the hotel lobby, the last sliver of sunlight had dipped below the horizon. She stumbled to a stop and slumped against the lobby doors. Her mind reeled as she became dizzy from reflecting on how everything seemed to spiral out of control, not just her marriage but her career as well.

As she recovered, she threw the doors open and stormed through the lobby. Her eyes took in the bookshelves filled with paperbacks. The hotel offered a selection of reading materials for guests. The sight triggers a reminder of the business crisis. An email from the office flashed through her memory. On the flight, she read how a key client was leaving her company for a different agency. Her business was already nearing bankruptcy, and she had just taken out a second mortgage on her and Mark's home to help cover the anemic expenses.

She marched toward the elevators, her mind still a storm of anger and self-recrimination.

"Lydia, wait!" Mark's voice called out. He caught up to her just as she reached the elevator doors.

"Leave me alone, Mark," she said. Her finger jabbing the elevator call button.

"Lydia, please, can we just talk about this?" His voice was pleading, but she could see the frustration in his eyes. Their tension-induced outburst had become well-practiced over the previous months.

"Talk about what? How you think you can control me? About how you can't stand the idea of me making my own decisions?" She spat the words at him, each one like an arrow.

Mark's face tightened. "That's not fair, and you know it. I just want to make sure you're safe."

"Safe? Or compliant?" Lydia's voice rose, drawing the attention of the other guests. "You know what, Mark? Get your own room. I'm done."

The elevator doors slid open, but she stepped back, turning towards the reception desk instead. The clerk, a young man with neatly combed hair and a nervous smile, looked up as she approached.

"Good evening, ma'am. How can I help you?"

"I want a separate room for my husband," Lydia demanded. "And put it on my bill, of course. As usual, the woman has to pay the way for the mindless men."

The clerk blinked, taken aback. "Ma'am, I ..."

"Don't 'ma'am' me," Lydia interrupted, her voice dripping with disdain. "Just get him a room. It's not that difficult. Or is it? Are men so incompetent that they can't even manage simple tasks?"

The lobby had cleared, and the tension was driving away the other guests. Even the piano player stopped, leaving only an uncomfortable silence hanging in the air.

"Ma'am, I'll need to check our availability," the clerk said. His confidence stammered.

"Check your availability? For God's sake, it's your job! Why is it that every time I need something done, it has to be me who takes charge? Men are useless." Lydia's rant extends. "Mark, you just stand there like you always do, letting me handle everything. Typical."

"Lydia, please," Mark said. His voice was barely a whisper now, heavy with embarrassment and sadness. "Let's just go to our room and talk."

She whirled on him, her eyes blazing. "No, Mark. I'm tired of talking. I'm tired of you. Get your own room and leave me alone."

The desk clerk's hands shook as he fumbled with the keyboard, eyes darting nervously between the screen and the chaos unfolding in the lobby. Sweat dotted his brow, and he cleared his throat. "I—I've got a room open, sir... ma'am." His voice cracked as if each word might trip him up. "I'll need a card for the payment."

Lydia's hand shot into her clutch, and the slap of the card hitting the counter echoed like a gunshot. "Charge it," she said, voice low and clipped, every syllable a punch. Her eyes never left the clerk's, daring him to question her authority. "Because being the only one who knows how to handle things means also having to foot the bill for everyone else."

The clerk swallowed hard, nodding as he rushed to process the payment. His fingers trembled, stabbing at the keys. The transaction beeped through, and with a hasty swipe, he pushed the key card toward Mark.

"Room 1421, sir," he said. His voice was just above a whisper. His eyes flicked to Lydia pleading one last time. Hoping for an acknowledgment that wasn't there. Then back down at the counter, eager to be rid of the moment.

Mark snatched the key from the counter, his jaw tight. The tension between him and Lydia wasn't something the clerk could name, but it was palpable. Lydia gave Mark a look that said everything—another mess, another crisis, but she was already ahead, as always.

Mark took the card and followed her, his eyes fixed on Lydia. "Lydia, I love you. Please, don't be like this."

But Lydia turned away, heading back toward the elevator. "Love me? You don't even know me."

As the elevator doors closed behind her, she leaned against the wall, the adrenaline slowly draining from her. The voice in her head, now louder, filled her with regret. Why can't I stop? Why do I keep pushing him away?

***

She threw every ounce of energy from the tempest that had grown within her into the door. The sound of it crashing against the frame behind her, the echo cutting through every corner of the hotel. Her block heels clicked against the marble floor as she strode to the living room, dropping her clutch onto the coffee table with a thud. The weight of everything—the business, the team, the pregnancy—pressed down on her, more suffocating than the stale air in the too-perfect room.

She collapsed onto the spacious sofa, the plush cushions offering no relief from the tension coiled tight in her chest and shoulders. Her eyes scanned the elegant suite—floor-to-ceiling windows, the skyline twinkling outside, the soft glow of designer lamps. It was beautiful. It was luxurious. And it was everything she couldn't afford to think about right now.

My business is struggling, and that newly commissioned market report reveals a harsh truth: most male readers are turning away from mainstream, traditionally published books—particularly those written by women for women. The report suggests that independent authors—often male—are capturing a significant portion of the male readership, especially in genres like thriller, suspense, and speculative fiction. What can I do? Should I flip the logo and business messaging? Doing so threatens the foundational core of my business model, I have always focused on female authors and female-centric narratives.

Her ongoing monologue spurred the memory of a recent conflict. Lydia was sitting in her meeting room. The entire team sat around the table. Lydia, reading through the research report. Her hands tremble as she scrolls through the data, which shows the decline in the male readership of her company's books. Charts and graphs highlight that indie authors are capturing male-dominated genres, while her agency's focus on women's literature is losing ground. The correlation to revenue loss was positive to the loss of male readership. The Senior Publishing Agent (Rachel) sat across from her. Her face was stern. Her voice was gruff and the back of her throat as if her voice traveled through a tin can. "These data could be wrong. Perhaps misleading?"

Rachel hisses. "We didn't build this company to pander to men. If that's where you're taking us, I'm done."

The room fell silent, then erupted into protests. One senior editor scoffed, saying, "So, we're supposed to abandon our mission and cater to men now? Just because they can't handle stories that don't center them?"

The night before flying to Mallorca for this vacation, Lydia recalled pacing her office late into the night, torn between loyalty to her team and the financial reality that demanded she take a new direction. She stares at her device, the market data still open on the screen. Her mind flashes to her unborn child, and she feels the pressure mounting. "What kind of future am I even fighting for?" She wonders aloud.

The agency was falling apart, and she was sitting in a hotel room halfway across the world. Every project back home was teetering on the edge of disaster. Contracts waiting to be signed, clients getting restless. Her team—the women she had handpicked, groomed, trusted with her life's work—were holding it together, but for how long? She'd seen the doubt in their eyes before she left. They knew the ship was sinking, even if no one dared to say it.

And then, of course, the pregnancy. The news that had blindsided her weeks ago, the one thing she hadn't planned for, couldn't control. Her hand drifted to her stomach again, an unconscious gesture that was becoming familiar. This wasn't part of the deal, not now. Not when the business was on life support, and every waking hour was consumed with trying to salvage it.

She leaned her head back, eyes closing for just a second. "What the hell am I doing here?" she said. Muttering under her breath. The words tasted bitter, the truth too big to swallow. This wasn't a vacation; it was an escape, a weak attempt at pretending she could walk away from the chaos she'd built around herself.

The hotel suite felt too quiet, too still. Her phone buzzed, vibrating on the table. She glanced at it—more emails. Another client demanded answers. Another fire needing to be put out. She ignored it, sinking deeper into the sofa, but the guilt gnawed at her like always.

Two years. Two years of working nonstop, no breaks, no time to breathe. Every decision, every risk, every sacrifice, had brought her to this point. She had thought she could handle it, that she was strong enough. But now, with the walls closing in, she wasn't so sure.

Lydia walked through the room, kicked off her heels, her footsteps muffled by the plush carpet, and headed to the small desk where her laptop sat. Outside, the sounds of vacationers drifted up from the terraces—laughter, and the distant sound of island music blending with the rhythmic crash of waves. The air was warm, carrying the tantalizing scent of BBQ mingled with sticky sweet tropical blooms.

With a sigh, Lydia opened her laptop and navigated to her email. She couldn't help herself; even here, miles away from her office, the pull of work was irresistible. The VPN connection hummed to life, encrypting her data, ensuring that her communications were secure, even in this distant resort. Security and privacy protocols were non-negotiable in her line of work—too many sensitive contracts and un-released manuscripts passed through her hands daily. She'd had the IT department set up a special server just for this, ensuring that nothing could be intercepted.

As she scanned her inbox for any emergency messages from the publishers and agents, she saw it. Another email from H.P. Kemper.

She rolled her eyes. Just another author submitting his novel. She received thousands of submissions every year, and her agency struggled to represent five or six new authors annually. It was grueling work, rarely yielding the discovery of a literary genius. The reality was harsh: it had been five years since her agency had made more than meager profits. It was expensive to represent an author, and the risks were costly. Even the very best agencies have a meager thirty percent success with the novels they publish.

This agency was more than a business. It was her statement, her way of proving women's voices mattered in a world that often sidelined them. But if she couldn't save it... if she had to make it something else to keep it alive ... wasn't it still hers?

But this H.P. Kemper didn't stop after she sent him the standard rejection letter. At first, she ignored his continued emails. One would arrive every two weeks. After ten or more, she began recognizing his from address. After many emails, she started telling the office agents about him, marveling at his persistence. For the staff, he had become a laughing point at the weekly meetings. "Email twelve," she'd say, and two weeks later, right on cue, he'd send her email number thirteen.

Lydia hovered over the email, number seventeen, her curiosity piqued despite herself. She had to admire his tenacity. But the thought of diving into another unsolicited manuscript from a male author right now, especially on vacation, was unbearable. She closed the laptop with a sigh and walked over to the terrace doors, opening them to let the fresh night air wash over her. The sea breeze rushed into the room like a swollen river cresting its bank. The sounds of the vacationers grew louder, their joy a stark contrast to the thoughts in her head.

An idea crossed her mind. Perhaps this was just what she needed on this holiday. What harm could it do? This could be a necessary distraction, a beach read from some unknown author. Nobody would care, and it wasn't as if she would have to read it like a working project. Maybe she could unwind and let go of the tension.

What if the story sucks? Her cynical side kicked in. What if she finds it impossible to get lost in the story? Another emotionless main character, stoic and unapproachable, boring. Or a story with no soul, no heart, and one that doesn't pull you into another world? She had seen too many of those over the years, and the thought of struggling through another one filled her with dread.

Still, there was a part of her that was curious. What if, against all odds, Kemper's manuscript was different? What if it was good? Lydia chuckled at herself. It was unlikely, but the possibility was enough to push her toward the laptop again.

She returned to the desk and opened the email from Kemper. The subject line read, "Manuscript Submission - IRRELEVANT." With a resigned sigh, she clicked on the attachment and read the email:

"Dear Lydia,

"Sorry to tell you, but I've done it again. Though I promised never to rewrite the beginning after the last time, this makes it the fourth. This is the final rewrite—I truly mean it this time. I hope you'll agree: the new opening is amazing. I've attached the manuscript and look forward to hearing from you soon.

"Best wishes and good reading,

"Philip

"A Male Novelist Writing Novels for Men."

Lydia couldn't help but smile at the email. His persistence was almost endearing. The mention of a fourth rewrite sparked a flicker of hope—perhaps this one would be the charm. The first ten pages were included in his email.

The sounds of laughter and music outside continued, but they faded as she got pulled into the opening paragraphs. The writing was surprisingly good, engaging even. She felt a spark of hope.

Maybe, just maybe, this wouldn't be a waste of time.

As she continued to read, Lydia found herself slowly relaxing. The story had a certain charm, a rhythm that was soothing yet captivating. She let herself get lost in it, the tension in her shoulders easing as she turned the pages. The subtle differences in styles that appeal to men oddly feel comforting to her. She felt as if she could sense that despite their differences in communication style and emotional triggers; it is these differences that combine to make men and women stronger when they work as one.

Perhaps this was what she needed after all. It was a distraction, a way to unwind, and a reminder of why she loved this work in the first place.

As the manuscript uploaded to her laptop, Lydia wandered out onto the terrace. The soft breeze rustled the palm leaves, and the distant sounds of someone with a peculiar laugh and music only deepened her sense of isolation. Memories of the fight with Mark flashed in her mind, each one like a dagger. She felt a lump in her throat and tears welled up, spilling over as she cried softly, self-loathing seeping into every sob.

Why am I like this? Why can't I just be happy?

She leaned over the railing, the drop below her both terrifying and tempting. The thought flickered briefly—an escape from the constant self-anger and tension. But then, the sound of the laptop signaling the file upload was complete broke through her dark thoughts.

Lydia stepped back from the railing, drying her cheeks with the back of her hand. She poured a glass of coconut water from the small refrigerator, savoring the cool, sweet liquid as it soothed her parched throat. Taking a deep breath, she gathered herself.

Curling up on the hammock with her laptop, she opened the file from H.P. Kemper. She adjusted the screen to block the glare of the moonlight and took another sip of coconut water. The hammock swayed gently as she settled in, a stark contrast to the turbulence within her.

With skepticism and curiosity, she began to read, Irrelevant by H.P. Kemper.

Chapter Two: Give Them War

Three Days before the concert, 08:00 AM

The haunting melody filled the room, each note stirring echoes of her past. She sat at the piano, inked symbols winding over the contours of her olive colored skin. Her fingers, steady yet burdened by years of battle, moved with purpose, each key a reminder of the ruthless arena she'd dominated and left behind. The years had sharpened her resolve and etched themselves into her bare skin. This was no quiet reflection; it was a reckoning; the notes striking against the silence, like an unfinished battle calling her.

The tattoos began across the tops of her cheekbones, swirling down her face and neck, over her shoulders, and across her entire form. Her eyes and forehead were uninked, giving her an ethereal appearance.

Her body was a canvas of whispery colored ink, each tattoo a depiction of demons and women being tortured in extraordinary ways. The tattoo on her right shoulder, TMSITE, was different and was more than just ink to her. It symbolized her hidden agenda, her unspoken mission to free the Earth from the grip of masculinity.

"The meek shall inherit the Earth" was her motto, but she kept this ambition carefully disguised. To the world, she had once been a politician but now she channeled her political ambition energy into music. A woman who had stepped away from the limelight and power because of stress and heartbreak, the equivalent of soul-crushing despair. Few knew this was the reason for her departure—the agony she felt when her fiancé, after many years together, chose to become a Neurotech Hybrid.

While she practiced the songs in preparation for the public recital, her thoughts raced from subject to subject. Her past was filled with regrets, and her plans for the future were filled with actions that she knew would haunt her even more.

She halted, her fingers pausing over the keys. The last bar of music felt off, the tempo not quite right. With a focused frown, she adjusted the tempo slightly, trying the bar again. "Tsk," she clicked her tongue in irritation as it still wasn't what she wanted. Another small tweak, her fingers moving with precision. This time, it clicked. Satisfied, she returned to the melody, her mind slipping back into the swirl of thoughts as the music carried her deeper into the echoes of her past.

The memory takes her back to the visceral moment. The odd smell of electronics mixed with organics. Off putting scents mixed with antiseptic chemicals. It combined and clung to the sterile corridors of NeuraSys Technologies. Dr. Laura Benton moved fast, ignoring the glassy-eyed hybrids passing by, each with that unnerving gleam in their eyes—a result of Victor Lang's latest "upgrade." She could feel Lang's influence here, in every indifferent glance and perfected stride. He'd mastered the art of stripping humanity down to raw data, then feeding it back in as something "enhanced." It made her sick. Doctor Victor Lang. The very name stirred her rage, a deep resentment that stayed like an old scar. He was the man she'd once tolerated for the sake of her fiancé, Marsal, and the man she now saw as the architect of her worst nightmares. NeuraSys wasn't just his empire; it was a shrine to his ego, a factory for churning out his abominations. He had promised Marsal liberation from human frailty, something Laura had seen as nothing but a seductive death trap for his soul. She'd watched Marsal change, watched him become one of them. Her gut clenched with the memory.

But there was no time for grief, no room for a broken heart in her crusade. The hybrids were spreading through sectors across the globe like a contagion, each one a bold statement of Lang's power, his vision of a post-human future. Her mission was simple but brutal—put an end to it all. As she walked, she didn't see hybrid humanoids; she saw what was left of those seduced by Lang's promises, hollow shells with something darker than circuits and blood in their veins. She could almost feel Lang's icy, detached gaze on her, even here in the corridor—his dispassionate eyes, always measuring, always calculating.

Back in her apartment, her sanctuary from his world, she let herself breathe. She poured a glass of Aragh Sagi, the potent, earthy liquor warming her throat as she sank into the heavy leather chair near the window. Outside, the city pulsed with life, unaware of the storm brewing within its quietest, most isolated corners.

Her hand drifted to an old Persian painting, the vibrant reds and golds whispering of Persepolis, tales her mother once told her. Resilience. She'd need it now more than ever.

During her twelve years at the World Liberty Congress, she and her team of skilled politicians accomplished more freedoms and seized control for women than anyone in history. Rising from the chair she crossed the room to the piano.

She unconsciously plays the last song for her recital while her conscious mind recalls a past event. Laura Benton stood at the podium of the World Liberty Congress, her presence commanding the room as if it were inevitable. The air was thick with the anticipation of history in the making. In her voice was an edge, cool and calculated, as she introduced the Women's Autonomy Act—legislation that would reshape society. With swift, relentless precision, she and her team of elite women politicians dismantled the old world's structures, pushing through reforms that redefined the roles of men and women.

They created hospitals exclusively for women, where they provided tailored care and groundbreaking treatments specifically designed for women's health. These reforms redefined single parenthood, granting only women the legal right to raise children alone, free from interference or dependency on men.

The changes didn't stop there. Military and judicial power, once the domain of a male-dominated world, is now firmly under the control of women. Laura, ever the tactician, knew this wasn't about fairness but survival—about securing power where it mattered most. What she created was more than policy; it was an empire. The room, full of murmurs and stunned silence, had no choice but to bow to her vision, whether or not they knew it yet.

The memory from politics faded and a tender smile in her eyes caused by a turn to the memory of Marsal and the love they had once shared. His Cuban accent still excited her libido. She could almost hear his voice.

As she played "Guantanamera," her thoughts wandered to her fiancé singing. The tune, his favorite, reminded her of the man who had once held her heart. They had dreamed of a future together, a life filled with love and shared ambitions. He was her anchor, the one who understood her deepest fears and highest hopes. But his decision to become a Neurotech Hybrid had shattered those dreams. The man she loved had been transformed, his humanity altered in ways she couldn't accept.

The transformation had been gradual, each enhancement a step further away from the man she had known. She remembered the nights spent discussing their future, his excitement about the possibilities of neurotechnology. He believed in the promise of transcendence. The ability to overcome human limitations and achieve something greater. But for Laura, it was a betrayal of the very essence of what it meant to be human. To be a woman.

Neuro implants had changed everything, revolutionizing the way people interacted with their own minds, bodies, and the world around them. Dr. Laura Benton loathed the technology, but she couldn't deny its efficiency, its seductive allure. The implants augmented sensory perception, heightening sight, sound, taste, touch, and smell to superhuman levels. Some people claimed to feel the vibration of sound waves in the air, hear whispers from miles away, or see ultraviolet light that had been invisible to human eyes for millennia. Those with neuro-implants no longer viewed reality as ordinary humans did; they experienced it in layers of augmented data.

The HUD—heads-up display—was their ever-present companion, a transparent interface hovering like augmented reality, controlled through thought. A flicker of intent and vital statistics appeared: heart rate, environmental data, atmospheric composition, incoming messages, or tactical information in combat situations. People could control their muscles with surgical precision, lifting objects three times their natural strength with ease, thanks to the muscle boosters embedded deep within their nerves. All controlled by thought through the HUD

For those connected to the Grid, a collective network, information flowed as fast as the brain could process it. Decisions became instantaneous, the world's complexity reduced to a neatly organized stream of raw data. It was efficiency elevated to an art form. But with that efficiency came a terrible price. The hybrids lost the subtle art of intuition, the unquantifiable sense of being human.

For Laura's fiancé, it had started innocuously—a small implant that helped him access the Internet without a device. Then came visual enhancements, amplifying his peripheral vision and giving him the ability to see in low light or extreme brightness. He could look at her and immediately detect the chemical signals in her body, see the dilation of her pupils, the slight rise in her pulse. The implants had made him omniscient, a walking god in a world of mortals.

But with each upgrade, he became colder, more distant. The man who once held her in his arms, warm and tender, was now a calculating machine, able to predict her every move before she made it. His touch had grown robotic, detached, as if he were analyzing the sensory feedback rather than lovingly touching her. The final blow was when he opted for the NeuroNet interface—a direct link to NeuraSys' centralized control system. His mind was no longer his own; it was part of the collective hive, regulated and optimized by Lang's design.

And that was the future Lang had envisioned—where humanity would evolve beyond its weaknesses, its messy emotions, its clumsy biology. Transhumanism, where all people would eventually plug into the network, shedding their organic selves in favor of digital transcendence.

Laura shuddered. She couldn't let that future take hold, not without a fight. The Neurotech hybrids were a direct threat to the essence of humanity, the beautiful imperfection that made life worth living. Dr. Lang calls us subhuman. She would see them undone, would expose the dark underbelly of NeuraSys Technologies, and dismantle Lang's empire piece by piece.

As the last note of Guantanamera lingered in the air, she realized that her mission wasn't just political. It was personal, a war for the soul of womankind. And she was ready for it.

The memory of their last argument still haunted her. He had stood in their living room, his eyes filled with a fervent determination that bordered on fanaticism. He wore metallic bracers on his arms, humming softly with each movement. Wearables that amplified his strength. Over his left ear, a neural interface glowed faintly, a signal to his connection with the NeuroNet Grid. "This is the future, Laura," he had said, his voice steady but laced with an underlying desperation. "We can be more than we are. Don't you see? This is the next step in human evolution."

She had felt a cold dread settle in her chest, a realization that the man she loved was slipping away. "At what cost?" she asked. Her voice breaking. "What will you become? What will we become?"

His response had been a chilling echo of Dr. Lang's rhetoric. His low, controlled growl, a brutal certainty in his words. "We'll become what we were meant to be—unbreakable. You can't stop what's already in motion. This is how we reclaim what was lost, how we men finally regain control."

Even when they joined in The Rite—that coupling, mechanical ritual meant to satisfy the primal need—she couldn't feel his kiss or his touch. Instead, it was as if the others from his hive were there with them. Shadow figures that bled into his presence. It wasn't just him inside her; it was all of them. Silent and watching. A collective hunger that smothered any trace of intimacy, turning the act into something darker. Something that made her feel less human.

Laura had turned away, unable to look at him. "I can't follow you down this path," she said. Tears streaming down her face. "I can't lose myself to this. This is a perversion of nature."

Their parting had been inevitable, a painful but necessary separation. Laura had retreated into herself, seeking solace in her music and her mission. Her tattoos became a shield, a way to bear her pain and her resolve for all to see. Each image was a merit badge from her struggle, a reminder of the suffering she sought to eradicate.

Laura stared at her reflection on the polished surface of the piano, her skin telling a story of pain and resilience. She couldn't afford to let her internal struggle undermine her mission. She would use the bitterness and revenge that threatened to engulf her.

She took a deep breath; the music shifted to a softer, more contemplative melody. Her mother's stories of Persepolis echoed in her mind, tales of a city that rose and fell but left behind a legacy of strength and beauty. Laura knew she had to channel that same resilience, to rise above her personal grief and focus on the greater good.

But the fear lingered like a shadow at the edge of her consciousness. What if she failed? What if, in her quest to protect humanity, she lost her sense of feminist values? The thought was a chilling one, a reminder of the fine line she walked. Her tattoos were not just proof of her resolve, but a constant reminder of what she stood to lose. Each

demon, each tormented figure, was a piece of her soul, a representation of the battle within.

The soft knock at the door jolted her back to the present, but the
depth of her thoughts lingered. She had to stay vigilant, not just
against the external threats, but against the darkness within herself.
Her mission was clear, but so were the stakes. The world was on the
brink of change, and she had to ensure it was a change for the better.
Her thoughts were interrupted again by the sound of a firm, more
urgent knock at the door. Laura stopped playing, her fingers lingering on the keys. She took a deep breath and rose from the piano,
wrapping a silk robe around her body. The smooth fabric caressed
her skin, a minor comfort amid the turmoil of her thoughts. As she
walked to the door, the intensity of her mission pressed heavily on
her shoulders.

***

Standing on the other side of the door was Noelle, her PA: a young
woman with cropped hair and piercing green eyes. Noelle was one of
Laura's closest allies, a trusted confidante who shared her vision of a
world led at every level by women. She stepped inside, her eyes scanning the room before settling on Laura.

"Any news?" Laura asked. Her voice steady, despite the undercurrent
of tension.

Noelle nodded, handing Laura a tablet. "Dr. Lang is preparing for
a major announcement. Something about a new phase of enhancements. It's happening tomorrow. He is appearing on the Starzel
World Show where he promises to make the announcement live."

Laura felt a surge of anger and determination. Dr. Lang's influence
was growing, and with it, the threat to her vision of the future. She
knew she had to act, to rally her allies and prepare for the next phase
of her mission.

"Thank you, Noelle," Laura said. Her voice firm. "We need to be ready. The world is on the brink of change, and we must be at the forefront, guiding it towards a new dawn."

Noelle nodded, her expression resolute. "I'll gather the others. We'll be ready. The day following your recital, as we planned. Everyone has agreed to be there."

As Noelle left, Laura returned to the piano, her mind racing with plans and strategies. She placed her fingers on the keys, closing her eyes, allowing the music to flow through her once more. Each note was a step towards her goal, each melody a whisper of her unspoken dreams. Music helped her plan, and she was searching deep within for a strategy that hadn't yet blossomed.

She glanced at the calendar pinned to the wall. Her debut piano recital was just two days away, a carefully chosen date that aligned with her next move. The recital wasn't merely a return to public life; it was a strategic maneuver designed to gather influential allies and set the stage for her mission's next phase.

Among those attending were the dark minds she had quietly aligned herself with. Women whose ideologies had long simmered at the edges of society, daring to challenge the old world's morality. One of them was Ingrid Valens, a shadowy figure whose writings on erasing the biological power dynamics between men and women had gained a near-cult following. Ingrid's vision was extreme—advocating for the genetic manipulation of future generations to ensure a society where physical dominance had no place.

Another was Nadira Holt, a political strategist known for her ruthless approach to dismantling male-dominated institutions from within. Nadira thrived on manipulation, her hands bloodied by the downfall of countless men in power, all framed as the natural collapse of their own corruption. She would help Laura weave her music into the political machinations that were just beginning to take form.

And last, there was Thalia Corvus, a woman so feared that her name alone sent ripples through the underground. Thalia, a former academic, had been exiled because of her controversial thesis. She argued that biological sex was an artificial construct that must be obliterated. Her theories on how to rewrite human biology made her dangerous, a figure who sought nothing less than the complete eradication of traditional gender.

Laura had spent months planning this event, ensuring that the audience included not just music lovers but also potential supporters of her cause. It was her chance to weave her message into the music, to craft a symphony that would subtly rally these influential women—and those who followed them—to her vision of a future freed from the grip of men like Dr. Lang.

The sun had set, and the room was now bathed in the soft glow of the streetlights outside. The city hummed with life, a hard rain falling and thunder mixed with distant sounds that mingled with the music. Laura felt a sense of calm wash over her, a brief respite from the chaos of her thoughts.

She thought of her parents, of the sacrifices they had made to give her a better life. They had faced adversity with courage and dignity, instilling in her a deep sense of justice and a desire to fight for what was right. Her Iranian heritage was a source of strength, a reminder of the resilience and beauty of her culture. The new generations forged in The Northern Heartland blending with the old.

Laura's journey was far from over. The transition from politician to pianist was merely a short chapter in her life. A strategic retreat to gather strength and resources. She had allies, hidden and scattered, waiting for the right moment to rise. The meek shall inherit the Earth, she reminded herself, and she would ensure it came to pass with her at the helm.

Chapter Three: The World Voice

Forty-eight Hours before the recital, 08:45 AM

A daily VoxCast, those streams of manufactured "public voice," engineered to reinforce societal control while pretending to represent the people's will. It was the dominant form of broadcast from the country of Starzel, hosted by the infamous team of Penelope Bradshaw and Galina Mikhailova—leading feminist talk show hosts who commanded the attention of millions. They had become the most-watched team in the world, their polished rhetoric wrapped in a thin veneer of progressiveness while subtly shaping a global narrative. Every broadcast was a carefully orchestrated performance, a psycho-social engineered to control minds masquerading as empowerment. There was no better place for Dr. Victor Lang to gain world attention for his much-publicized announcement. He paces in the green room while the early show wraps up with their last guest before moving to the world broadcast. He is a towering figure, both physically and intellectually. Standing at six feet five inches, his slender frame was often a striking presence in any room he entered.

Adam Cole watched the monitor in the green room on the other side of Doctor Lang's pacing. Adam was half consciously observing Lang's restless movements. His heart pounded in his chest, not from fear, but from the strain of responsibility. He wondered if Lang was responsible for the missing scientists and engineers that repeat over and again. Last count had the number missing at nine. In the past three days, nine, mostly civil engineers and environmental scientists, have disappeared.

The introduction to the show played, and Adam knew this was his cue and the moment was approaching. It was time to go on stage.

"Our next guest is someone who writes articles that change minds," Penelope said. "His literary prose reveals the depth and reach of both his resources and his mind. His iconic signature is well known and at the end of his articles, he writes: Mae'r byd wedi cael ei droi tu mewn allan.

"This is a Welsh statement that means the world is turned inside out. Adam Cole is a man driven by a relentless pursuit of truth, standing as a beacon of journalistic integrity in a world rife with deception and power struggles. But first, let me tell you what you may not know about Adam."

Adam took a deep breath, steeling himself. The door to the green room opened, and a production assistant signaled for him to get ready. His heart pounded, and he glanced at the monitor, seeing Victor Lang still pacing, a stark reminder of the confrontation to come.

"At five feet ten inches, he is only average height. His athletic build is a reward for his years as a lettered footballer, a passion he maintains today by playing semi-professionally in Boston. The capital city under NATO control where he now lives.

"Off the record, Ladies," Galina looks into the camera, The camera zooms in tight on her face. "His deep blue eyes, often described as piercing, made people feel as if he could see right through the facades they present. Making him a formidable presence in any investigative endeavor."

Adam stepped onto the stage, the intensity of the lights hitting him like a wall of heat. Overhead, the LuxNova beams—each light emitting a staggering 200,000 lumens—bathed the entire set in pristine, hyper-real clarity. These lights weren't just bright; they were first used on the Moon base and later on the colonies. Developed by Ukraine Optics to mimic natural sunlight in environments where none existed. Originally designed for harsh extraterrestrial conditions, these lights brought the power of a distant sun to even the darkest corners of space.

Powered by photonic plasma cores, the LuxNova fixtures operated at 6,000 Kelvin, the equivalent of direct sunlight, with an ultra-precise beam that left no room for shadows. On Earth, they had found a new purpose: making every 3D Tri-View television broadcast impossibly vivid. The audience could see every detail, from the texture of the fabric to the microscopic imperfections on a performer's face, as if they were sitting just inches away. Adam felt the heat of the lights on his skin, aware that the stage's unforgiving illumination would magnify his every move.

Blinking against the glare, he refocused on the familiar figures of Penelope Bradshaw and Galina Mikhailova. Their faces, perfectly highlighted under the relentless beams, were as composed and clinical as the stage's stark brightness, betraying nothing of the ruthless minds behind those poised expressions. Just like the lights, they left no room for a shadow of doubt. The set designers meticulously planned this moment for precision and control.

The studio air carried the faint scent of makeup and the sterile smell of high-intensity electronic equipment. The hum of untethered monitors and the murmur of the studio crew created a backdrop of white noise, intensifying the sense of being in a high-stakes arena.

As Adam took his seat, gripping the armrests of his chair, he could feel the unexpected cool metal providing a sense of stability as he prepared for the upcoming confrontation. A bitter taste lingered in his mouth, a reminder of the hastily consumed coffee that fueled his resolve. The countdown to the broadcast ticked away, each second amplifying the importance of his responsibility. This was more than just a televised interview—it was a battleground for the future of humanity.

The camera switched over to Penelope. She stood to the side of an enormous wall plastered with articles, awards, and images of Adam's investigative reports. "Born and raised in Southern England, Adam's distinctive Southern British accent carries a subtle lilt of Welsh, a nod to his heritage and his fluency in the Welsh language. His academic journey took him to Cardiff Metropolitan University, where he earned a degree in journalism. His education honed his natural talent for uncovering the hidden and the overlooked skills that would become the cornerstone of his career."

After showing several seconds of shorts of previously recorded interviews, to the national audience the live shot returned to Galina. Pacing the show with her deliberate slow narration, the camera panned back and angled away, keeping her in the frame as it expanded to reveal Adam Cole seated in the guest chair next to Penelope.

"Despite his attractive face and figure, with his lack of hair only stressing the intensity of his blue eyes, Adam remained notably detached from romantic pursuits. Women often clamored for his attention, drawn to his charisma and the quiet confidence he exuded, but Adam, like sixty-five percent of men these days, is asexual.

"His focus was singular and unwavering: to discover and then expose the truths others preferred to keep hidden."

As Adam braced himself for the interview, his thoughts briefly wandered to Dr. Laura Benton. Not only did Dr. Benton make groundbreaking scientific advancements, but she also had a powerful vision for a future where humanity's survival depended on a deep ethical foundation. Laura's mission was far more than just a technical or biological evolution—it was a moral crusade, a reclamation of dignity and balance after centuries of patriarchal dominance. She believed that the next great transformation wasn't just about rewriting humanity's biology; it was about carefully steering morality, ensuring the scales tipped in favor of justice, equality, and sustainability.

Adam admired that vision, and in it, he found clarity for his role. He had always understood that men, like him, were no longer the center of power in this emerging world, but instead, they were the supporters, the stabilizers. To Adam, the strength of a man was not in dominance but in understanding, in lending his voice and efforts to a greater cause led by the authority of women like Laura. Feminist authority had become a guiding star, not just for societal progress, but for survival itself. And his duty was clear—stand as a pillar, help shoulder the burden, and fiercely protect the future that Laura and her allies were building.

He reflected on this new order with profound insight. True strength, as Adam saw it, lay not in challenging or undermining the new hierarchy but in embracing it fully, supporting its leaders with unwavering loyalty. The world was evolving beyond the tired old structures that men like Dr. Lang clung to, desperate to maintain their fading grip on control. What men offered now was resilience, dependability, and the willingness to fight for a future that wasn't theirs to lead but theirs to defend.

Adam's efforts to expose the truth about Dr. Lang's unchecked advancements were vital to this grand vision. If he failed, it would mean more than his own ruin—it would jeopardize Laura's delicate mission, one that aimed to prevent the unraveling of humanity under the diseases of greed and recklessness. Men like him, men who understood the greater good, had a unique place in this new world. They were the protectors of that balance, ensuring that the dangerous legacy of patriarchal chaos didn't seep into the future that women like Laura were working tirelessly to create.

As the interview approached, Adam felt the magnitude of that responsibility pulsing through him, and he welcomed it. He drew his strength from supporting others, serving as the solid foundation for a new, more ethical society. Laura counted on him not just to act, but to understand. This wasn't a fight between genders—it was a fight for the survival of civilization itself, and Adam was determined to play his part.

The keen listener may have heard Galina switch to past tense in her last sentence, hinting at their romantic relationship. Adam felt a slight twinge at her mention of his asexuality, but he knew it was part of his story, part of what made him relentless in his pursuits. His life took a pivotal turn when he became deeply involved in investigating the radical societal changes that had swept through the world.

As Adam sat in the glaring lights of the stage, bracing for the interview, a deeper truth gnawed at him—one that most of the world remained oblivious to. His mind drifted back to an ominous conversation he'd once overheard in hushed whispers, something buried far beneath the surface of public discourse. The names of powerful men who had met in secret on Jekyll Island centuries ago held a chilling relevance even now. These men weren't merely the architects of financial empires; they were the unseen puppet masters, pulling the strings of political and social movements to suit their interests.

Adam understood now that feminism, conservatism, liberalism—it was all part of the same web. Carefully spun, designed to keep society fractured, distracted. Every division, every political clash, was fuel for the men behind the curtain. The very men who had shaped history since the days of Jekyll Island. Pulling strings from the shadows while the world danced on their invisible marionette lines.

His breath quickened. He'd been blind, just like everyone else. And Dr. Lang? A pawn in a far deadlier game than anyone could have guessed. The game was older than democracy. His advancements weren't just dangerous; they were the keystone in a plan centuries in the making. Bio-enhancements, neuro-tech—they weren't the future. They were the yokes. The ultimate step in permanently enslaving humanity.

As Adam stared out into the bright lights, his resolve hardened. This interview wasn't just another spectacle. It was a minefield. One wrong word and the truth could stay buried forever. But if he played it right, if he could just keep control long enough, maybe—just maybe—he could tear open the veil and show the world what was really happening. He could unmask the men who had built the system, brick by invisible brick.

He felt his pulse hammering in his throat. "There's something Adam and Galina want everyone to know," Penelope said, her tone dripping with jealousy. The game was already in motion.

Adam took a breath, readying himself. "There's a lot Galina and I share," he said, locking eyes with the camera, his voice steady despite the storm of insecurity inside him. "And what we've uncovered goes beyond anything the public has been told. The development of bio-memory and bio-devices isn't progressing. It's an existential threat. And we're running out of time."

"Sorry to stop you from telling us more about the existential crisis, Adam." Penelope asserted her interruption with a firm tone. "There is already too much fear and misunderstanding in the world today where these cyborgs are concerned. In many parts of the world, governments are executing cyborgs on sight. At the same time, millions of people believe bio-enhanced humans are a natural next step for mankind.

"On our World Show, which begins in fifteen minutes, we have as our guest the man behind the technology himself. Dr. Victor Lang will join us. Can I ask you to stay with us? Adam, will you join us as we interview Dr. Lang? I've put you in the hot seat and I want you to know it is alright if you cannot stay for another hour."

The camera zoomed in tight on Adam's face as he digested the bomb she had just thrown into his lap. All of Starzel waited for his answer.

"This is unexpected and I'm not prepared."

"We have years of research and every detail outlined," Galina said. "It's the world show. Everyone will hear your words and the truth."

"He has not one protocol to protect humanity," Adam said. "In his carelessness in inventing bio-enhancing software, there are no limits. The biokernel is wide open to each person who undergoes a transformation.

"It is reckless and should be criminal." The camera panned away until the three of them could be seen on the screen.

"Then this is your hour," Penelope said. "Stay with us for the World Show and confront Dr. Lang."

While the ending credits cascaded across the monitors, Adam Cole nodded. "Yes. I will stay for the World Show."

Fifteen minutes felt like a heartbeat. The quiet chaos moved in perfect rhythm, transforming the local stage into the polished, hyper-modern set of the World Show. Adam could feel the air change around him, a cool, artificial draft brushing his skin in stark contrast to the lingering heat radiating from the lights above. The subtle hum of uplinks connecting, each one sending a faint vibration through the floor beneath his feet, added to the growing tension. The energy of the broadcast, like invisible static in the air, buzzed against his skin, heightening his awareness of every movement, every shift around him.

The touch of the makeup devices was mechanical but precise, cold metal applicators lightly grazing his face, applying layer after layer of a fine powder. A quick, sterilized mist of air followed, ensuring the makeup adhered seamlessly under the harsh lights. The sharp, sterile scent of the studio clung to the staff as they moved around him—clean, efficient, almost metallic. Behind that, faint traces of perspiration mixed with synthetic perfumes as the crew worked at a relentless pace.

Penelope Bradshaw and Galina Mikhailova sat beside him, their faces still as makeup artists swept soft, velvety brushes across their skin, careful not to disrupt the perfect layer of powdered finish. Their hairpieces clicked into place with mechanical precision, hands adjusting strands with quick, deft motions. The air around them felt tense, charged, as if the life forces of the world pressed against them, and the entire stage.

Adam's pulse thudded in his ears. He tried to focus, but the sounds and sensations crashed over him—distant uplinks syncing in place with a heavy clunk, the low hum of servers linking to satellites, ready to broadcast their every word. He could taste the sterile air, dry against his throat, a reminder of the artificial world he now sat in. The world beyond the studio was watching, and the audience would soon be tuned in.

He shifted in his seat, the fabric of his freshly tailored suit cool against his skin, but the pit in his stomach grew. There was no turning back now. The screen flickered to life, the introductory sequence flashing across the massive display. The lights blazed hotter, washing out every shadow, while the artificial chill of the air fought to keep the studio in balance.

The world was about to watch. Every breath he took felt heavier, every second stretched longer. The final countdown began.

The man's voice was deep and resonant, carrying an authoritative yet approachable tone. His enunciation was crisp, and his pacing deliberate, drawing the listener into the story. There was a subtle warmth in his delivery, making the audience feel as if they were being guided through a personal journey by someone who knew the subject intimately.

"Born in Saudi Arabia, Victor had grown up in the bustling city of Riyadh, where the traditional met the modern in a complex dance of culture and progress. From an early age, he displayed a prodigious intellect, outshining his peers and captivating his educators with his insatiable curiosity and innovative thinking."

While the announcer spoke, a video played running highlights from Dr. Lang's past. Black and white footage of a modest house, a young boy playing with building blocks, and then running through a lush green park under a cloudless sky. Color footage of a young Victor in a classroom, answering questions with enthusiasm, and later, leading a group project with other students. Victor in a football jersey, scoring a goal, celebrating with teammates, and practicing tirelessly on the field. Footage of Victor at university, attending lectures, engaging in debates, and working on a student vlog. The announcer continued speaking.

"Victor's academic journey led him to the prestigious King Abdullah University of Science and Technology, where he immersed himself in the fields of neuroscience and biotechnology. His groundbreaking research on neural interfaces earned him international acclaim, and it wasn't long before he envisioned a future where humanity could transcend its biological limitations.

"By the age of thirty-eight, Victor Lang had become a renowned scientist and a polarizing media personality. He was the visionary behind the Transhuman Race, a movement that sought to enhance human capabilities through advanced Neuralink technology. His innovations promised superhuman strength and intelligence, with followers capable of processing information thousands of times faster than ordinary humans. However, these advancements came with significant ethical and societal questions, which Victor often brushed aside with his persuasive rhetoric and charismatic demeanor."

Visual archives streamed out from the Pluto TV Studio in Starzel to the people of the world showing Victor presenting his inventions at tech expos, working late nights in his lab, and him receiving many accolades for his inventions of BioSynaptics with their TissueLink Synaptic Nodes, hailed as a groundbreaking leap in human augmentation. These microchips, designed to seamlessly merge with the brain, nerves, and muscles, offered unprecedented control over the human body, enhancing everything from motor function to cognitive processing. Practical applications spanned across medicine, allowing paraplegics to walk and amputees to control advanced prosthetics as if they were natural limbs. Plans for the military not yet implemented and industrial sectors, BioSynaptics would produce elevated human performance, creating workers and soldiers capable of superhuman strength, precision, and reflexes. The technology promised to reshape humanity's relationship with its own biology—merging man and machine into one.

This recognition led Victor to even more speaking engagements. Video archives showcased Victor on talk shows, speaking at tech conferences, and interacting with fans and fellow inventors. As the announcer came to the end of the narration, the video showed a montage of Victor's career highlights, ending with a close-up of him looking thoughtfully into the distance, surrounded by his transhuman creations.

"Victor's philosophy was rooted in the belief that humanity's frailty was its greatest weakness. He saw the current societal reforms, aimed at achieving gender equality, as a distraction from what he considered the true path to progress—technological evolution. To him, the elimination of gender distinctions was a superficial fix for deeper, more systemic issues. He believed that true equality and advancement lay in transcending human limitations altogether.

"Despite his controversial stance, Victor has an enormous following. His eloquent speeches and a magnetic presence that drew people to his cause characterized his public appearances. He envisioned a world where enhanced humans will lead society, prioritizing efficiency and progress over outdated human values.

"Victor's ambition did not stop at technological advancement. He harbored aspirations of becoming the first world leader-dictator, a position he felt uniquely qualified for because of his superior intellect and vision for the future. His critics, however, saw him as a dangerous figure, one whose quest for power and control threatened to undermine the foundational rights of human society."

The video faded to black and then out of the center of the visible field an image grew until it filled the screen with a final image of Victor's signature and a caption that read, "Doctor Victor Lang: Pioneering the Future of the new era AnthroGenesis at the end of the era of humanity."

In the complex and often contentious world of Dr. Victor Lang, there was a blurred distinction between visionary genius and tyrannical despot lunatic. His presence loomed large over the global stage, as did the potentially perilous power of his ideas. Society grappled with the implications of his technologies and philosophies. Victor Lang remained steadfast in his belief that he was leading humanity toward its next great evolutionary leap.

***

"We celebrate together the end of the era of homo sapiens and herald the dawn of AnthroGenesis," Victor said, still standing off-stage in the doorway leading from the green room. The cameras fixed on him switched from camera one, tight focus on his face, camera two, framing him standing over the threshold of the door, and camera three, panning between the audience and the three on stage: Penelope, Galina, and Adam.

Outside, a storm raged, lightning illuminating the darkened sky, mirroring the tempestuous debate within the studio. The wind howled, a harbinger of the ideological storm brewing inside. The scent of damp asphalt and concrete filled the studio, signaling to all in the studio that the rain had begun.

Victor walked to the stage with a blend of scientific gravitas and passionate advocacy, explaining the profound transformation humanity is undergoing. As he approached the guest chair, his mind briefly wandered to the deeper motivations driving him.

"AnthroGenesis," he said, "is derived from 'anthropos,' the Greek word for human, and 'genesis,' signifying a beginning or creation. This term captures the rebirth of humanity into a new era, where traditional gender roles and sexual reproduction become obsolete. We're witnessing an evolution in human identity and consciousness, leading to a society that transcends conventional boundaries. In this new era, we are not merely enhancing our biological capabilities with technology but rethinking what it means to be human. Our identities, previously anchored in gender and biological reproduction, are now liberated, paving the way for a more inclusive and advanced state of existence."

As Victor continued speaking, he couldn't help but think about the legacy he wished to leave behind. The significance of his vision was immense, not just for its scientific implications, but for what it meant for his place in history. He was driven by a mix of altruism and ego, believing that his work would solve long-standing issues related to gender and identity while cementing his place as a transformative figure. The fear of failure was not just about the rejection of his ideas, but about his achievements and legacy fading into irrelevance. He needed this to succeed, not for humanity, but for himself.

Doctor Lang's vision for AnthroGenesis was both exhilarating and deeply controversial. He painted a bold picture of a society where technological and biological integration would eliminate the need for sexual reproduction, replacing it with advanced methods of creation and identity formation. In Lang's future, procreation would no longer hinge on the union of two sexes but on the precise manipulation of genetic material, allowing for the design of new humans with enhanced capabilities. This transformation promised to dissolve long-standing gender distinctions and societal roles, ushering in an era where human potential was no longer defined by biology.

For seven centuries, world governments fought against the rise of cloning technology, terrified of what it would mean for the masses to understand that the existence of two sexes was no longer a necessity. The fear of losing control over the most basic foundation of human identity—the male-female dynamic—kept these technologies at bay. But Lang's AnthroGenesis wasn't just about reproduction; it was about reshaping human identity itself, offering individuals the power to redefine who they were, untethered from the limitations of birth or gender.

The implications of this shift were staggering. The shift would have an irreversible impact on ethics, culture, and personal identity. The creation of life would no longer be a private, biological affair but a carefully controlled process overseen by scientific principles and advanced algorithms. As humanity stood at the precipice of this new epoch, AnthroGenesis challenged the very foundation of human existence.

Doctor Lang's vision compelled society to ask troublesome questions of itself: What happens when there is no longer a need for men or women in the traditional sense? What becomes of family, relationships, and the essence of who we are? For Lang, the answer was obvious. This was not the end of humanity, but its next great evolution. In this future, only imagination will limit the boundaries of human potential. Pushing us to redefine not only our roles but our place in the universe.

"Welcome to The World Stage," Galina said.

The studio audience erupted into loud applause, and whistles intermixed with whoops and cheers. Victor, wearing traditional Saudi attire, bowed deep. His thobe, a long, flowing robe that extended to his ankles, was tailored from high-quality, lightweight fabric. The thobe was immaculately white, symbolizing purity and reflecting his country's preference for light colors because of the tropical climate. The garment featured subtle alabaster embroidery along the cuffs and collar, adding a touch of intricate artistry to the otherwise simple design.

Draped over his shoulders was a bisht, a cloak often worn on formal occasions. The bisht was made from luxurious black fabric with gold trim, signifying his status and the importance of the event. The gold embroidery along the edges of the bisht highlighted his distinguished presence and complemented the simplicity of the thobe underneath.

On his head, Victor wore a ghutra, a traditional headscarf, neatly folded and secured in place by an agal, a black cord. The ghutra was predominantly white, echoing the color of his thobe, and was arranged in the classic style, cascading smoothly over his shoulders. The agal, with its understated elegance, added a final touch of authenticity to his attire.

Victor's choice of footwear was a pair of traditional leather sandals, comfortable yet appropriate for the formal setting. These sandals completed his outfit, ensuring he maintained cultural authenticity from head to toe.

"We have asked the award-winning journalist, Adam Cole, to join us today," Penelope introduced Adam as she spoke to Victor. But before she could seize control of her show, Dr. Lang interrupted.

"While waiting backstage, I watched the brief interview you provided, Adam. Everyone knows your work, and I especially enjoy your vlog where you keep the world aware as you search for the documents from Jekyll Island."

Adam tried to speak, but the ever-charismatic Victor Lang continued, seeming to never pause for a breath.

"You accuse me of criminal action because I have not included protocols in my bio-enhanced neural implants and exoskeleton wearables. What protocol should I put in place that will make you stop claiming that I am a dangerous-criminal?"

The audience chuckled, some applauding, their attention locked on the exchange. Adam didn't flinch. He'd heard those dismissive responses before and knew exactly where they were leading.

Without hesitation, Adam leaned forward, his voice cutting through the noise. "Simple. The most basic protocols—do not harm humans. Even your predecessors—those executed for crimes against humanity, whose cyborgs were hunted to extinction hundreds of years ago—implemented human safety protocols. You, however, seem to celebrate the end of humanity, ignoring these protections as if they were relics of a bygone era."

A ripple of boos scattered through the audience, but Adam saw it—the tension, the anticipation. Most of the audience sat on the edge of their seats, leaning in, waiting for the next move. Adam held his gaze on Victor Lang, who briefly acknowledged him with a moment of eye contact before turning to address the camera. The world watching.

"This accusation," Dr. Lang began, his voice steady and controlled, "has three parts that I want to address."

He raised a finger. "First, you said my predecessors had cyborgs. I assume you are referring to the late Elon Musk and his robotic ambitions. Neuralink, his brain implants, were indeed dangerous—recklessly dangerous—and his cyborg culture grew into a counterculture that became a threat to world governments. But even they followed the simple human-safety protocols you mentioned."

Lang paused for effect, the camera panning to the audience, capturing the tension in the room. "But as you said, despite those protocols, Musk's cyborg society followed what all human civilizations have done since the beginning of recorded history: kill and declare war. It wasn't just a technology problem. It was a human one. Humans are programmed for conflict, for war, driven by the madness of power-hungry, greed-fueled leaders. Despite being called safeguards, they could not prevent the inherent urge for violence and dominance."

He lowered his hand, gesturing to the two feminist hosts of the show—Penelope Bradshaw and Galina Mikhailova—both seated prominently, their over-the-top, exorbitantly expensive wigs glinting under the stage lights, framing their carefully crafted appearances. With thick and flawless makeup, they enhanced every visual cue of femininity, deliberately alluring. Their outfits left little to the imagination: tops that barely covered their breasts, exposing cleavage and skin far below their midriffs. Their hips accentuated, pants hugging tightly to show the deliberate separation of their bottoms, revealing curves designed to captivate. It was more than spectacle—it was strategy. They were weapons, projecting control through sexuality, manipulating the power structures of society, bending laws, courts, and even governments to their will with a visual dominance few could resist. This wasn't new; it was ancient, feminism power and control repackaged.

"Second," Lang said, ignoring the image of the hosts flashing behind him, "you misunderstand AnthroGenesis. It's not the end of humanity—it's the next stage. A natural evolution. The end of the human as we know it, yes. But not the end. It's not an extinction, but evolution, a transcendence. If you think that by clinging to outdated safety protocols, you are preserving something sacred, then you are the one living in the naïve past."

Lang pointed toward the audience, his tone sharpened with authority. "Look out at the people here." The camera panned again, scanning the audience: some engrossed in Lang's every word, others more skeptical, sitting silently as if grappling with the gravity of what they were hearing.

"These people, these pioneers, they aren't afraid of what comes next. They embrace it. AnthroGenesis is not about killing what was; it's about accepting what we've become. We are not bound by the rules of old civilizations. Those protocols, those limitations—they're the remnants of a dying species. We're here to evolve beyond that. You accuse me of abandoning human safety, but I'm offering humanity a way forward where safety protocols are unnecessary. We won't need them because the era of conflict is ending with the human as we know it."

Adam felt the power of Dr. Lang's words sinking into the crowd. The man was skilled—too skilled. Every word calculated, every pause a strategic move in a greater game. But Adam wasn't backing down. He knew what Lang's vision truly meant: the erasure of humanity, dressed in the language of progress. And beneath that slick rhetoric, Lang's refusal to implement basic safety protocols screamed of something far more dangerous—unchecked power in the hands of those willing to redefine humanity for their own purposes.

Victor knew most studios provided a few rows of comfortable chairs for the studio audiences. The Starzel World Show had two rows of five and a second section with two rows of five chairs. The other three hundred people stood. A corporate cost-cutting measure on maintenance and the price of replacing chairs.

The cameras blurred the low-light standing audience and focused instead on the two well-lit sections. The cameras briefly captured shots of the audience, and after a live shot, the event organizers rotated the seated individuals out to the standing area to create the illusion of showcasing different sections of seats with different people.

Everything in Starzel was a deception and an effort to boost ratings and cut costs.

"The people in this studio audience today are Enhanced Beings, or what many of us are calling ourselves, transhumans. None of them pose any threat, nor are they any more violent than unenhanced beings."

"Nor are they any less violent," Adam said, pointing an accusatory finger at Dr. Lang. "But they are significantly stronger and faster than people. So, by your very definition, they are a danger to society and an existential danger to humanity."

"Did you say that you live in Boston?" Dr. Lang asked.

"Yes, that's correct. I'm the son of Welsh parents, but I have lived in Boston for many years."

"That's in the northeast coastal area and inside the NATO-occupied territory, isn't it?"

"Yes," Adam nodded. "Since the second American Civil War, NATO has occupied the area going on three centuries. What's your point?"

"Are there still daily bombings and sniper attacks?" Dr. Lang asked, his face and body expressing empathy for the tragic conditions. "You needn't answer the question. We all know about the ongoing tragic violence in the area. Neurohumans, as you call them, are responsible for none of it."

As Dr. Victor Lang spoke about the transformative potential of An-throGenesis, a flicker of determination glinted in his eyes. He was not merely advocating for a scientific breakthrough; he was laying the foundation for a legacy. The drive to be remembered as a vision-ary, one who liberated humanity from the constraints of biology and societal norms, fueled his every word. This vision was more than a professional achievement; it was his life's mission, born from a pro-found desire to push the boundaries of human potential. A libera-tion.

Yet, a fear also propelled him forward. Serving as the crucible that forged his resolve. He needed this to succeed, not just for the ad-vancement of humanity, but for the validation of his life's work. As he looked out over the audience, his heart beat with a mix of hope and trepidation, knowing that the future he envisioned was within reach, but precariously balanced on the edge of acceptance and rejec-tion.

"Have you heard of Dr. Laura Benton?" Galina asked. "She was the Heartland and Northeast Canadian ambassador to The World Lib-erty Congress."

"She is much more than an ambassador," he said. "I remember her long before she was Prime Minister, winning the gold medal in the Summer Olympics.

"She was just twenty years old and the Fencing Champion of the world. She took silver in the women's twelve hundred meters. And now she is a pianist."

As Victor continued speaking, he couldn't help but run his fingers along the intricate embroidery of his thobe, the familiar texture grounding him amidst the storm of skepticism.

"Her debut concert is at Walt Disney Concert Hall in Los Angeles the night after next. Sadly, I cannot attend because I have to be at the NBA finals that night. Coach Sam Taylor reserved court-side seats for me in San Antonio. Game six of the conference. If the Spurs lose, his season is over."

"Sorry to tell you, Dr. Lang," Penelope said, "she is not a fan of you in the same light as you hold for her. You see, when she heard we were having you as a guest on our World Show, she sent us a statement she wants us to read to you on her behalf."

"For me?" His words expressed the anticipation he felt. The famous Dr. Laura Benton sent a message just for him. "I can't wait to hear it." The teleprompter displayed the message while Galina read the words for everyone to hear. "Genesis chapter 2 verse 18 - 24: The Lord God said, 'It is not good for the man to be alone. I will make a helper suitable for him. Now the Lord God had formed out of the sea all the wild animals and all the birds in the sky. He brought them to the man to see what he would name them; and whatever the man called each living creature, that was its name. So the man gave names to all the livestock, the birds in the sky, and all the wild animals. But for Adam, no suitable helper was found. So the Lord God caused the man to fall into a deep sleep; and while he was sleeping, he took one of the man's ribs and then closed up the place with flesh. Then the Lord God made a woman from the rib he had taken out of the man, and he brought her to the man. The man said, 'This is now bone of my bones and flesh of my flesh; she shall be called woman, for she was taken out of man. That is why a man leaves his father and mother and is united with his wife, and they become one flesh.

"From the Quran, Surah Al-Hijr (15:26-28): And We did certainly create man out of clay from an altered black mud. And the jinn we created before from scorching fire. And [mention, O Muhammad], when your Lord said to the angels, 'I will create a human being out of clay from an altered black mud.'"

Dr. Benton told the story of the creation of men and the creation of women from the Hindu, Chinese, Greek, Zoroastrianism, and Native American Navajo traditions. After she had completed the reading from them the cameras focused on Dr. Victor Lang.

"Do you have a reply for Dr. Benton?" Galina asked.

"No," Dr. Lang said. "I will not argue with someone who is not here to defend themselves. It is an interesting debate and her intention is gender-related. My work is not gender-related. I do not find it valuable to argue the ancient, failed, and trivial feminist pursuit.

"You invited me here to tell you about my recent achievements. Then you ambush me with Adam Cole and his Russian girlfriend, Galina. Now you strike at me again with Laura Benton, who isn't in the studio but is, according to you, supposed to have sent a message.

"Before I leave and never return to this World Show, I will tell you what I was invited here to tell you. We have Boundarian Creators. Four of the transhumans have developed the ability to detect harmonic balance between Class M planets. Through the balance, they open a portal and we have sent transhumans and supplies to occupy other planets."

"By whose authority have you sent people and supplies to other planets?" Adam Cole stood and threw his arms to express his surprise and challenge Dr. Lang. "Do you have any proof or scientific data to verify this claim?"

Victor Lang didn't look back. He exited through the stage door and out of the building, while the audience cheered and applauded his announcement. Penelope and Galina sat stunned. Adam chased after him.

Chapter Four: Recitals and Returns

Twenty hours until the recital, 11:58 PM

As Doctor Laura Benton addressed the Feminist Militia leadership, her mind sharpened with a singular focus: eliminating Dr. Lang and his neurohumans. For years, she had warned about the dangers of his unchecked advancements, how they threatened not only the balance of power but the very fabric of human existence. Lang's vision wasn't just dangerous; it was a perversion of everything she fought to protect. His creations—bio-enhanced, soulless, and detached from the vulnerabilities that made humanity valuable—represented the last step toward a dystopia she couldn't allow to come to fruition.

From the moment Laura activated the link to begin the meeting, the world around her fractured, then reassembled into layers of augmented reality with a precision of a machine executing a program. The comfortable home office faded to the edges of her awareness, replaced by a rugged war room suspended over a Martian canyon, cliffs streaked with veins of crimson ice. Beneath her fingertips, the steel desk was real, but everything else was the EcoSphere — a seamless fusion of reality and augmented reality (AR). The women assembled around her blinked into sharp relief: some stationed on Earth, others projected from Moon bases, and a few from Mars colonies. The AR tech was relentless in its authenticity; the Martian dust clung to one attendee's boots, while Earth's golden sunlight slanted through another's window. Each flicker of movement sent ripples of data cascading through the air — charts unfurling, reports dissecting, voice commands snapping information into place.

Laura's gaze triggered tactical readouts, the AR layers anticipating her needs with ruthless efficiency. Bio-feedback bled into the stream: the tension in a jawline, the barely perceptible tremor of doubt. The EcoSphere didn't just project people; it stripped them down to their mental armor, exposing the undercurrents beneath every word. As she pinned a key point to the virtual wall with a curt gesture, a ripple of acknowledgment flashed across the group. Here, on the knife-edge between reality and simulation, decisions struck with the significance of worlds — Earth, Moon, Mars — all converging in this gritty nexus where presence, data, strategy and truth fused.

As she addressed the Feminist Militia leadership, a new phrase slipped from her lips. "Lang's vision is a blirant, an egregious blurring of the natural and the artificial, where men believe they can transcend their humanity by becoming bionic machines." The word had a peculiar ring to it, a cross between blight and arrogant, capturing the absurdity and the danger of his vision.

She saw the quizzical looks from her colleagues, but didn't pause to explain. They'd understand soon enough. For now, blirant was hers—a label for the cold, misguided pursuit of perfection that threatened to dismantle everything human and precious in their worlds.

Deep inside, Laura's true motivation burned with an intensity that had only grown stronger since her departure from political leadership. She had left the world stage to focus on her health, to build the family she had long neglected, but she knew she couldn't walk away from the fight entirely. Her purpose was greater than herself. It was about the meek—the "mama's boys," the men who were willing to give everything, even their lives, for the women they loved and revered. These were the men Laura believed could help rebuild society after the impending collapse. They weren't the warriors or conquerors. They were the nurturers, the protectors—the ones who understood that strength lay not in dominance but in devotion.

Lang's neurohumans, with their cold, calculated efficiency, represented the antithesis of this ideal. They were designed to be perfect, superior, but they lacked the humility, the tenderness, that made humanity worth saving. For Laura, Lang's creations were a direct threat to the world she envisioned—a world where men who loved deeply, who will sacrifice everything for women, would thrive. These men were the backbone of the future she fought for, not the domineering or power-hungry, but those who cherished the power of cooperation, empathy, and care.

"We must act decisively," Laura said, her voice firm and steady. "The neurohumans are a threat to everything we stand for, but more than that, they threaten the very essence of humanity. It's not just our survival at stake—it's the survival of those who will build the world after us. We owe it to them, to the meek, to ensure that the future belongs to those who understand the true meaning of sacrifice."

She looked at the faces on the screen, knowing that the fight ahead would be long and brutal. But Laura was ready. She would not allow Dr. Lang's twisted vision to destroy the world she believed in. She would fight for the men who would give everything, even their lives, for the women they loved—and she would stop at nothing to see that vision become a reality.

"In the beginning, the universe, in its vast complexity, created man in its own image, designed for perfection and higher consciousness. Later, the universe introduced the woman as an afterthought, considering her a temporary utility. She was required to inspire men to evolve and replace her inferior purpose with a new era of man."

Laura paused, watching the tension ripple through the faces on the screen. The Feminist Militia leadership, hardened and fierce, sat in silence, their expressions taut with unspoken questions. She pressed on, knowing the weight her next words would carry.

"Dr. Victor Lang has identified three ways to propel humanity into this new era: medical prosthetics, neural implants, and exoskeletons. These technologies promise to enhance human capabilities beyond natural limits. However, these advancements must not include women. Women do not need to evolve. We are perfect as we are, and we own this planet. We must prohibit these alterations on our celestial sphere."

The silence thickened, almost suffocating. Laura scanned each face on the screen, feeling the complexity of her statement settle like a heavy stone in the pit of her stomach. The room fell still. Her resolve, however, was unshakeable.

"Dr. Lang's announcement during the World Show threatens to upend this delicate balance. We must act decisively to prevent these technologies from being misused. Our mission is to safeguard our society, to ensure that the natural order remains intact."

Her words echoed through the digital space as she reached for her glass, taking another sip of Aragh Sagi. A potent warmth, flavored with anise, spread through her chest, momentarily dulling the strain of the dangerous path ahead. The recent violence from earlier in the day weighed on her—eighty-three lives lost. Five of them women, in a genre-organized militia shootout in Berlin. The urgency of their mission had never been more clear.

"The World Show brought international attention to our struggle," she continued, her voice steady but edged with iron. "Yet, it also underscored the deep divisions we face. The shootout was a stark reminder that the violence was escalating, and we must be prepared for what comes next. We must escalate defense protocols to wartime. Now is the time to vote—do we approve these protocols or reject them?"

Laura tapped a button on her desk, activating the VeraVote 5000—an advanced, impenetrable voting mechanism designed to prevent any possibility of voting fraud. Developed by top-tier cryptographers and quantum computing experts, the system relied on neural biometric verification, scanning each participant's brainwave patterns and combining it with their DNA imprint to ensure absolute authenticity. After casting their votes, the system used quantum-level security protocols to encrypt participants' choices, which would destroy the data if anyone interfered with it. The quantum-level security protocols made it impossible to fake, alter, or intercept the vote.

Each of the militia leaders placed their hands on their respective biometric devices, the faint hum of the system filling the air as it processed their inputs. Laura watched the digital display on her screen: names flashing green one by one, confirming their ballots. The technology was flawless—instantaneous tallying, a true ballot count displayed before anyone had time to doubt the results.

A soft tone sounded, and the results flashed up in front of her: Unanimous Approval.

It was official. They were at war.

Laura let the tension drain from her shoulders, allowing herself a brief celebration in a moment of reflection. The screen faded back to the familiar faces of her comrades. Her mind wandered to Dr. Aylin Kaya, the brilliant scientist whose achievements in reproductive DNA cloning had been a beacon of inspiration.

Kaya had been right. Her voice whispered through Laura's mind, a reminder of the responsibility she now carried.

"You have the power to change the world, Laura. Never forget that."

Laura nodded slightly to herself. The die was cast, and there was no turning back. Lang and his neurohumans were the last obstacle, and she would stop at nothing to see their end. For the women who had fallen. For the meek men who would sacrifice everything. For the future, she had sworn to protect.

The screen filled with the faces of her colleagues flickered. A symbolic visual of the global reset. Allies in this unprecedented struggle. Laura felt a surge of determination. She would honor her legacy by continuing to fight for what she believed in. Her unwavering commitment paved the way for the future she envisioned—a world where women lead without fear and where the natural order was respected.

The meeting ended, but Laura's work was just beginning. She turned back to her computer, her fingers flying over the keyboard as she drafted the next steps of the plan. The moonlight outside her window cast a serene glow over the city, a stark contrast to the turmoil within her.

Laura reached for the glass again, taking a hard sip of the Aragh Sagi. As Laura reached for the drink she desired, a memory of her mother surfaced, vivid and familiar. Laura's mind drifted back to her younger days, the stories her mother used to tell her about Iran. She remembered the scent of saffron and rosewater in their kitchen, the taste of her mother's homemade baklava, and the sound of Persian music that filled their home. Those memories were bittersweet now, reminders of a time when life was simpler and her biggest concerns were school and friends, not the fate of the world. Her mother used to say, "A river doesn't carve its path through stone by strength, but by persistence."

Laura's upbringing instilled in her the wisdom of that simple truth, teaching her to value the power of unwavering determination over brute force. It wasn't the flash of a moment that shaped the world—it was the relentless determination to keep going, even when the way seemed impossible.

The historic value of her mother's words echoed through Laura now, as she faced the long, inevitable fight ahead. Like the river, she would persist. The world would change, and she would carve her way through, one decision, one battle, at a time.

The path ahead was fraught with more bloodshed and challenges, but Laura Benton was ready. The meek would inherit the Earth. And she would ensure it came to pass.

As Laura continued to draft her plan, her thoughts drifted to the piano recital. Music had always been her refuge, a way to process her emotions and find clarity. She had been preparing tirelessly for this performance, perfecting each piece through endless practice. The recital was more than just a personal passion; it was a strategic maneuver to get back into the media's eyes, and to gather strength and resources.

Laura often thought of Dr. Kaya, her second hero after her mother, especially when she needed inspiration. The head of Turkey's reproductive sciences. The two women had crossed paths during Laura's political career, and Dr. Kaya had become a mentor and a friend. Her unwavering commitment to her work and her ability to balance multiple passions were qualities Laura deeply admired and sought to emulate.

But the burden of her mission quickly returned, pressing on her shoulders like an invisible hand. She rose from the computer and moved to the window, looking out at the city that stretched before her. The lights of the city twinkled like stars, and the sounds of distant traffic and occasional sirens created a hum that was both comforting and added stress

"In our country we don't call it stress," Her mother said. Laura's head was in her mother's lap as she laid stretched out on the picnic blanket and watched the clouds changing their shapes in the sky. "Our people have a different word for stress, we call it sin. It's a sin to worry. A worse sin to make someone worry. It's a sin to be afraid. A worse sin to cause someone fear. Do you understand, Laura?"

Laura turned away from the window and walked toward a small shrine set up in the corner of her apartment. The candles flickered softly, casting shadows over the photographs of her parents and a few cherished trinkets from her childhood. She pulled a fresh candle from the drawer. When she lit the candle, the flame wavering as if uncertain. She whispered a prayer for guidance and strength. The war was coming, and she knew she would need every ounce of resolve.

Stepping onto the terrace, she found herself caught between the present and the swirl of memories pulling her backward. The cool night air, stinging, and felt like sharp teeth biting her skin, a stark contrast to the warmth of the glass in her hand. Beyond her apartment, the city sprawled in dystopian fashion, a mass of towers and smoke, the once vibrant skyline now dominated by surveillance drones humming like mechanical wasps, weaving between colossal billboards that blared propaganda. The neon glow of advertisements reflected in the distant haze—flickers of distorted family images, slogans promising a return to values under the new Chinese-Russian alliance. It was a strange war: Family Values clashing against feminist-led governments, each side claiming to save the soul of humanity while tearing it apart.

"War!" she shouted into the night, her voice swallowed by the city's hum. She took another sip from her glass, closing her eyes against the overwhelming tide of memories. After today, she might never again have the freedom to recall the people who had shaped her, those whose inspirations and dreams had brought her here. She had just finished drafting the last section of her war plan. Preparations; knowing there would be a day after the fighting ended. Though that day felt impossibly far away, and she wondered if she would still recognize herself when it finally came.

Her thoughts drifted to her fiancé, a figure both vivid and ghostly in her mind. She gripped the railing of the terrace, the cold metal stung her palms. She leaned forward, the liquor in her glass turning milky white as the ice melted into it. But it wasn't the drink alone that made her stumble. The memory—so heavy, so raw—pulled her down, forcing her to confront the pain she had long tried to bury. She vowed this would be the last time she allowed herself to relive it. His transformation into a Neurotech Hybrid had shattered her, as much as it had fueled her determination to destroy the technology that had stolen him from her. She could still see his face, feel the warmth of his hand on her skin, hear the way his voice filled with hope when they spoke of the future. They had been so certain of their path—vacations on Mars, a family, the quiet life together they had dreamed of building once their missions for humanity were complete.

Their relationship had begun at a conference just south of Beijing, in a city once known for its historical significance. But now infamous as the epicenter of the long and often terrorist fought Family Values War. The Chinese-Russian Alliance had risen there, casting a shadow over the rest of the world. The conference on cancer cures had been a bright moment in those dark times, where the best minds gathered to discuss humanity's last great medical frontier. Laura, with her many cancer cures, had been a keynote speaker, a rising star in the fight against disease.

He had approached her afterward, Marsal's eyes alive with admiration, his curiosity palpable. They had talked for hours, their connection instant and magnetic.

Later that night, they sat together at an expensive restaurant, the atmosphere tense, heavy with the weight of unspoken threats. A few bodyguards lingered nearby, ever-vigilant, ensuring her safety. As Prime Minister of the World Liberty Congress, Laura was never truly alone in public. Marsal, though visibly uncomfortable with the presence of armed escorts, tolerated it because being with her came with its dangers. His wary glances scanned the restaurant. He was on edge.

Laura offered him an alluring smile, trying to bridge the distance, but her thoughts, as usual, were elsewhere—swirling in the joy of their shared ambitions, haunted by the war that was tearing everything apart. She raised her glass to toast their newfound friendship, but the romance came crashing down in an instant.

The first shot rang out, shattering the tranquil hum of the restaurant with a deafening blast. Laura's lead bodyguard took the first hit. Something so powerful it tore his upper body from his legs, blood and tissue spraying violently across the restaurant's glass windows.

The sickening red splatter, sending the patrons inside into panicked screams, their voices rising in a cacophony of terror.

Before she could process the horror, the guard inside—just to her left—collapsed, his chest obliterated by another round. Blood pooled around his lifeless body, mixing with the metallic tang in the air, the scent mingling with the cooked food in the background. Laura's heart pounded, her breath coming in sharp gasps as the world around her descended into chaos.

Then Marsal sprang into action. Instinctively, he grabbed her, pulling her from her seat with a fierce grip, his arms around her waist as he shoved her toward the back of the restaurant. "Run!" he shouted, the urgency in his voice slicing through the panic.

They bolted into the kitchen, dodging overturned pots and pans, the clatter of metal hitting the floor adding to the pandemonium. Flames burst from abandoned stoves, the acrid smell of smoke filling the air. Laura's heart raced, her feet barely keeping pace with Marsal as they crashed through the back door into the cold alleyway.

The night air was a shock to her system, cutting through the adrenaline flooding her veins. Shadows enveloped the alley, with only the weak glow of a flickering neon sign breaking the darkness. The distant gunfire echoed in her ears, growing faint as they fled deeper into the night. But it wasn't over. They weren't safe yet.

Protective and determined, Marsal pulled her behind a stack of crates, pressing her against the cold brick wall. "We need to get to my hotel," he whispered, breathless but certain. "It's just a few blocks from here. Stay with me."

Laura nodded. Her breath ragged. Fingers trembling in a mixture of fear and rage as they hovered over the gun concealed in her handbag. As footsteps echoed in the distance, she pulled the weapon from her bag, the weight of it familiar, comforting. She spotted the first assailant emerging from the shadows, creeping toward them, his gun drawn. Without a second thought, she raised her HK USP Tactical and fired.

The assailant crumpled to the ground, blood pooling beneath his body.

At almost the same moment, Marsal had drawn his FNX-45 Tactical from a rear holster, turning swiftly to take out another attacker from behind a corner. His shot rang out, sharp and deadly, the man falling instantly.

They moved quickly, darting from one dark hiding place to the next, their steps in sync as they navigated the maze of the back alley. Every sound felt amplified—the distant wail of sirens, the hurried footsteps of those hunting them, the pounding of their own hearts. Sweat dripped down their skin, their breaths shallow and urgent, but they pressed on. The world had become a battlefield.

Finally, they reached the hotel—its façade casting long shadows in the moonlight. They slipped into an alcove, hidden from sight. The moon hung high above them, casting an eerie glow over the alley. Marsal stood close to her, pressing her against the wall, the tension in the air keeping their bodies barely separated. His chest rose and fell rapidly against her back, their guns still drawn, the metallic taste of fear lingering in her mouth.

For a moment, they were still—both catching their breath, their hearts hammering in unison. His breath was warm against her neck, mingling with the frigid night air. "Creo que todo esta bien." Laura turned slightly, their eyes meeting, and in that single glance, everything shifted. The adrenaline, the fear, the overwhelming rush of surviving together — it all twisted into something else. Something primal.

"Que bonita." He leaned in, and she met him halfway. Their lips collided in a kiss that was anything but gentle. It was fierce, urgent, filled with the raw need to feel alive after teetering on the edge of death. Her fingers tangled in his hair, pulling him closer, as his hands gripped her hips, pressing her against the wall. Their bodies were slick with perspiration, the heat between them undeniable, and their breath came in ragged, hungry gasps as they devoured each other.

The world faded away—there was no war, no death, no fear. Just the two of them, bound by passion and survival, their kiss deepening with every passing second. It was a kiss filled with lust, with desperation, and an unspoken promise that no matter what came next, they would fight for each other. His hands roamed her body, their need palpable, as the moonlight bathed them in its icy glow, a stark contrast to the fire burning between them.

As their relationship blossomed over the years following that night in Bejing, so did their dreams. They planned a future that balanced their careers and their love for each other. He supported her political ambitions, and she encouraged his scientific pursuits. They were partners in every sense until the allure of becoming more than human tore them apart. His decision to undergo the transformation had left her feeling betrayed and alone. She couldn't understand his willingness to sacrifice his humanity for the promise of something she saw as wrong.

Breath by breath, her throat felt like it was closing with the thoughts of the Feminist Army declaring war. Her decision, the votes cast, and now bombs and bullets from her militia, would take the lives of the opposition. Men and women would die.

Laura took a deep breath, trying to calm the storm inside her. She walked back to the piano, letting her fingers rest on the smooth ivory keys. The music had always been her refuge, a way to express her emotions and find clarity. She played again, the melody of Ey Iran filling the room. It was a patriotic anthem, embodying national pride and heritage.

She closed the piano lid softly, the last echoes of Ey Iran lingering in the air. The concert later was an important milestone. It was not just about music; it was about making a statement, rallying support, and showing the world that her resolve was unbreakable.

Laura moved to her desk, where stacks of notes and plans lay organized but daunting. She took another sip of Aragh Sagi, letting the warmth infuse her with a momentary sense of calm. Her communicator buzzed with a message from Noelle, confirming the last details for tomorrow's meeting. Everything was in place.

The shootout between the gender-organized militia still haunted her thoughts. Eighty-three lives lost, including five women. This violence was a direct consequence of the societal upheavals they were navigating. Laura knew that controlling this chaos required more than just tactical prowess; it required winning the hearts and minds of the people.

She opened her laptop and began typing, crafting a message to her Feminist Militia leadership. Her words needed to inspire, to reassure them that their sacrifices were not in vain.

Comrades,

Our world is at a crossroads, and we are the vanguard of a movement that will define the future. Dr. Victor Lang's appearance on The World Show was a repugnant reminder of the danger to our cause, and it also highlighted the fierce resistance we face.

The tragic loss of eighty-three lives in the recent shootout is a somber reminder of the stakes and the advancing enemies. We mourn the loss of our five sisters, and we honor their memory by doubling our resolve.

Tomorrow's recital is more than a performance; it is a beacon of hope and resilience. I urge you all to attend, either in person or through the EcoSphere, and to use this moment to strengthen our unity. Fear and violence will not deter us. Our mission is just, and our purpose is clear. Together, we ensure that the meek, led by women, inherit the Earth.

In solidarity, Laura Benton

She sent the message and leaned back, closing her eyes for a moment. The mass of outing her true ambition, her tough leadership, was otherwise crippling, but she carried it with tested and seasoned pride and determination. Laura knew that each action she took, every word she spoke, had the power to influence the course of history.

The piano recital will be her chance to reach them, to speak to their hearts through the music. Each piece she had chosen was deliberate, each note carefully crafted to convey her message. She would play with all the passion and intensity she could muster, using her art to touch souls and inspire action.

Laura turned back to her small shrine and lit an incense cone. The flickering smoke rising was a symbol of her undying hope and resilience. She knelt and placed her hands together, whispering, "For you, Mother. For you, Father. For you, my love. Ahura Mazda, guide me."

She stared at her reflection in the window and called Dr. Lang. The device rang, a sound that seemed to echo her own rising anticipation and dread.

"Hello, Dr. Benton. I'm glad you called," Victor said.

"Tell me about the Boundrin Creator, Victor. What the hell are you up to?"

Chapter Five: The Recital

Long before the piano recital event, Dr. Laura Benton meticulously researched the best concert halls on Earth. She had found one in Starzel that struck her as matching the prestige of Carnegie Hall—a place where the pioneers of Feminism had once risen to prominence. Her excitement mounted as she neared the venue. This was her first trip to California. The Walt Disney Concert Hall in Los Angeles, with its stainless-steel exterior gleaming against the city's skyline, stood as a testament to twentieth century architectural and acoustic perfection. The hall's state-of-the-art design made it one of the most acoustically advanced in the world, drawing performers from across the globe. Yet, what captivated Laura was its intimate seating arrangement for 2,265 people, offering both grandeur and closeness, the perfect setting for her performance.

On the night of the recital, as Laura arrived on stage, the scent of clean fabric and fresh flowers filled the air, mixing with the distant rumble of a storm rolling over Los Angeles. The taste of Lagavulin, which she had sipped backstage, still lingered on her tongue, grounding her amidst the electrifying anticipation of the night. Every step toward the piano felt measured, each beat of her heart echoing the storm outside.

Laura had always used her body as a living canvas, a statement for the complexities of her life. Since graduating with a PhD in oncology, she had adorned herself with tattoos that were extreme in their detail, remarkable in their intricacy, and almost hypnotic in their allure. These weren't mere images—they were pieces of art that demanded the viewer's attention, each miniature scene meticulously layered to draw the eye deeper into its labyrinth.

From a distance, her body appeared like a kaleidoscope of colors and shapes, but upon closer inspection, the art revealed its haunting narrative: demons tortured women caught in the clutches of sinister forces, shadows consuming light in a twisted horrific dance. These tattoos told a story, one of internal struggle, deception, and a dark, unrelenting battle with the world she saw around her. The grotesque and beautiful images within the tattoos shifted and blended as she moved, the figures seeming to hide within one another. Her tattoos were her armor, a living chronicle of the pain she and all women since the beginning of time had endured and the dark visions etched into her soul.

Laura intended for the tattoos to serve as both a shield and a weapon, allowing her to wear her past, her pain, and her mission on her skin. However, those who did not understand their true meaning found them shrouded in mystery. Vivid, swirling colors and dark, foreboding images covered every inch of her skin, creating a stark contrast between her outward appearance as a refined pianist, a world leader and media celebrity, and her inner turmoil and determination.

The cameras locked in, capturing the breathtaking scene unfolding on stage. Every screen across the globe illuminated with the image of Dr. Laura Benton, her bare, ink-covered body displayed under the stark stage lights. Within seconds, the television anchor's voice filled the airwaves, seamlessly guiding viewers through the surreal moment.

"Ladies and gentlemen," he began, his voice smooth yet reverent, "what you are witnessing is far more than a performance. Dr. Laura Benton, once the Prime Minister of the World Liberty Congress and visionary leader, has just discarded not only her gown but the conventional boundaries of identity and power. Her body, adorned with exquisite, intricate artwork, now stands before us as a living tapestry—a chronicle of her past, her pain, and her relentless pursuit of a future that challenges everything we think we know about ourselves."

The camera zoomed closer, lingering on the swirling designs etched across her skin, vivid images that seemed to come alive under the spotlight. "These tattoos, far from mere ornamentation, are a relic and placeholder to Dr. Benton's journey. Each color, each symbol, woven into the very fabric of her flesh, speaks to the battles she has fought, the scars she carries, and the mission that drives her forward. This is not the unveiling of her body—it is the unveiling of her soul." The anchor paused, letting the significance of the moment sink in, before continuing, "Tonight, this concert hall transforms into more than a venue for music—it becomes a global stage for defiance, for courage, for a new way of thinking about power, art, and humanity itself. Dr. Benton, standing here as both leader and artist, reminds us that sometimes the greatest weapon we have is our vulnerability. In this moment, she is both warrior and masterpiece, merging the lines between art and rebellion, leaving the world transfixed."

As Laura turned and approached the piano, the audience erupted once more with applause. The cameras zoomed in on her hands poised over the keys, but the anchor's voice lingered in the minds of millions: "The world may never forget this night, for it is rare that we witness not only history but the embodiment of change itself."

Taking her position on the piano bench, she played the opening piece, "Morghe Sahar" (Dawn Bird), sung by the artists and singing phenomena of the day. Meanwhile, the cameras swept over Laura's body, revealing the intricate portrait for the world to see.

Upper Body

Her right shoulder, where the tattoo TMSITE was etched, featured a scene of demons with elongated limbs and twisted expressions, symbolizing the corrupting influence of power and deceit. The surrounding area showed women in various states of agony, their faces contorted in silent screams, representing the suffering caused by men in power.

Arms

Laura's arms were a blend of intricate patterns and chilling depictions. One arm showcased a spiral of figures, each one more grotesque than the last, trapped in a nightmarish dance of torture and manipulation. The other arm featured scenes of betrayal and anguish, with shadowy figures lurking in the background, eyes glowing with malice.

Back

Her back was a sprawling mural of chaos and torment. A central figure, a demonic overlord with wings outstretched, dominated the scene, surrounded by writhing female bodies in various forms of torture. This image was a stark representation of the oppressive forces Laura fought against, both externally in the world and internally within her mind.

Chest and Torso

The chest and torso were a palimpsest of pain and resilience. These dark images portrayed demons inflicting suffering while also intertwining symbols of resistance and strength. Hidden within the chaos were subtle motifs of women giving birth and nursing babies and children, suggesting that even in the darkest of times, there was a spark of defiance.

Legs

Her legs depicted a descent into the abyss, with figures falling into dark, bottomless pits, their expressions frozen in terror. This imagery signified the downward spiral Laura feared for women in a male-dominated humanity if her mission failed. Yet, near her ankles, the scenes showed a glimmer of light and redemption, hinting at the possibility of salvation and a brighter future.

Hands and Feet

The ink nor the camera didn't spare even her hands and feet. On her fingers, as they danced over the keys, were small, intricate designs symbolizing control and manipulation, reflecting her own strategies and plans. She adorned her feet with symbols of stability and endurance, grounding her tumultuous journey.

Face

Her face was a myriad of tear-filled eyes, each one reflecting a different aspect of her sorrow and determination. The eyes told silent tales of loss, suffering, and unwavering resolve, making her visage both haunting and captivating. They served as a reminder that despite the horrors etched into her skin, Laura's spirit remained unbroken, her vision undeterred.

Laura's tattoos were more than just art; they were a visual manifestation of women's lives, missions, and the inner demons they battled daily. Though grotesque and horrifying, each image was a step in her path toward achieving a world where the meek survive and thrive in peace. Her body thus became a powerful chronicle of her resilience, her vision, and the complex duality of existence.

Her playlist for the evening was a compilation of Iranian musical classics, interpreted through the rich and expressive medium of the piano, representing a heartfelt message from Iran to the world. Each piece was a tribute to the enduring spirit, cultural heritage, and the profound emotional landscape of the Iranian people.

Playlist:

- "Morghe Sahar" (Dawn Bird)—A traditional Persian song, often adapted for various instruments, including the piano. Accompanied by Leyla Amini on vocal.

- "Gol-e Gandom" (Wheat Flower)—A famous folk song with deep roots in Persian culture.

- "Soltane Ghalbha" (King of Hearts)—A classic love song that resonates deeply in Iranian popular culture. Accompanied by Dariush Esfandiari on vocal.

- "Ey Iran"—A patriotic anthem, embodying national pride and heritage.

- "Baroon Barooneh" (It's Raining)—A beloved song often associated with nostalgia and cultural memory.

- "Bahar" (Spring)—Celebrating the Persian New Year (Nowruz), this piece is full of joy and renewal.

- "Kojaei" (Where Are You?)—A melancholic yet beautiful piece reflecting longing and separation. Accompanied by Shirin Rahmani on vocal.

- "Shabe Mahtab" (Moonlit Night)—A romantic and evocative classic often performed in various arrangements. Accompanied by Arash Khodadadi on vocal.

- "Raghs-e Shotor" (Dance of the Camel)—A traditional piece with a rhythmic and engaging melody.

- "Azari" (Azeri)—Reflecting the rich Azerbaijani influence within Iranian culture, often performed with vibrant energy.

Before the final song began, noises and a commotion backstage filled Walt Disnet Concert Hall with immediate tension. Raised voices echoed through the back halls, and the hurried footsteps of security guards reverberated like distant thunder. The air, once calm, turned electric. Several armed security personnel rushed to the stage, forming a protective perimeter around Dr. Laura Benton, their weapons drawn, scanning the room for any threat. Through the labyrinth of equipment and shadows, more security darted toward the source of the disturbance, their coms crackling with frantic updates.

The muffled chaos continued to escalate, and even the crew, usually invisible and calm in their professionalism, were on edge, their eyes darting toward the corridor where the noise originated. On stage, the MC, trying desperately to maintain a sense of order, adjusted the microphone with trembling hands. His voice, though steady, carried an unmistakable note of unease as he addressed the audience.

"Ladies and gentlemen, please remain seated. We will continue the program shortly," he announced, his words met with a murmur of confusion rippling through the audience, uncertainty hanging thick in the air.

Suddenly, from the back of the hall, a figure emerged from the shadows and strode confidently toward the stage. The tension in the room spiked as the audience collectively held its breath. Amy Goodman—the infamous leader of propaganda for the World Liberty Congress—appeared at center stage, cutting through the tension like a spotlight at midnight.

Her arrival sent a ripple of disbelief through the concert hall. Dr. Laura Benton stood frozen, her eyes widening in shock as recognition dawned. Her hands instinctively covered her mouth, a mixture of surprise and excitement lighting her features. The commotion backstage seemed to melt away, all eyes locking onto the two women as they embraced in front of the packed hall.

Security forces returned to their stations. Like a soft whisper and shadows in the night, they disappeared back into their positions. The danger resolved.

The audience, sensing the gravity of the moment, began a slow, hesitant applause, a few scattered claps that soon swelled into a thunderous ovation. The delight of the world seemed to hover in that singular, suspended moment.

Amy stepped forward, her commanding presence undeniable as the microphone boom descended from above, her voice cutting through the applause with calm authority. "Good evening, everyone," she began, her tone measured yet charged with urgency. "And to the world, good evening—or whatever time it may be where you are."

The room fell into a profound silence, each person hanging on her every word as she continued, "This beautiful composition of Iranian folk music played for us by Dr. Benton tonight, the brilliance of her talent on display, serves as a reminder of how much she has already given to the world. We are all aware of her exceptional gifts, her intelligence, and the profound ways in which her abilities have bettered our lives." Amy paused, letting the significance of her words sink into the audience like the retreat of a slow-moving fog.

"But I am not here to lecture, nor to remind us of the debt we owe her," Amy added, her voice softening to an almost pleading tone. "I am here with a plea—for her to return to the World Liberty Congress. The world is on the brink. We need her. The world needs her help."

Amy Goodman paused, her eyes locking onto Laura's, the words hanging in the air. The audience, now silent, felt the surprise in the excitement of the moment.

"Laura," Amy continued, her voice resonating with a rare blend of authority and warmth, "the beauty of your music tonight has moved us all. But beyond these walls, a world in turmoil awaits. A world where the scars of our gender divide run deep, and the cries for equality and justice grow louder each day. Your talent has the power to heal, to inspire, but it is your courage and intellect that the world desperately needs now."

She stepped closer to Laura, her hand outstretched, a gesture of both request and solidarity. "We stand at the precipice of a new era, where we must let go of the remnants of old prejudices and construct a harmonious future. I ask you, not just as a friend, but as a representative of the World Liberty Congress, to lead us once more. Lead a team to research, to forge the path forward, and establish the means to end this gender war once and for all."

Amy's voice rose with conviction, echoing through the concert hall. Cameras froze on each of them, alternating the broadcast image. "The task is monumental, but so is your strength. The world needs a leader who can navigate these treacherous waters with wisdom and compassion. Laura Benton, will you accept this mantle? Will you help us shape a future where gender distinctions are not chains, but the colors of our diverse humanity?"

The audience erupted into applause, the sound a thunderous affirmation of Amy's plea. Laura stood there, her body a canvas of pain and resilience, her heart beating in sync with the hopeful rhythm of the crowd's applause. She took a deep breath, knowing that her answer would change the course of history.

As Laura's fingers danced over the piano keys, she sat to play the last song as the melody of "Azari" filled the hall, vibrant and pulsating with the rich values of Azerbaijani and Iranian heritage. Each note seemed to carry the weight of her thoughts, the music a conduit for the swirling storm of decisions within her mind. Her eyes remained closed, her body moving in perfect harmony with the piano, yet her mind was far away, grappling with the monumental choice before her.

Meanwhile, Amy Goodman had exited the stage, leaving Laura alone to face the crescendo of her performance and the storm of her inner conflict.

Could Dr. Benton turn her back on the Feminist militia? Having received a unanimous vote to declare war only hours ago. Or could she somehow merge the World Liberty Congress and the militia into a single cohesive force?

Remaining spellbound, the audience continued to stand. The beauty of the music, the rawness of Laura's artistry, and the anticipation of her decision held them in rapt attention. The final chords of "Azari" resonated through the hall, the last note lingering in the air like a breath held in suspense.

Laura's eyes opened slowly, the intensity of her unflinching gaze meeting the expectant faces before her. She tied the robe over her shoulder and around her inked neck. As she stood, the room seemed to hold its breath, the compass of the world on her slender, inked shoulders.

She looked out at the audience, her jaw clenched, the magnitude of the task ahead etched into her features. The silence was profound, the moment heavy with significance. Finally, she nodded, her expression steely with determination.

"Yes," she said, her voice clear and unwavering. "I will accept the assignment and end the killing and the war of genders on Planet Earth."

The hall erupted into applause, a deafening roar of approval and hope. The world outside waited with bated breath, the message of her acceptance spreading like wildfire through the global networks. Dr. Laura Benton, with her extraordinary talent and indomitable spirit, had taken up the mantle once more, stepping into the breach to lead humanity toward a future where the divisions of the past would be no more.

Chapter Six: Above The Rim

The day of the recital, 16:20 PM

The recent purchase and renaming of Starlink Center in San Antonio was a cauldron of tension and excitement, with 80,000 fans packed into the arena, creating an electrifying atmosphere that sparked with anticipation. The roar of the crowd was a living entity, a wave of sound surging and receding, fueled by the pounding bass of the warm-up music reverberating off the rafters. Every corner of the stadium buzzed with energy, from cheerleaders launching shirts and hats into the stands to vendors hawking drinks and food, their calls blending into the chaotic symphony of the night.

The excitement in the stadium was electric, rumors spread in urgent whispers: Dr. Lang's bio-enhanced humans had infiltrated the NBA. Illegal for players and coaches alike, bio-enhancements should have had no place here, yet the conspiracy theories multiplied. Fans traded anxious glances, recounting stories of athletes with inhuman reflexes, unnatural recoveries from devastating injuries, and movements that defied belief. Some swore they'd seen eyes glinting a shade too bright, muscle tone too defined, and game records broken with a precision that felt chillingly flawless.

"Have you seen the way he moves?" One fan muttered to another. "That's not normal—he's got to be one of Lang's hybrids."

"I heard they're testing them, but it's all under the radar," another whispered, glancing nervously at the holographic Starlink ads glowing above. "No one's gonna say it out loud, but we all know something's up."

Although rigorous testing protocols were in place, and league officials publicly denied any involvement with Neurotech enhancements, the rumors persisted. Conspiracies demanded more stringent testing, with some claiming that Lang's creations could seamlessly bypass the leagues outdated detection methods. Fans weren't just there for basketball anymore—they came to watch for the next potential controversy, speculating about which players might already be altered.

The Starlink Center loomed, casting its high-tech glow across the city like a beacon. Once celebrated as a hub for sports and entertainment, it had since morphed into a focal point of unease. The arena's vast, automated surveillance flickered from one enhanced player to another, while fans, oblivious to the ever-present scrutiny, came to cheer their team to victory.

Beneath the surface, however, everything was shifting. Neurohuman athletes moved with a precision too sharp, too flawless—striking an uneasy contrast against their human counterparts. Spectators couldn't know it, but the air hummed with anticipation and tension, as if each game, each elimination, was one step closer to the inevitable clash of human versus enhanced.

The familiar smells of popcorn, hot dogs, and nachos mingled with the sharp tang of sweat and the faint scent of the rubberized court. Intermingled with these timeless stadium scents was the pungent, earthy aroma of marijuana drifting in subtle waves from the stands. New, high-potency vape strains added sweet, fruity notes to the sensory mix, their faint haze creating a heady backdrop to the electric atmosphere. It was a hometown vibe, complete with contact-highs infused with euphoria, yet emphasized by an undercurrent of something darker—a tension that rifled through the air.

Above the din of the crowd, towering, draconian armed security robots patrolled the concourse, their glowing red optics scanning the fans. Standing at eight feet tall, their mechanical limbs and metallic bodies cast eerie reflections under the fluorescent lights. The robots' presence reminded everyone of the new era: order must be maintained at all costs. Alongside them, human security guards, equally imposing in their black uniforms, moved with cold precision, watching the crowd for any hint of disruption.

Prior to her early retirement, Dr. Laura Benton, for fifteen years while leading The World Liberty Congress, put forward many feminist advancing laws and changes to society. But men's sports were always an obstacle for her. Each time she tried to end them in favor of women's sports, her attempt failed. Everyone seemed to want men's basketball more than woman's and men's soccer, etcetera. Her team tried to invent new sports for women so they didn't have to copy men's sports or try to compete with men. But in the end she resorted all her attempts to stifle men's sports with draconian regulations. But no matter how much she tried to make it not fun, people still preferred men's sports.

As always happens at these events, the air shifted when a fan in section 302 began hurling violent, slurred words at the Cavaliers' bench. Within moments, one of the security robots, well timed and perfect execution of mechanical motion and silent, zoned in on her. Its sensors detecting the escalating aggression. Without warning, a crackling sound echoed as the robot extended a taser, sending volts of electricity surging through the unruly fan. The woman collapsed, convulsing briefly before being dragged from her seat by a pair of guards. Her stunned friends helpless to intervene.

Further up, in the nosebleed section, two fans erupted into a physical fight, punches flying over spilled beer and crushed nachos. The audience barely had time to react before two more robotic enforcers closed in. One tasered the first offender while the other restrained the second, their movements coldly efficient. Security hauled away the aggressors, their shouts quickly drowned out by the crowd as security escorted them out of the stadium. They will likely be banned from attending future games.

This wasn't an isolated event. Throughout the Starlink Center, the scene repeated itself. Any display of violence or disruptive behavior was swiftly and ruthlessly quashed, a reminder to all that the game could be passionate, but not chaotic. The armed robots and their human counterparts ensured that tension wouldn't spill into an uncontrollable frenzy, their presence a looming threat to anyone who dared step out of line.

Still, for those not on the receiving end of the draconian enforcement typical of Texarkana, the air remained dense with excitement. Every practice shot, every dribble carried the weight of a season. But the underlying threat of control, of order being maintained by these robotic enforcers, added a dystopian edge to the otherwise electric environment. This wasn't just a game; it was a glimpse into the future—where technology kept a tight grip on society, and moments of passion were closely monitored, swiftly crushed if they crossed the line.

This was more than a championship battle. A game played under the shadow of authoritarian control, where even joy and fury had limits enforced by cold, unfeeling machines employed by the wealthy elite. The announcer's voice boomed through the speakers, a deep baritone that added to the sense of gravity. "Ladies and gentlemen, welcome to game five of the NBA semi-finals! Tonight, your San Antonio Spurs in a must-win game, face off against the Cleveland Cavaliers. Let's make some noise!"

The response was immediate—a wall of sound that rattled the arena to its core. Excitement and raw desperation battled for dominance, making the energy volatile. The crowd roared, but there was an undercurrent of something darker—anxiety, fear. It gripped everyone in the building. This game felt like a last stand.

On the court, the Spurs players exchanged glances, eyes hard with silent determination. They knew this was it—do or die. The roar of the crowd pressed down on them, the desired expectations of an entire city on their shoulders. But something in the air made everything feel sharper, more dangerous. The armed security robots at the edges of the stands, scanning the crowd, created a tension that ran deeper than just the game. One wrong move, one burst of anger from the fans, and the robots would act without hesitation.

The stakes weren't just on the court. A world at war on every front. Fear rippled through the seats. Everyone was one step away from boiling over, and the sense that everything could break—here, tonight—hung in the air like an unspoken threat.

For the Spurs, for their fans, the game was survival. But the danger that lingered just beneath the surface made it feel like something far worse.

Victor Lang sat courtside, just behind the Spurs' bench, his eyes sharp and calculating. The chaos of the arena—roaring fans, pounding drums—barely registered. Victor's eyes were glued to Coach Sam, who was huddling with his team, furiously sketching last-minute plays. Victor had spent years perfecting the art of reading lips, and while the cacophony drowned out the coach's voice, he deciphered the hurried adjustments, the desperation in each command. But what Victor truly noticed wasn't the strategy. It was the coach's face—the tightness in his jaw; the doubt buried beneath the mask of determination. He could sense the coach's fear, the uncertainty clawing at him from within.

Victor, however, felt none of that. His focus shifted to the visitor's tunnel, where Eli Johnson emerged, moving through the dim corridor like a predator stalking its prey. Eli's eyes found Victor's immediately, and in that instant, a mutual nod passed between them—a gesture loaded with history, trust, and a shared understanding of what lay beneath the surface of this game. Eli was not just another NBA star. He was Victor's creation.

As Eli approached, Victor's mind flashed back to the day it all began, years before Eli became a phenomenon. He had been just another rising star then, with raw talent but a body broken by relentless injuries. It was in those fragile moments—when hope seemed lost—that Victor had introduced Eli to the world of enhancement through voluntary transformation. The lab was sterile, cold, as Victor explained the process that would make Eli more than human. The first implant was small, barely noticeable beneath the skin, but it set off a chain reaction inside Eli's body, knitting together torn ligaments and rebuilding muscle faster than any natural recovery could accomplish.

Eli had returned to the court after that, and what followed was a miracle. His performances defied logic. He shattered records, made plays that seemed impossible, and his recovery from near-career-ending injuries had become the stuff of legends. The media hailed it as dedication and perseverance, but Victor and Eli knew better.

Victor recalled one game in particular. Eli's first after the transformative bio enhancements. The world watched as Eli tore down the court, faster than he'd ever been, his movements almost too fluid, too precise. That night, he broke five records in one game. Victor, in his lab, had rebuilt Eli's body, each operation making him a new kind of human—a fact unknown to the world. A transhuman, capable of feats the average player could never hope to achieve.

Now, as Eli approached, the triumphs of their shared secret hung in the air between them. Eli wasn't just here to watch the game; he was a living testament to Victor's vision for the future. A future where humans, enhanced with biotechnology, could outpace, outfight, and outlast any natural competition.

Victor's attention snapped back to the present, watching as Eli took a seat next to him on the sidelines. The game on the court seemed almost irrelevant compared to the larger game they were playing. Eli's nod wasn't just a greeting; it was a signal. They both understood the stakes of the situation—the delicate balance between pushing the limits of human evolution and the risks of exposure.

The crowd's roar ebbed and flowed, the sounds of the arena a chaotic madhouse. Victor's senses were heightened, every detail around him etched into his memory.

Coach Sam finished his final instructions, clapping a hand on the shoulder of one of his players before turning away, his expression grim. Victor's eyes followed him, noting the tight set of his shoulders and the resigned slump in his posture. The coach's doubt was a silent specter, hanging over the team like a dark cloud.

As the clock ticked down to game time, Coach Sam approached Victor and Eli, the tension in his face only barely hidden by a stoic front. The roar of the arena faded just for a moment, the din of 80,000 fans simmering to background noise as the three men stood together, linked by more than just the upcoming game.

Eli, dressed in civilian clothes, wasn't playing tonight. His team, the New York Knicks, had already advanced. Eli was here to support his husband. He reached out, clasping Coach Sam's hand in a firm grip, their eyes locking on a silent exchange that spoke of trust and something more intimate. The look between them was quick, but carried the experiences of countless battles fought together, both on and off the court.

"Take it to them early and don't let them breathe, Coach," Victor said, his voice steady but firm, always the strategist. His gaze shifted between them, knowing that, despite the stakes, this game wasn't only about basketball. It was about Sam, about Eli, and the connection they shared, both of them moving in a world Victor desired to reshape.

Coach Sam nodded, his tension easing just a little as he drew strength from the familiar presence of Eli and Victor. "We will," he replied, his voice resolute but laced with the weight of the moment. "We'll give it everything." But the look in Sam's eyes said more. He didn't just want to win this game—he needed to, for reasons that went beyond the scoreboard.

Eli gave a nod so discreet it was unnoticed by all but the most discerned observer, stepping closer to Sam, their hands still clasped, lingering in the moment of calm before the storm. "You've got this," Eli said softly, offering more than just encouragement. He was the rock that kept Sam grounded, the one who knew him better than anyone. "Play it like you always do. Aggressive, early. Don't give them a second to catch up."

Sam's eyes flickered with the weight of his husband's words. He nodded, squeezing Eli's hand once more before turning his focus back to the court. "You'll see what we're made of," he said, his voice carrying just enough confidence to mask the nerves gnawing at him. The sport was their zest for life, the nerves and adrenaline were their life's blood. He walked back toward the bench, his shoulders squaring as he shouted instructions to the team.

Victor watched the exchange with a keen eye. Though Eli wasn't playing tonight, his presence was undeniable. He could see the way Sam pulled strength from his husband, and Victor respected that. The man sitting next to him wasn't just a top-tier NBA player—he was the lifeline that kept Sam grounded in the madness of this high-stakes world.

As Coach Sam walked away, Eli turned to Victor. "He'll do what needs to be done," Eli said, his tone calm. "He always does."

Victor nodded. "He's a fighter. But the game's bigger than just tonight, Eli."

Eli glanced at his husband again as Sam rallied the team, his voice blending with the roar of the crowd. "I know. But tonight, it's about him."

Victor leaned back, his eyes scanning the arena. "For now," he muttered, his thoughts already running past the game.

Eli settled into his seat beside Victor, his focus on the man he loved as Sam squared his shoulders, preparing to lead the Spurs in their do-or-die moment. Whatever happened on that court, Eli knew Sam wouldn't go down without a fight.

Victor's pride and ambition for Eli's future were always simmering beneath the surface, but tonight, as the game unfolded, a darker current of apprehension churned within him. The truth about Eli's bio-enhancements hung like a guillotine, waiting to drop. If it ever came to light, everything would unravel—Eli's dominance on the court, Victor's carefully calculated plans, the control he'd worked so hard to maintain. But that day hadn't come yet. For now, Eli was safe, and his athletic feats remained unmatched, sparking awe and reverence from those who were none the wiser.

That day will come, Victor reminded himself, when the truth breaks free. When he no longer has to hide behind the veil of secrecy. When men would finally rise and take back their lost dominion—when they would break the curse that had shackled them for millennia. Paradise Lost would be completed, not by the hand of divine justice, but by Victor Lang's hand, by his bio-enhanced vision of man's true potential. Men, no longer slaves to a natural order dictated by the past, would evolve beyond their weaknesses, beyond their suffering. Victor's eyes flicked to the court. The game was tightening—every point counted, every second mattered. But this, too, was only a part of the plan. Victor's testing ground was the sports world, a key to the future. Bio-enhanced athletes like Eli would soon break through every record, shatter every ceiling, and push human achievement into realms never imagined. But tonight's focus wasn't on Eli or records; it was on survival. On the Spurs, and on, a far more immediate threat looming in the distance. The war declared by the feminist militia.

The first half of the game had been a brutal tug-of-war, but in the last five minutes, the Cavaliers had unleashed a run that left the Spurs gasping. A gap had opened, one that felt insurmountable as the players trudged into the locker rooms, their faces a mirror of the crowd's growing tension. The air in the arena was thick, not just with perspiration and adrenaline, but with the kind of collective fear that seizes a city when hope slips through its fingers.

Then, the screens above center court flickered. The sound of the game faded, replaced by a somber voice. The crowd fell into stunned silence as Amy Goodman appeared on screen, standing at the Walt Disney Concert Hall, her face grave.

***

Victor's pulse quickened. He knew what this was—he'd been expecting it, dreading it. Laura Benton. The woman whose very existence was a threat to everything Victor had built.

"Ladies and gentlemen," Amy began, her voice cutting through the charged atmosphere, "we interrupt this broadcast for an urgent announcement. We are requesting Dr. Laura Benton, a pivotal figure in global leadership, to return to the World Liberty Congress.

Victor's stomach clenched. Laura Benton, the woman who had stood in his way for years. She was more than just an opponent. She was a force—a leader whose vision for the world directly opposed his own. To her, bio-enhancements were not an advancement but a dangerous perversion of humanity. Her influence was vast, and her return to power could spell disaster for Victor's plans. She'd always championed a feminist vision of the future—one where natural evolution, guided by women, would lead humanity. A world where Victor's vision—his transhumans, his dream of reshaping the world—would be destroyed.

The screen shifted to show a nude Laura walking to the piano at center stage. The crowd in the arena fell into a hushed silence, as if caught in her spell. Her fingers brushed the keys, producing a haunting melody that reverberated through the space, a chilling contrast to the violent, frenzied atmosphere of the game. Even the players returning from the locker rooms for the second half paused, mesmerized by the performance unfolding on the screen above them.

Victor's mind raced. Laura's return was a catastrophe in the making. Her influence was global, her convictions ironclad. She wouldn't stop at philosophical opposition—she would fight to dismantle everything he'd created. And with her back in power, she had the means to do it. Bio-enhanced athletes, his technological breakthroughs, Eli—everything was now at risk.

The last note from Laura's piano hung in the air, a haunting reminder of the stakes. Amy Goodman returned to the screen, her voice solemn as she spoke. "Dr. Benton, the world awaits your decision."

Then Laura stood, her eyes sweeping over the audience, and delivered the words Victor had dreaded.

"Yes," she said, her voice clear and unwavering. "I will accept the assignment and end the killing and the war of genders on Planet Earth."

The arena erupted into applause, but Victor's hands remained frozen in his lap. The screen flickered back to the NBA logo. Returning to the court, the players sensed the world had just shifted beneath their feet. Dr. Victor Lang knew it had. Laura's return was a declaration of war on his empire.

As the ball was tipped to start the second half, Victor felt the weight of impending battle settle on his chest. This game, this moment—it was just one skirmish in a much larger war. One that would decide the future of humanity itself.

He leaned back in his seat, eyes cold and calculating. Laura's influence, her control, could threaten everything. But Victor wasn't going to let her win. The battle for the future had begun, and he would do whatever it took to ensure the future of humanity bent to his vision. He would need transhuman generals.

The game raged on before him, but Victor's mind was already in motion. Calculating. Planning. Preparing for the war that was coming.

With her back in control of World Liberty Congress means his actions to capture the 44 will have to happen sooner rather than later.

Three Months into The One Year Position
10:00 AM

The gavel in her hand felt rigid and archaic. As she looked at it, she questioned the validity of the power it symbolized. "What a testament to where we have come from," she spoke with a tone of epiphany. "Men hammered their demands and their objectives beaten into society. Not with love nor with care, but with force and backed by systems of power and oppression."

The assembly of feminists and women activists cheered and acknowledged her display as she tossed the gavel into the rubbish. Followed by the anvil. She slid the contents on the tabletop with her left arm, sweeping everything onto the floor.

The first meeting of the World Liberty Congress appointed End Gender War task force took place in an expansive auditorium near Brussels, its grandeur reflecting the significance of the occasion. Vibrant feminist decorations adorned the walls, showcasing the movement's history and future. Banners hung high, emblazoned with slogans like "Equality for All" and "Empowerment is Now." Posters featuring prominent feminist icons from around the world stood as sentinels, their eyes seeming to watch over the proceedings with approval. The stage featured a backdrop of intertwining symbols of unity and strength, a kaleidoscope of colors that seemed to pulse with the energy of the assembled crowd.

Dr. Laura Benton stood at the podium, her presence commanding and resolute. Her hair, a cascade of meticulously styled waves, framed her face with an air of elegance and determination. With bold red lips, perfectly complementing her flawless makeup, hinted at both passion and authority. Her dress, a striking deep-blue tailored piece, hugged her form perfectly, exuding power and poise. The hemline fell just below the knee, a balance of professionalism and femininity. On her feet, she wore sleek black heels that clicked against the polished floor, each step resonating with purpose.

As she addressed the assembly, Dr. Benton's emotional state was almost tangible. Her voice, though controlled, quivered with the intensity of the moment. She had fought long and hard to reach this point, and the magnitude of that journey shone through her now. The act of throwing away the gavel symbolized a powerful rejection of the old systems of authority and control, particularly those tied to patriarchal structures that have historically oppressed and dictated societal norms.

When Laura said, "Men hammered their demands and their objectives beaten into society," she was directly addressing the violent and authoritarian legacy of patriarchy. Tossing the gavel into the rubbish bin is an intentional rejection of that tool of enforcement, signaling that the time for such rigid structures was over. By following the gavel with the anvil—another tool of force—it amplifies the message: the era of hammering and shaping society through force and coercion has ended.

The assembly of feminists and activists, responding with cheers, reflects the collective recognition that this symbolic act is more than just a gesture. It's a declaration of a future where leadership and governance are built on principles of care, inclusivity, and mutual respect, rather than hierarchical and oppressive systems. Laura's sweeping of the remaining contents from the table onto the floor further drove home the message that the entire system of control is being discarded, making way for something radically different.

The gathering erupted in cheers. The World Liberty Congress and the Feminist Militia were united as one.

Her eyes scanned the room, locking onto the faces of countless women who had gathered, each one a symbol of resilience, defiance, and the hope for change. This wasn't just another meeting—this was a revolution. The grand hall, with its high ceilings and echoing walls, seemed to breathe with the collective energy of their shared struggles and triumphs. Laura felt the ecstasy brought by this new world order. The weight of history lifting from women's shoulders. She stood taller, her resolve crystallizing into something unshakable. This was their moment, and she was ready to lead them through humanity's most radical transformation yet.

With a subtle gesture, she called for the applause to quiet, and the room buzzed with anticipation, the air thick with both tension and excitement. The scent of fresh flowers adorning the tables mingled with the faint, metallic scent of adrenalin perspiration, and the palpable thrill of what was about to unfold. Laura took a deep breath, the rise and fall of her chest mirroring the epic embarkation of the task before her. The future lay ahead—uncharted, filled with both promise and peril. She glanced at the discarded gavel, now a forgotten relic of a bygone era, and turned her focus back to the audience, her voice cutting through the air with clarity and purpose.

"In our streets, across the planet, the war rages on," she began, her hands gripping the sides of the podium with the force of her conviction. "For three years, our military has fought against the oppressive forces, and still, victory eludes us. But we are not here to declare war against men. Our message must be unified and clear: We are not here to end men."

A brief silence followed as her words sank into the room. Laura's gaze swept over the sea of faces, and her resolve was reflected back at her, etched into every steely expression that met hers. She continued, her voice unwavering.

"Let us be clear: there are, and always have been, men who love, respect, and protect women. These men have existed since the beginning of time—men who would give their lives for us, who value our existence. These men are good. These men are decent. They are the type of men the world welcomes, and their presence is vital to our shared future."

The room was hushed, but the tension in the air was electric. Then Laura's tone hardened, her voice cutting through like magma on dry grass. "But the oppressive man—that man is what we fight against. These men wrote history to suit their despotic rule, to serve their tyrannical agenda, a book of fiction and lies. They filled history with tales of women's betrayal and unworthiness, poisoning the truth. But now we stand in authenticity, and the universe has brought us full circle. It was the man who lied and created the deceptions that have condemned humanity. Today, we are free at last from the oppression of men's lies."

The chamber erupted. A tidal wave of cheers crashed against the walls, the roar of the crowd deafening, each voice rising in unison like a battle cry. The energy surged through the room, as fists were raised high, and bodies stood in solidarity. The overhead lights gleamed off banners and posters, casting the room in a warm, golden glow that seemed to embody the new era they were all so close to grasping.

When the cheers subsided, Laura stepped forward again, her voice stronger now, charged with the power of the moment. "Our mission for this task force is to end the gender war. I believe we can achieve this by defining the good man—a man who embodies respect, compassion, and strength—and establishing a lawful society that allows the good man to prosper. This task is daring, and it is long overdue."

The gender war tore the world apart, leaving shattered cities and fractured societies in its wake. With every battle, the boundaries between man, woman, and other identities blurred further. In the chaos, new weapons were developed, some targeting genetic markers related to gender. Missiles were fired not just to destroy physical structures but to wipe out ideological threats. Drones, bioweapons, and psychological warfare became common in an attempt to decimate opposing forces.

In the early years, gender itself became a battleground. Propaganda machines worked overtime, categorizing citizens not just by their political beliefs but by their gender identity or fluidity. As the conflict grew bloodier, the lines became less clear—who was a woman, who was a man, and who existed somewhere in between? Loyalties splintered. Friendships and families disintegrated under the crushing weight of the war. New genders rose, collapsed, and redefined themselves daily. Some warriors changed allegiances as often as they changed their gender identity.

The 20th through 22nd centuries witnessed a seismic shift in the very concept of gender, which had once been a relatively simple binary. As social constructs began to evolve, gender became an ever-expanding spectrum. Men could be classified as women, and women could be classified as men. Transgender identities blurred lines even further, but that was just the beginning.

By the 22nd century, the gender landscape exploded into a vast array of classifications—ELGBTQSDR, and beyond—a spectrum so wide and fragmented that a person could claim multiple gender identities simultaneously. This once theoretical expansion became the grounds for a violent and bitter cultural clash, and eventually, war.

At first, these tensions erupted in ideological skirmishes—heated debates on human rights, gender identity, and equality. But the conflicts escalated, spilling out into the streets. As factions grew more entrenched, their battles became literal. What started as localized protests turned into coordinated, violent strikes. The first casualties numbered in the dozens. Victims of targeted assassinations and strikes aimed at eradicating political opposition. The gender war had begun, and it quickly spiraled out of control.

By the 22nd century, cities became battlegrounds. Bombings, missile strikes, and tactical warfare left devastation in their wake. Skyscrapers lay in ruins, and the death toll soared—hundreds perished in each engagement. Craters and wreckage, remnants of the bitter war marked entire regions. Entire governments crumbled, their leaders caught in the crossfire, their cities divided by warring factions driven by conflicting visions of gender and power. Three major factions of the gender war emerged and soligified.

1. *The Feminist Militia*

   Born out of a fight for freedom and equality, the Feminist Militia was led by women from North America, Europe, and the United Kingdom, but the bulk of its soldiers were men—men who had rejected traditional roles and saw themselves as allies in the struggle for gender liberation. These men, driven by a fierce desire to create a world where women could flourish unimpeded by patriarchal oppression, formed a tight and loyal military force.

   The Feminist Militia employed guerrilla warfare, ambushes, and tactical strikes that left their enemies disoriented. They were strategic and precise, using speed and intelligence to their advantage, knowing that they were often outnumbered. What they lacked in brute force, they made up for with dedication and a singular, relentless goal: to dismantle the structures of male-dominated power. These strikes took the form of explosions in government buildings, kidnappings of key figures, and stealth missions to destabilize patriarchal regimes.

2. *The Male Military*

   A reactionary force, the Male Military grew from the backlash against gender progressivism. Supported by Russia, China, and the Middle East, this faction was built on preserving traditional male dominance, fighting to maintain a patriarchal order. Their soldiers, equipped with the latest technology and driven by a desire to crush the multi-gender uprising, executed brutal and merciless campaigns.

The Male Military moved in large formations, using their numbers and strength to overwhelm their enemies. They employed shock-and-awe tactics, bombing cities and obliterating opposition forces with overwhelming firepower. Their goal wasn't just victory—it was annihilation. They wanted to eradicate the very idea that women could ever claim equality, let alone power, over men. Wherever they marched, they left cities smoldering in their wake, their brutal efficiency unmatched. Battles were fought on a grand scale, often with catastrophic civilian casualties.

3. *The Family Military*

While the Feminist Militia and the Male Military battled for control of gendered power, a third force rose from the defense of traditional family values. Backed by India, South America, and Africa, the Family Military fought to preserve the structures that had defined their societies for centuries. They believed in the complementary roles of men and women within the family unit, and they fought with a fanatical devotion to protecting what they saw as the natural order of the world.

The Family Military employed more defensive tactics, holding their ground in entrenched warfare. They believed in resisting the extremes of both the feminist and patriarchal forces, aiming instead to maintain a balance rooted in traditional cultural and religious norms. Their soldiers were often religiously devout, fighting with a conviction that bordered on zealotry, believing that their way of life was worth any sacrifice. They built massive defensive fortresses and strongholds, their battles often long and bloody, marked by trenches and stalemates. They believed that their way of life—centered on family, duty, and religious order—was worth preserving at any cost.

By the middle of the 22nd century, the war had ravaged the planet, with near two billion dead, governments destroyed, and society crumbling. There were no victors. The battles between the Feminist Militia, the Male Military, and the Family Military had dragged the world to the brink of collapse. Entire regions of the globe were nothing more than wastelands, populated by remnants of the old world, struggling to survive in a landscape marked by the ghosts of what had been.

In the words of Dr. Victor Lang, as quoted by Adam Cole in his blog post about the Lang Empire: "They exiled humanity from paradise. Original sin, they called it, brought an end to man's original condition. Cast out, mankind was set adrift in a void he called the universe, condemned to pay an eternal price, floundering through the universe in search of something it couldn't name. Evolution became a desperate search for identity, a species seeking itself like a fish in the ocean searching for water—blind to the very thing it swims in.

"The gender war is the ultimate expression of that search, but it had evolved into something far greater than a battle for rights or power. It was a war for control over the most fundamental question of all: Who are we?"

The conflict that had once been about gender equality, liberation, and preservation of cultural values had spiraled into a brutal contest for control of identity itself. Man, woman, and all identities in between had their boundaries stretched, twisted, and eventually collapse. The war's bloodshed wasn't just physical—it was philosophical, a tearing a part of the seams that once held human understanding together.

***

A beautiful G800, Laura's personal jet aptly nicknamed "The Valkyrie," sat ready on the runway, gleaming under the midday sun. After the feminist meeting, Dr. Laura Benton, accompanied by her personal assistant Noelle, and three prominent political leaders, boarded the aircraft. Their flight from Brussels to Toronto was a carefully orchestrated maneuver, while in flight they would lay the groundwork for legalizing and rolling out the Good Man plan as the major step to ending the Gender War.

The jet sliced through the sky with ease, but inside the cabin, the atmosphere was thicker than the clouds they pierced. Dr. Laura Benton sat at the head of the table, her eyes locked on the surrounding women. This wasn't just a meeting. It was a battlefield of ideas. The Good Man Initiative was no longer an abstract discussion; it was about drawing blood and breaking bones—redefining a world too long bent under the weight of old expectations. Laura wasn't here for compromise. Neither were they.

The interior of the jet was an opulent luxury, but the conversation inside was anything but soft. Noelle, Laura's ever-efficient PA, sat quietly, her fingers flying across her tablet, eyes darting between the women, tension humming beneath her composed exterior. To Laura's left, Evelyn Cross, President of the European Council, had her lips pressed into a thin line, ready to pounce. On her right, Fatima Rahmani, the United Nations Minister of Global Gender Equality, radiated barely contained intensity. Isabella Fernández, the South American ambassador whose speeches could level nations, sat forward, in coiled energy and brutal pragmatism.

Laura didn't mince words. "The Good Man Initiative isn't some feel-good, soft-peddled, educational program. We're talking about reshaping men from the ground up, stripping out the rot. We either redefine men or we let them go. There is no middle ground. This isn't a debate about human rights anymore—this is about who will survive the next phase of human evolution. Either they evolve our way, or they die."

Evelyn jumped in, her voice sharp. "And what do you think happens when they resist, Laura? We're not asking for minor changes. This will spark rebellion. These men, they've built their identities around the very things we're telling them to burn down. You want them to accept that without a fight?"

Isabella's laugh was dry. Dangerous. "I don't give a damn if they fight. Let them. You push hard enough, they'll fall in line. We don't need every man to stand up and salute. We need the ones that matter. The rest? Collateral damage."

Laura didn't blink. "We're not interested in half measures. We can't afford it. There's no going back. We've seen the damage—cities burning, bodies stacking up. The Gender War didn't start with men and women politely disagreeing over coffee. We're past the point of conversation. You want to see a man kneel? You must be ready to break his knees."

Fatima's voice cut through, sharp as a dagger. "We've been too polite for too long. The Male Military, the Family Militias, they've shown their hand. They'll burn the world to keep their power. What we're proposing? It's not equality. It's dominance. Let's be honest about that. We will take over, and the Good Man will stand to defend and support us or be crushed. The days of playing nice are gone."

Evelyn leaned in, her face hard. "So we make it clear—evolve, or get left behind. But if we push too fast, too hard, we risk mutiny. The key isn't in scaring them—it's in showing them there's no place left for them in the old world. The new world has already begun. They either adapt or become extinct."

Noelle, for once, raised her head from her tablet. "But if the initiative is nothing but punishment, it will backfire. What we need isn't fear—it's conversion. We're not just remaking them, we're reprogramming them. A war on every front isn't necessary. We need the right men in the right places to spread this like a virus. You make an example out of the first wave of resistance, then let the rest fall in line."

Laura smiled a cold flash of teeth before she said. "That's exactly what I mean. We don't just reshape them; we make them obsolete unless they play by our rules. You build a system where the only way to survive is to comply. No room for rebellion. Good men thrive, wicked men burn."

Fatima leaned back, her dark eyes glittering. "What do you say to the women who still cling to old ideas of family, of men as protectors, nurturers, and leaders? You know they'll stand in our way too."

Isabella snorted. "Let them. They're as much part of the problem as the men who've clung to power. Women who don't evolve get left behind too. There's no room for half-assed loyalty. You either fight for the new world or get destroyed with the old."

Laura's voice turned icy. "The initiative isn't about just punishing men—it's about giving them one last chance to stay relevant. The Family Militias, the Male Military—they'll fight. They'll push back. That's fine. We need a war to finish this. Feminism didn't survive by asking permission. It survived by taking what it deserved."

Evelyn's voice was dark, like smoke curling through the room. "We don't need a utopia. We need control. You say the word, and I'll have the legal framework to make this initiative global. The Good Man Initiative will be the law. Refuse it, and they'll face a world they don't recognize. The world will have no place for the old breed."

Fatima's gaze was intense. "Then we make sure we don't stop until it's global. Let there be no sanctuary for men stuck in the past. Every society, every corner of the planet must succumb."

Isabella grinned, fierce and wild. "Let them fight. If they want war, we'll give them their final war."

Laura's eyes gleamed as she surveyed the women around her. This wasn't about reconciliation. It wasn't even about peace. It was about power. Undeniable power that reshaped the world by force. She leaned forward, her voice snapping through the air like a whip.

"The Good Man Initiative is a revolution. It's not about balance or compromise. It's about winning. Men will fall in line, or they'll fall entirely. The world is changing, and those who refuse to adapt will disappear. We're not asking them to evolve—we're forcing them. And if that means breaking them to rebuild them better? So be it."

The jet hum surrounded them as the Atlantic stretched out below. The Gender War was raging on the ground, but in this cabin, 25,000 feet above, the final battle lines were being drawn.

As "The Valkyrie" descended toward Toronto, the gleaming jet slicing through the clouds, the unthinkable happened. A flash of light streaked across the sky, and in an instant, a guided missile found its mark. The explosion was deafening, tearing through the fuselage with brutal force. The detonation ripped through the tail nacelle, turning the pristine cabin into a storm of debris and flames as the jet spiraled downwards. Blown out of the clouds.

The impact obliterated three passengers. In an instant, their bodies disintegrated leaving only twisted metal and smoldering remnants. A violent shudder racked the jet. Thick black smoke filled the cabin. Suffocating, the air unbreathable, with its acrid stench.

Noelle, ever the stoic by Dr. Laura's side, lay unconscious amid the wreckage, her leg torn from her body. Blood pooled beneath her, the crimson stark against the shattered luxury of the jet's interior. Dr. Laura's body was battered by the force of the impact, throwing her against the cabin wall and snapping her collarbone with a sickening crack. The pain was immediate, searing through her with every breath.

The jet slammed into the Earth with a vicious crunch, the remains of the aircraft skidding along the ground before coming to a halt. Fire and smoke billowed into the sky as emergency sirens wailed in the distance, a desperate race against time to save the few who survived.

When the first responders arrived, they found a scene of carnage. The once-opulent G800 was now a twisted mass of metal debris scattered across the field like a war-zone. First responders pulled charred, unrecognizable bodies from the wreckage. Blood, smoke, and the stench of burning fuel filled the air.

They worked frantically, pulling Noelle's mangled body from the rubble, the stump where her leg had been still bleeding heavily. Carefully, they removed Dr. Laura, her face pale with shock and pain, her collarbone screaming with every movement. Despite her agonizing pain, her thoughts remained focused on Noelle.

The survivors were taken to the nearest hospital, but for Noelle, the nightmare had only begun. As they wheeled her into the emergency room, the hospital staff hesitated, their faces stiffening as they reviewed her medical records.

The doctor entered Laura's room, flanked by two nurses, his expression tight with tension. "Dr. Benton, we need to talk about Noelle."

Laura struggled to sit up, her face twisted in pain. "Where is she? How is she?"

He hesitated, glancing toward the nurses before speaking. "She's alive, but there's a complication. She's undergoing hormone treatment for Swyer Syndrome—her chromosomes are XY."

Laura's eyes narrowed. "What does that have to do with her receiving medical care?"

Visibly uncomfortable. "Our hospital has strict policies. We're not permitted or equipped to treat patients with XY chromosomes here."

The room seemed to freeze in that moment. Laura's breath hitched, and then her fury erupted like a volcano. "Are you telling me you're refusing to treat her because of her chromosomes? She's lost a leg, for God's sake! She's dying, and you're spouting bureaucratic bullshit about chromosomes?!"

The doctor struggled to maintain his composure as the tension in the room thickened. "Dr. Benton, the board's directives are clear. Following guidelines that your policies stipulated years ago. We are a gender-specific hospital. We cannot provide care to individuals with male chromosomes. She has to be transferred to a gender-free facility."

"No!" Laura's voice cracked with rage and desperation. "You're condemning her to die because of your idealistic policies! She won't survive the transfer in her condition. You have the facilities, the expertise right here, and you're refusing to treat her because of some legal mandate? I demand she be treated."

The doctor flinched, clearly torn. "There's nothing we can do," the doctor said, looking troubled. "The policies are in place to maintain the hospital's ethical guidelines. We've arranged for an ambulance—"

"Moral guidelines?!" Laura spat, eyes blazing. "What kind of morality lets a person bleed out on a hospital bed because of their chromosomes? She's a woman, and she deserves the same care as any other patient here!"

The nurses exchanged glances, clearly uncomfortable with the unfolding confrontation, but neither of them moved. The doctor, his face tight with internal conflict, exhaled. "We've done everything we can within the limits. She's already en route to the other facility."

Dr. Laura's fist clenched so tightly that her knuckles turned white. The pain from her broken collarbone was nothing compared to the rage boiling inside her. "This is why we fight. This is why we risk everything. Your hospital's policies are a death sentence for people like Noelle. If she dies because of this, I will personally see to it that your hospital, your board, and every corrupt institution like it are burned to the ground."

The doctor's face fell, his resolve shattered. He could only mutter, "I'm truly sorry."

"Sorry doesn't save lives," Laura said. Her voice trembling with the weight of her fury. "If she dies, her blood is on your hands."

Outside, the ambulance carrying Noelle sped through the streets, but Laura knew. She knew it was too late.

Two Weeks Later: Four Months Into The One-Year Appointment at The World Liberty Congress.

Adam Coles' journalistic prowess once again captivated the globe, his latest investigative report shaking the core foundations of society. For hours, it appeared the universe itself paused, engrossed in the profound revelations detailed within his words.

In their opulent highrise apartment overlooking Central Park, in the NATO-occupied regions of North America, Coach Sam and Eli were deeply engaged with the report. The apartment, a harmonious blend of particular modern contemporary design and personal touches, was a showcase of their lifestyle and their love for one another. Every corner told a story of shared moments, from the framed photos of vacations and milestone athlete accomplishments to the maximalist eclectic mix of artwork they had collected together. The scent of freshly brewed expensive coffee mingled with the faint aroma of Eli's cologne, adding to the intimate atmosphere.

The recent disappointment of the San Antonio Spurs' playoff elimination lingered in the air. The taste of defeat was bitter in the back of his throat, yet the aroma of the rare roasted coffee beans offered a slight comfort. As Coach Sam devoured every word of Adam Coles' article, Eli packed his bags for an impending road game, his movements efficient and purposeful. Eli felt a swirl of emotions—excitement to be playing in the semifinals, sorrow for his husband's team's early exit, and a constant gnawing anxiety about the possibility of someone exposing his secret.

The article was a comprehensive exploration of the Moon and Martian bases, delving into the political landscapes that defined these new worlds. On the Moon, a fragile balance of power existed, with various factions vying for control. The Martian bases, in contrast, were a hotbed of tension and unrest. Cole laid bare the intricacies of the legal systems on both celestial bodies, each struggling to establish a semblance of order in the harsh environments.

In contrast, the article took an unexpected step to the side from gender politics. There is a colony called Suffragette City.

"Suffragette City: The Mysterious Martian Colony,"

By Adam Cole

Coach Sam's voice echoed softly in the quiet room, as Eli came over to lie next to him, eyes closed, listening intently to the article being read aloud. The rhythmic hum of the city outside their window provided a stark contrast to the strange world Adam Cole had described. Sam's voice was steady, deep, as he narrated, pausing every so often to glance at and take in Eli's expression.

"Listen to this, Eli, it's like something out of a dream," Sam said before continuing.

I had heard rumors of Suffragette City for years, but never imagined unnamed sources would take me there. I was now aware of a colony on Mars, a place previously whispered about in hushed tones, in all its mysterious beauty. As I descended toward the surface, what lay before me was nothing short of a marvel—a city, gleaming against the familiar red Martian landscape, impossibly pristine. The architecture seemed ancient and futuristic all at once, leaving me to wonder: Who built this place? Were they Egyptians, as some whispered? Or perhaps, Iranians? The truth, as always, remained hidden.

From the outside, Suffragette City is an enigma, a shimmering oasis in the barren expanse of Mars. There are no markers, no inscriptions to reveal who constructed it. It was as if the city had simply emerged from the planet itself, silently waiting to be discovered. And yet, for all its external beauty, the exterior offered nothing in terms of answers. Who colonized it? Why? No one would tell me. Most of my questions went unanswered. Perhaps no one really knew.

But the moment I stepped inside, the mystery deepened. The interior of the city is lush—almost impossibly so. Grand gardens flourish under artificial sunlight, with plants and trees that have no right to exist on such a desolate planet. Waterfalls cascaded down marble walls, filling the air with the soft trickling sounds of water, while the smell of exotic flowers and sweet perfumes wrapped around me like a lover's whisper.

The people of Suffragette City seemed to live in some kind of utopian paradise. Their clothing was revealing but elegant, draped in such a way that celebrated the human form without cheapening it. Men and women walked together through corridors, smiling and laughing, their interactions free from the tension that seemed to plague Earth's societies.

It was simply opulent. Every corridor and room I passed through exuded wealth, luxury, and, most surprisingly, joy. These weren't the faces of a people burdened by war or conflict. These were cheerful people, living as though they had transcended the struggles that have torn Earth apart.

"I can't imagine it, Eli," Sam said softly, pausing in his reading to look at his husband. "A place where people don't fight over anything—especially not gender."

Eli opened his eyes, meeting Sam's gaze. "It sounds impossible," he whispered.

"It does, doesn't it?" Sam said. He smiled faintly before continuing.

What struck me most was the philosophy at the heart of Suffragette City. In this place, gender had become irrelevant. The exploitation of women as tools and weapons in power struggles, something we know all too well on Earth, is absent here. Suffragette City has neutralized gender distinctions, which have shaped and divided humanity for centuries. I felt as though the city had outgrown the need for gender conflict, rendering those old wars meaningless. They embraced their differences. A balance that keep them united as one.

Women are no longer pitted against men in societal or biological battles. There is no manipulation, no struggle for dominance or equality. Instead, the people of Suffragette City exist in a state of balance, free from the cultural baggage that has weighed down Earth for so long.

In this colony, both men and women are allowed to simply be without the pressure to conform to outdated expectations or roles. This wasn't just equality—it was something beyond that. A society where gender was not a factor at all. The people here didn't fight over it. They refrained from weaponizing it. They just lived, free from the burdens we've all carried.

"That's what you'd want, right?" Sam paused, glancing over at Eli, who lay silent next to him. "A world where we don't have to fight over something like that?"

"A world like that would be worth everything." Eli smiled, but there was a sadness behind it.

Sam sighed. His fingers brushing lightly against the screen before reading on.

Suffragette City defies explanation. I don't know who built it, or how it came to exist. There are no markers of history here—no statues of founders, no plaques commemorating or weaponizing the past. It's as if the city has always been here. Suspended in time. A secret that Mars has kept hidden from the rest of us.

But as beautiful as it is, I can't shake the feeling that this city holds a dark secret—something that goes beyond the surface of its perfection. Perhaps it's the way the people smile, too easily, too blissfully, as though they know something I don't. Perhaps it's that there's no sign of struggle, no hint of the hardship people must have faced to build such a place. And to maintain and sustain it on a remote baron planet.

For now, though, Suffragette City stands as a testament to what humanity could be, if we could leave behind the wars of gender that have plagued us for centuries. This city is more than just a colony. It is a vision of the future—a future free from the chains of division, where men and women are no longer enemies but partners in a greater, more harmonious existence.

Sam's voice grew softer as he finished the last line, setting the reader aside.

"What do you think?" Sam asked. Quietly, looking down at Eli, whose eyes were still closed, a faint smile on his lips.

"I think," Eli began, his voice barely above a whisper, "I think it's the kind of place you never want to leave."

Sam leaned back, staring out the window as the sounds of the city below mingled with the words Adam had written. In this world, where they fought every day for survival, for equality, for peace, the idea of a place like Suffragette City felt like a distant dream.

"Maybe one day, we'll find a place like that," Sam said softly, his hand resting gently on Eli's.

"My plane leaves in two hours. I have to finish packing," Eli said. He sprang to his feet and went to his bag. Thoughts of the colony mixed with his excitement for the game ahead.

As Sam read the article aloud, the words jumped off the page, grabbing the attention of both him and Eli, just as they had captivated diplomats, politicians, and warriors across the globe. Adam Cole had a way of bringing his reports to life, weaving fact with a sense of mystery and danger that left his readers on the edge of their seats. But this latest piece wasn't just about the mysterious Martian colony. It struck something deeper—a truth that resonated with the personal struggles Sam and Eli were navigating in their own lives.

Suffragette City, the fabled Martian colony, had become a symbol of Earth's long struggle, playing out in a distant, alien landscape. But what startled Sam wasn't just the beauty and opulence of the colony, but the gender dynamics Adam described, dynamics not so different from Earth. Sam's voice grew tense as he read the next line.

"Just like on Earth, issues of gender equality divided the other martian colonies. On the Moon and Mars, men fight against a tide that threatens to render them third-class citizens. Women, holding most legal and political power, have done little to improve the overall quality of life. Their grip on power has become a source of deep division."

Sam's words hung in the air like a toxic cloud. Eli sat for a moment on the couch, his brow furrowing as the realization of the power struggle sank in.

"The tension is palpable," Sam continued, his voice lowering, "Cole says it's like an open wound—rebellion could break out at any moment."

Sam glanced at Eli, noting the shift in his expression. "But listen to this, Eli. This next part—it took me by surprise."

As Sam read on, Adam Cole's article took a twist.

"There are growing numbers of male-only colonies on Mars," Sam read, his voice picking up pace. "Entire settlements of men—heterosexual and homosexual—living without women. They've established rogue governments and hybrid laws, separated from Earth's morals and judicial structures."

Sam paused, his mind racing with possibilities. "Can you imagine that, Eli? Men living together, governing themselves, creating something entirely new?"

Eli's packing halted as the article seized his attention. "What laws? What kind of society? No women!"

Sam grinned and continued, excitement building in his voice. "They've established a community where resources and responsibilities are equally distributed." No wealth hierarchy, no status. Get this—both straight and gay men live together, raising children in a way that defies everything we know on Earth. It's not traditional parenting. A group of men, all sharing the responsibility of caregivers, raise the children.

Eli's eyes widened. "An entire community of men raising families together? It sounds like they've created their own utopia. A society free from the... I'll be polite and say, the constraints that hold us back here."

Sam leaned forward, his pulse quickening. "Exactly! They're breaking away from the old rules and building something entirely different. What if we did that? What if we took our sports to Mars and raised a family there?"

Eli stared at Sam, considering the magnitude of the idea. "You mean... leave Earth? Start over on Mars?" He shook his head, a mixture of disbelief and intrigue in his voice. "It's bold. It's an enormous step. But... imagine what we could build there. We'd be free from the bullshit we face here. Our kids could grow up without the pressure of these gender wars."

Sam could already feel the idea taking root in his mind. "Exactly. No more constant fighting for space or recognition. Just... living. In a community that accepts and supports us. A place where our kids can grow up without feeling like they have to fight for every scrap of self worth."

Eli zipped up his duffel bag, his eyes shining with a glint of hope. "What if that's our future, Sam? Mars. Starting over, raising our family there, in a place that makes sense."

The new dream feel of the moment settled between them, charged with the potential for something worthwhile, something liberating. Sam's mind raced, but as the words of Adam Cole's article faded, the world around them snapped back into sharp relief.

Sam stood on the terrace, staring down at the burned-out city park below. The charred trees rustled in the breeze, their leaves—what few remained—blackened by the fires of unrest. Soldiers patrolled the paths below, their presence a constant reminder of the conflict that defined the streets of the city. Birds darted between the branches, their song a faint echo in the air, while the rumble of drones and military planes roared overhead. The smell of wet dirt and burnt rubbish filled the air, thick and acrid. Sam's eyes lifted, searching the dusk sky for the faint glow of Mars.

"I'll sue the World Liberty Congress for denying men the rights we deserve," Sam muttered, his jaw tightening. The injustice of it burned inside him, an unquenchable fire. He needed to act, to fight for something bigger than himself. But who could stand beside him? Who had the power and the influence to go against the world and its systems?

There was only one man who came to mind—Victor Lang, the brilliant mind behind bio-enhanced humans and one of Sam's closest allies. He had been at the Spurs game with Sam and Eli recently, and their conversation still lingered in Sam's memory. Victor was the only one who could help him launch this fight.

As Sam turned back toward the apartment, his steps deliberate, the communication system flashed with a news alert.

"Breaking news: A missile attack has been launched against Dr. Laura Benton. The Russian government has claimed responsibility. Initial reports show multiple casualties, including Dr. Benton's personal assistant. Further details to follow."

Sam's heart sank. Laura Benton wasn't just another political figure—she was central to the efforts of navigating the gender cataclysm. Her influence. Her work, had been crucial to preventing total societal collapse. This attack wasn't just on her—it was on everything she represented. Fear clung to the air, mixing with the smell of Eli's fresh coffee and turning bitter in Sam's mouth.

Torn between the need to process the shocking news and the burning resolve to move forward with his own fight, Sam made his decision. He needed Victor Lang to champion his cause.

The screen flickered to life, and after a few tense moments, Victor's face appeared, his usual calm demeanor cracked with concern.

"Sam, I heard about Laura. This is devastating," Victor said, cutting straight to what he imagined was the purpose for Sam's call.

Sam nodded, his voice steady despite the weight of the news. "It is. But we can't let it stop us. I need your help, Victor. I want to sue the World Liberty Congress for denying men's rights—on Earth, and in the colonies. This is a fight that needs to go all the way to Mars. Men can't be left behind. Not again."

Victor's face spoke of surprise. "You're asking for a battle, Sam. The political landscape has never been more volatile. This attack on Laura—it's going to make things worse. They'll use it to clamp down on everything—on men's rights, on my transhumans. But you're right. If anyone can make noise about this, it's you."

Sam explained everything he'd learned from Adam Cole's article. He described the male-only colonies, the potential for new beginnings, and the future he and Eli dreamed of. As the words left his mouth, they no longer felt like fantasy. They felt like reality waiting to happen.

Victor's eyes narrowed, considering Sam's plan. "You've got a compelling argument. We'll need to gather testimonies, legal precedents, build a case that shakes the foundations of the World Liberty Congress. But it's doable. It won't be easy, and I'm with you."

Another alert buzzed on the screen, more updates about the attack on Laura. Sam's heart ached at the news, but his resolve only strengthened. He looked back at Victor, his voice filled with the challenge of the fight ahead.

"This is about more than us, Victor. It's about creating a world where everyone has a fair chance. No matter the cost."

Victor nodded, his face softening. "Then let's get started."

***

Dr. Laura Benton winced as she adjusted the brace supporting her broken collarbone. The pain—like the sleepless nights haunted by the memories of the explosion—was a constant reminder of the attack that had nearly killed her and claimed Noelle's life. The sterile scent of antiseptic clung to her skin, mingling with the harsh industrial smell of smoke and burnt metal, a sensory echo of the fiery wreckage she had narrowly escaped. Her once pristine face, now marred with cuts and bruises, felt raw and tight, and her hair—formerly a symbol of her poise and authority—was a singed, unruly mess, the aftermath of flames licking too close for comfort.

She sat at her desk, the frosty edge of the wood pressing into her good arm, the polished surface mocking the pain it couldn't soothe. Across from her, Noelle's parents sat in the sterile, tension-filled silence, their faces reflecting a maelstrom of grief and rage. It was her last meeting after the aircrews families and three prominent leaders. The hum of distant machinery outside the room, paired with the steady beeping from her communicator, offering a mix of incoming messages and updates, created an unnerving rhythm—life going on as normal, despite the devastation to which she sought to bring closure.

Dr. Benton forced a strained smile, though the effort tugged at her bruised face, sending a fresh ripple of pain through her body. "I'm so deeply sorry for your loss," she began, her voice heavy with exhaustion and rough from the medications dulling her physical agony but not her guilt. Each word felt like it cost her. "Noelle was more than just an assistant. She was—she was a vital part of everything we are working for."

Noelle's mother dabbed her swollen eyes with a lavender-scented tissue, her sobs soft but continuous. Meanwhile, her father, his face taut with controlled fury, leaned forward, the leather of his jacket creaking as he placed his elbows on his knees. His eyes burned into Laura's, his body brimming with barely contained rage.

"Sorry doesn't bring her back, Dr. Benton," he said, his voice hard and low. "This wasn't an accident. It was murder."

Laura's heart thudded painfully in her chest. She nodded slowly, feeling the ache in her collarbone intensify as though her bones were gnawed at with the fangs of the truth. "You're right."

Her words stretched out between them like a thin layer of smoke—heavy, suffocating, impossible to ignore. Noelle's death had not only shattered her sense of purpose but had also ignited a flame of vengeance inside her that burned with a relentless hunger for justice. The promise was not empty; it was a vow.

The parents sat in silence for a moment longer, Noelle's mother's quiet sobs the only sound in the room. Then, with a resigned look, they stood. Noelle's father hesitated at the door, his eyes lingering on Laura, as though searching for some unspoken assurance she couldn't offer, before finally exiting. The soft click of the door as it closed behind them sounded like finality.

Laura sat in the silence, her breath uneven, a swirl of regret and determination in her breast. Noelle's absence left a deep, raw void, one that Laura couldn't fill with promises of vengeance or the cold comfort of retribution. Yet Laura knew, without question, she had to end this war, had to end the Men's Militia—if not for Noelle, then for everyone caught in this spiraling madness.

Turning back to her desk, Laura Benton picked up Adam Cole's latest investigative report from the Turkey Hürriyet Daily News, her fingers trembling slightly from both strain and the seriousness of the content. The paper had the faint, sharp scent of ink and toner, the sound of the rustling pages an oddly comforting contrast to the storm of thoughts brewing in her mind. Her eyes locked onto the section on Dr. Aylin Kaya, and her pulse quickened—a strange mixture of anger and urgency overtaking her.

Dr. Aylin Kaya—a Turkish scientist whose name had become synonymous with controversial reproductive technologies. Kaya's work had recently made headlines for suggesting that men, in fact, might evolve better without women. But what disturbed Laura most was Kaya's use of religious texts to support her claims.

Laura's eyes hovered over the printed words. Dr. Aylin Kaya: A scientist working on the forefront of reproductive research, proposing that men could evolve beyond the need for women. Her theories, based partly on interpreting Islamic scripture, claim that men are central to reproduction and societal progress. Chapter 4, verse 34 of the Qur'an states, 'Men are the maintainers of women,' a passage Kaya suggested hints at men's divine role as caretakers, providers, and ultimately, the drivers of human evolution.

Laura's grip on the paper tightened, a flare of sharp pain radiating through her injured collarbone. Her mind churned—this kind of twisted rhetoric wasn't just pseudoscience; it was a dangerous weapon that could stoke the fires of extremism she had spent her life trying to quell. Kaya's arguments, based on a misinterpretation of the Qur'an, could inspire the kind of male-centric ideologies that threatened to undo all the work Laura had fought for.

The verse Kaya referenced—"Men are the maintainers of women"—was a common citation in certain religious debates. But Dr. Kaya had skewed its meaning. To interpret it as a justification for men's dominance over reproduction was not only an abuse of religious doctrine, but a distortion of both science and faith. It wasn't just about women's rights anymore—it was about redefining humanity's place in the universe.

Laura had long understood the importance of men's reproductive rights—her work had been dedicated to striking a balance. There were genuine discussions to be had about the role of men in the future of reproduction, especially as technology evolved. In fact, recent advancements had allowed men to carry pregnancies to term with synthetic wombs, and other technologies allowed for reproduction without the traditional female role. Laura supported these breakthroughs, but not in the oppressive, patriarchal vision that Kaya and others like her promoted.

For Kaya to intertwine such scientific research with religious beliefs—particularly from the Qur'an—and claim it as a justification for a future without women was a dangerous precedent. The Qur'an, after all, upheld the spiritual importance of both genders, their roles complementary in the eyes of God. Yet here was Kaya, advocating for a future that could wipe out half the population's biological significance.

Laura set the paper down, the pain in her body intensifying as she contemplated the implications of Kaya's claims. The rise of these ideas would only embolden the Men's militia, adding religious validation to their brutal campaign for male dominance. And that would mean war—unending holy war.

Her decision came swiftly, borne from the fierce determination that always ignited in her when she sensed the world teetering toward chaos. She couldn't sit idly by while someone like Kaya spread ideologies that could destroy everything she had worked for.

Dr. Kaya needed to be confronted—challenged directly. Laura wanted to look her in the eye and tear apart the foundation of her dangerous beliefs. There was no time to waste; the world couldn't afford the spread of this toxic narrative.

With the sting of pain as her constant companion, Laura made a series of quick calls, arranging immediate travel to Turkey. Despite the lingering injuries, she couldn't take time for herself to heal while the world continued to fracture. This was her fight, and every moment spent resting was another moment lost in the battle for humanity's future.

Men are the key to God was not a new belief. Laura reflected on the long, historical focus on men in religious texts. In the Qur'an, there were passages that undeniably placed men as protectors, providers, and, in some interpretations, as those closest to God. But these texts also spoke of balance, mercy, and responsibility—something Kaya and her ilk conveniently ignored.

In truth, the notion that men had a special role was ancient, but people always meant it as a spiritual guidepost, not a justification for subjugating women. Kaya's argument warped these sacred teachings into a means of asserting biological and political dominance.

Women have value beyond pregnancy. She thought.

As the flight preparations clicked into place, Laura put the last steps into the plan as she strategize the addition to the war. She wasn't just fighting for women's rights anymore—she was fighting for the truth, for balance, for the future of humanity itself.

The jet's cabin was an organized frenzy of bodies and tasks, each one aimed at erasing the physical and emotional wreckage left by the explosion that had nearly killed Dr. Laura Benton. Inside the humming aircraft, the scent of fresh shampoo mingled with the lingering odor of burnt flesh and jet fuel, creating a heady, unsettling atmosphere. The quiet murmur of voices faded into the background as Laura sat still, letting them transform her from victim to victor, from survivor to leader.

The blast had singed her hair, once a symbol of pristine authority, beyond recognition, but a stylist worked to restore it. The sharp snip of scissors punctuating the silence. Strands of burnt hair fell like dead leaves to the cabin floor, the rhythm of it familiar, mechanical. The sensation of the needle buzzing as it retouched her tattoos, drawing life back into her vivid, dark ink, was a grounding presence. Each stroke of ink, each swirl of color, was both armor and expression, a reminder of the battles she'd survived—and the ones still to come.

Her wardrobe was no less of a challenge. The tailor's hands moved swiftly, snipping and adjusting the fabric with practiced efficiency. She needed something that maintained her air of authority, something sleek and ruthless, but that wouldn't pull at the brace supporting her broken collarbone. The result: a tight, tailored outfit, black as midnight, cut to perfection, designed to hold her together even when everything inside her felt fractured. She looked like power incarnate, a visual rebuttal to anyone who dared question her resolve.

The icy burn of Aragh Sagi lingered on her tongue, a bracing, bitter sweet reminder of her roots. It mixed with the faint medicinal taste of painkillers that kept her body functioning, even though every movement screamed in protest. The alcohol numbed her broken, burnt and bruised body. It was calming and uplifting her in equal measure. This mission was too important, too personal. She would confront Dr. Kaya—and crush the insidious beliefs threatening to tip the world even further into chaos.

As the plane descended into Istanbul, the jet's cabin fell silent, save for the faint hum of engines and the whir of the landing gear hydraulics locking into place. Laura stared out the window. The sprawling city below illuminated in the fading light, and her memories of previous visits cause a distant recollection of the smell of spices and hard physical work.

Once inside the bustling airport, the change in atmosphere was instant. The air felt heavy, thick with the scents of grilled meats, spices, and the salt from the Bosphorus. Yet there was something more—a tension. She could feel eyes following her, suspicious, curious, hungry eyes. Whispers followed her like ghosts, swirling in the air, but her focus remained razor sharp.

Then the paparazzi descended. The clicks and laser flashes shattered the ambient noise like glass. They surrounded her, desperate to capture the woman who had narrowly escaped death.

"Dr. Benton! Over here!"

"What happened in the explosion?"

"Are you meeting with Dr. Kaya?"

The questions came rapid-fire, shouted over one another, the crowd moving like a swarm of vultures. The stench of desperation hung around them, sweat-soaked bodies, cameras thrust forward, their eyes gleaming with the thrill of the chase.

Her team moved swiftly, forming a protective barrier, but the swarm was relentless, their bodies pressing in, their words sharper than the bright lasers that stung her eyes. The taste of anxiety grew bitter on her tongue, the strong anise of the sagi doing little to calm her rising tension.

Just as they neared the exit, a black van screeched to a halt. Doors burst open and masked figures emerged with swift precision. Before Laura could react, the Feminist Militia had surrounded the paparazzi, moving with a militaristic efficiency. The insignia on their uniforms flashed unmistakable in the dim light.

Laura's pulse quickened, but not out of fear. These were her people—and they were taking no prisoners.

In a matter of seconds, the paparazzi were subdued, their protests silenced with brutal efficiency. One of the masked women, her movements fluid and determined, approached Laura and lowered her scarf to reveal a hard-set face. Her eyes burned with righteous resolve.

"Dr. Benton, we apologize for the disturbance," she said, her voice sharp but respectful. "We will handle this. Your safety is our priority."

Laura, breathless, nodded, her eyes flickering between the subdued paparazzi being dragged into the van. It was over in moments—the doors slammed shut, the engine roared, and the van disappeared into the night.

"I didn't ask for this," Laura said, though there was no genuine conviction behind the words. The adrenaline still coursing through her veins made her pulse throb in her temples.

"You didn't need to," the woman said, her voice laced with the unspoken truth. "We protect our own. Especially our commander and chief."

Without another word, the Feminist Militia vanished as quickly as they'd appeared, leaving Laura standing in the suddenly eerily quiet airport, her team around her, tension fading.

The cool night air greeted her as she approached the waiting car. Though Istanbul's bustling streets whirred in the background, Laura focused solely on the confrontation ahead. She could feel the stakes rising, the anger building inside her—the world was on the edge, and extremism was the key to attention.

She sank back into the seat of the car, the rush of adrenaline still singing in her blood. Dr. Aylin Kaya and her twisted theories were on the horizon.

***

The better part of an hour's drive had been long and winding, a quiet journey that allowed Laura Benton to mentally prepare for what she knew would be a confrontation—not just with Dr. Aylin Kaya, but with the very future of human reproduction. Though nestled in the city's heart, the modern design of the facility they arrived at stood in stark contrast to the ancient architecture surrounding it. A stone lintel boldly stretched above the steel-framed glass doors, engraved with the words Institute for Advanced Reproductive Technologies.

As Laura stepped out of the car and approached the entrance, a surge of anticipation mixed with unease churned in her gut. The cold, sterile scent of the lab hit Laura as soon as she was ushered inside. It was a mixture of faint traces of disinfectant and chemicals, the kind of smell that carried an unsettling sense of clinical precision. The white walls reflected the harsh fluorescent lights, making everything seem sharper. Cleaner—too clean.

Dr. Aylin Kaya's presence was disarming at first glance. She stood at about five feet five, her slender frame giving her an almost delicate appearance. Her long, dark hair framed a face that could only be described as oddly adorable. Soft, rounded features betrayed none of the sharp intellect hiding behind her striking silver-grey eyes. These eyes—hypnotic and unsettling—constantly blinked against the brightness of the sterile lab lights, as though they were too sensitive for the world she worked in. They glistened, not with tears of sadness but with a watery, iridescent sheen that only made her look more innocent, more vulnerable, and somehow, more dangerous.

Her skin, pale to the point of looking anemic, was smooth but tight, giving her a strange ageless quality that made it hard to place her within any specific decade. Her nose was small and slightly upturned, balanced by a pair of full lips that always seemed to hover on the edge of a smile—calculated, knowing. It was a face that didn't quite match the intensity of the ideas and controversies she wielded with such precision.

But her voice—her voice shattered the illusion of fragility. It was low and smooth, like velvet over steel, with a calm, almost hypnotic lilt that carried a quiet power, a hidden edge. When she spoke, there was a measured control, a confidence that didn't need to raise its volume to command attention. Her words wrapped around you, pulling you in, only to reveal the sharpness of their meaning when it was too late to resist.

"Dr. Benton," Kaya greeted smoothly, her accent lilting, though her smile was slight, almost dismissive. "I must admit, I didn't expect you to come all this way."

Laura's eyes narrowed as she took in the woman's sight, responsible for one of the most dangerous scientific breakthroughs of their time. "I needed to see it for myself," Laura said, her voice edged with steel. "Your claims are not only scientifically questionable, but socially divisive."

Kaya raised a brow, her lips curving into a smile that was both secretive and knowing. "The Qur'an is only the tip of the iceberg, Dr. Benton. The real breakthrough is much larger than religious interpretation. Come, let me show you." There was a barely contained glee in her voice, a tinge of dangerous excitement in her eyes.

Laura followed as Kaya led her through the facility, passing rows of blindingly sterile corridors and rooms filled with unrecognizable equipment—machines that hummed and pulsed with a low, constant vibration, their purposes a mystery. There was something alien about the setup, as though she had walked into a world that had evolved beyond human understanding.

Finally, Kaya stopped outside of a sealed door. A soft hiss sounded as it slid open, revealing the heart of her research: rows of artificial wombs, each containing a developing fetus suspended in fluid. Tiny and fragile, yet astonishingly real.

The sight made Laura stop dead in her tracks. The room itself was dimly lit, the only sources of light coming from the glowing womb chambers, their surfaces softly illuminated in shades of blue and white. A soft hum of incubation filled the space, blending with the rhythmic pulse of life as the machines worked tirelessly to grow and sustain the fragile beings within.

Laura stepped closer, her curiosity driving her to touch one of the chambers. The surface was cool and smooth under her fingertips, but beneath it, she could feel a faint vibration—the sensation of machinery working in tandem with organic life. Inside, the fetus floated in an amber-colored liquid, bathed in a soft, ethereal glow that made the delicate features of its developing body angelic.

The air was thick with the smell of cleanliness and synthetic life, but underneath it, Laura could detect something else—something primal. The faint scent of newborns, that unmistakable scent of human life in its earliest stages. It hit her harder than she expected, drawing her into the gravity of what was happening here.

"These are... artificial wombs," Laura whispered, her voice betraying a mix of awe and dread.

"You see, Dr. Benton," Kaya began, her voice as smooth as silk, yet laden with the lead of her resolve. The subtle accent in her speech only deepened the sense of mystery that surrounded her. "Men are meant for this—reproduction without depending on women," Kaya said. "They no longer need us. Women are irrelevant. The universe is made clean."

Her smile widened, but it wasn't warm—it was a smile of victory, of someone who knew they had just revealed a truth you couldn't escape from. It made Laura's skin crawl, as if a predator had just shown its fangs while still wearing the mask of charm.

Up close, Kaya's face was an exquisite mask—beautiful, yet hollow. It was as though she had perfected the art of being pleasant and endearing, while the real her, the one with grand visions of human control, lurked just beneath the surface, waiting for the right moment to strike. And now, surrounded by the glowing artificial wombs, with the hum of machinery vibrating through the sterile lab, Laura could see the true depths of Kaya's ambition.

Kaya nodded, her silver eyes gleaming in the low light. "Yes. Each one is an independent incubator, designed to nurture a developing fetus. What you're looking at is the future of reproduction. No female egg required each child the product of sperm enhanced with superhuman xxx chromosome."

Laura's eyes flickered from one chamber to the next, trying to comprehend the scope of what she was seeing. The hum of the machines was almost soothing, yet the implications of these glowing chambers sent a chill down her spine. These were not human births, as she knew them. The births were manufactured, with their development controlled down to the molecular level.

She leaned in closer to the womb, tracing the outline of the fetus with her eyes. It was unsettling how perfect the creature inside looked. No flaws, no imperfections. A perfectly engineered male human. The womb glowed faintly, casting an otherworldly halcyon light on the skin of the fetus as it floated in its artificial environment, suspended in time and space.

"How is this possible?" Laura asked, her voice tight with disbelief.

Kaya smirked, stepping to one of the nearby machines—its purpose immediately unclear, but its importance obvious by the way it hummed and blinked with lights. "Through semen regeneration and biological manipulation, we have found a way to bypass the need for traditional female reproduction. The machines you see here take genetic material—specifically male semen—and convert it into viable embryos. Fertilization is immediate. The embryo grows in these bioengineered wombs."

Laura's stomach twisted into a knot as she stood in the heart of what felt like the end of humanity as she knew it. The sterile glow of the artificial wombs pulsed with an eerie rhythm, each one filled with a tiny, developing life—life born without love, without warmth, without a woman's touch. It was as if the room itself had become an alien womb, birthing something unnatural, something that defied everything humanity had ever understood about itself.

The unfamiliar machinery vibrating with power that seemed to come from some deeper force, something beyond technology—a force that was evolving human life into something unrecognizable. Screens displayed data on growth cycles, vital signs, and genetic compositions, revealing the man-made process of life creation, where scientists spliced life in this mechanical, sterile void where nature was no longer needed. No longer wanted.

Laura could barely breathe, her throat tightening as she stood at the crossroads of a future no one had ever imagined. Here, in this lab, scientists had reduced creation to numbers and tubes, a place where they ripped the human soul from the act of birth. A void filled the space, a silence so profound it felt like the universe itself had turned its back on what was happening here.

Dr. Aylin Kaya stood beside her, eyes glowing with the pride of a god who had reshaped the world. Her voice cut through the hum of machinery, smooth and calm yet dripping with conviction. "Dr. Benton, this is what men are meant for," Kaya whispered, her words seeping into Laura's ears like poison. "Reproduction without dependence on women. Men as the primary creators. The Qur'an hinted at it, but now science has fulfilled it. It is not a unique soul inside every human, as some religions teach. Rather, the universe is the soul and men are the incarnate representation inside the soul."

The chilling certainty in Kaya's voice sent a shiver down Laura's spine. This wasn't just science. It wasn't progress. It was a declaration of war on the essence of humanity—on love, connection, and everything Laura had ever believed about a woman's life. Kaya's world, this world, was something darker than any dystopian vision.

"This is madness," Laura's voice cracked as her heart raced, pounding in her chest with both fear and fury. "You can't seriously believe that eliminating women is the answer. This isn't evolution, Kaya—this is destruction. It's ... demonic!"

Kaya's smile widened, her face suddenly cold and unyielding. Her silver-grey eyes, once so disarming, now gleamed with a terrifying sense of superiority.

"You don't understand, Laura. We're not eliminating women—we're freeing humanity. The Y chromosome was always the degraded human state. It diluted and poisoned the superman chromosome. Once we repaired the male genome, we realized it could replicate itself, creating life without the need for the female counterpart. We have returned to Eden, Laura. A world where man is in harmony with the universe, where gender is no longer a burden."

Laura's mind raced, trying to process the enormity of Kaya's words. This was not about progress. It was about rewriting the fabric of existence, stripping away the natural balance of life. Kaya wanted a world where women were obsolete, where the delicate dance of creation, of male and female, would be replaced by the cold sterility of machines and tubes.

"Destroy this technology," Laura's voice trembled, but her conviction was steel. "You've gone too far, Kaya. You've broken the fundamental rules of life. We're not gods. We don't get to rewrite the universe."

Dr. Kaya's expression darkened, her eyes narrowing as her voice took on a sinister edge. "It's already beyond you and beyond me, Dr. Benton. Turkey's government is considering the implications of this technology. Soon, this lab will be impenetrable, protected by forces you can't comprehend. The world is changing, whether or not you want it to."

Laura felt an icy dread creep over her. Kaya truly believed what she was saying. The implications of this technology weren't just confined to a lab—they were already in motion, already part of a larger plan. But Laura knew better than to believe in government power. World governments—including her own—would soon learn of Kaya's vision, and they would fight over it. Escalating the violence. Fostering a holy war.

Laura's voice was calm, but her mind raced as she asked, "Do you really think the Turkish government is more powerful than the World Liberty Congress?"

"You're naïve. You've created something far more dangerous than you can control."

Kaya's face twisted into a cruel smile. "No bombs or lasers or armies can harm this lab, Dr. Benton. You're already too late. The world of men is about to return to its natural state."

The words hung between them, thick and suffocating. Laura's blood boiled. She knew what this meant. The fall of women, the fall of balance, the fall of everything. This wasn't just about science. This was a revolution, and it was one she could not let succeed.

Laura left the lab, the cold evening air rushing into her lungs like a relief, but the battle she just lost and the fate of the world pressing harder than ever. The scent of spices and city smoke filled her nose as the distant call to prayer echoed through the streets—a reminder of faith, of strength, of what humanity had held onto for melania. She paused, closing her eyes as she breathed in the chaotic sounds of life outside the lab, far removed from the sterile life inside.

As she stepped out, armored vehicles surrounded her convoy, the low rumble of engines like a war drum. She could feel the tension in the air, the silent battle between those who would cling to the old ways and those who sought to reshape the world in their image. It was inevitable. A holy war required a change in protocol.

"It's time to exterminate the bio-humans," Laura whispered to herself, her voice filled with the cold resolve of someone who knew exactly what had to be done. "Dr. Lang be damned—there's no place for his superior men and women or Kaya's twisted vision of a man-only universe."

Her words fell on no one, but she didn't intend them for an audience. They were a statement of self-conviction, a rallying cry for the battle ahead. She stood there, surrounded by the machines of war, her mind churning and blending the strategy she would need to end this madness before it consumed the world.

Chapter Nine: Consequence Of Eden

Six Months Into The One-Year Appointment at The World Liberty Congress.

The Good Man Initiative, a series of policies designed to incentivize men to align with feminist values, had been at the heart of the World Liberty Congress' agenda. Dr. Laura Benton spearheaded its implementation, believing it would create a society where gender equality was not just a goal, but a reality. Bold moves often come with unforeseen consequences. Tension was growing.

The Good Man policies were designed to reward men who actively contributed to feminist causes. These policies offered lower medical insurance premiums to men working in jobs that directly improved women's lives, such as nurses, caretakers, teachers, and other professions considered essential to the feminist society. Men who chose to serve in the Feminist Militia were given reduced interest rates on loans and the opportunity to purchase homes after a decade of service. The World Liberty Congress believed these incentives promoted gender cooperation.

But beneath the surface, the world was fracturing.

Adam Cole's investigative report had peeled back the layers of a brewing storm. His exposé highlighted how these policies, while outwardly progressive, were alienating large swaths of the male population. Cole's sharp journalistic lens revealed the dark side of the Good Man Initiative: violence, riots, and a growing male rebellion. Traditional roles shifted, men felt pushed out, marginalized by policies that demanded subservience.

In one of his vlog articles, Adam had spoken:

Previously, the world championed gender equality, but now we find ourselves caught in a novel form of oppression, where men are valued only for their ability to serve women.

His words resonated with men trapped by pressure to comply with World Liberty Congress policies. The unrest began in small pockets—men burning insurance certificates and holding protests outside loan offices—but soon it escalated into nationwide riots.

In the early days of the Good Man Initiative, the first sparks of violence flared in cities like Berlin, Istanbul, and New York, where men took to the streets, clashing with police forces and feminist militias alike. What started as peaceful demonstrations quickly spiraled into bloody conflicts, with thousands of men storming government buildings, setting fires, and looting stores. Cole's articles further inflamed the situation, revealing that benefits like home ownership were withheld from men unless they served for years under feminist command—a service many saw as forced indoctrination.

Adam's investigation uncovered even more troubling details. In Italy and Greece, Chinese-backed Masculine Army forces had taken control of large territories, declaring them independent of feminist rule. These occupied territories stood as decades old victories to the growing global divide. In one particularly graphic exposé, Cole detailed the recent Feminist Army's counterattack in the north of Italy—a brutal operation aimed at reclaiming the land from Chinese-backed forces.

The Feminist Army took back Greece at the cost of four thousand soldiers. A toll many questioned for what gain.

Dr. Laura Benton sat at the head of the beautiful polished steel modern conference table, her sharp gaze sweeping across the room. The mood was palpable—tense, electric, a sense of urgency hanging in the air like the rumble of thunder before a storm. A wildfire of social unrest, sparked by the Good Man Initiative, threatened to consume the world. The feminist victory was in reach, and the value of it pressed in on the entire room like the inside of an instapot.

Across the table, Jacob, her chief analyst, scrolled through his tablet, his brow furrowed in concern. Carla, a renowned sociologist and expert on gender relations, sat beside him, her fingers drumming on the table, betraying her usual calm. Nadia, the legal expert, adjusted her glasses and leaned forward, her face tight with frustration. To Laura's left sat Gwen, the media strategist, scribbling notes, her lips pressed into a thin line.

Laura broke the silence, her voice cutting through the tension. "Let's get to it. We need to discuss the public's reaction to the Good Man Initiative and the growing unrest. Adam Cole's exposés are gaining too much traction. We need a response, and we need it now. We bring peace to EASLGTBQ+ genders and the diversity, equanimity, and inclusion of every one. Everyone, Asexual, Straight, Lesbian, Gay, Transgender, Bisexual and Queer. + Encompasses other identities, such as Intersex, Two-Spirit, Nonbinary."

Jacob glanced up from his tablet, his expression grim. "The metrics aren't good, Dr. Benton. We're seeing a massive spike in male discontent—especially among the working-class men who feel marginalized by the policies. Cole's vlog posts about Turkey's government courting Dr. Lang to move his bio-enhancement labs there are fanning the flames. Men feel like they're being pushed out of every aspect of society—from jobs to reproductive rights."

Carla chimed in, her voice steady but intense. "It's more than just economic dissatisfaction. Men are feeling like they've lost their traditional roles, and the Good Man Initiative, while well-intentioned, is perceived as coercive. These incentives—lower insurance premiums for men in feminist-supporting jobs, home loans for militia service—they're backfiring. Men feel like they have to earn basic rights, like owning a home, by first submitting to feminist control."

Nadia scoffed, unable to hold back. "Submitting? Are you serious? We're offering them opportunities they wouldn't have otherwise. These men want traditional roles back? What? They want to keep women under their boot like they did before the 20th century? They want to keep us chained to the kitchen. Pumping out kids while they play like they're the victim?" Her voice was dripping with sarcasm, her frustration obvious.

Carla shot her a sharp look. "That's not the point, Nadia. The perception is what's causing the problem. They see these policies as a way to strip them of their masculinity. The protests are turning violent because these men feel like they're being dehumanized."

"So what? We cater to their egos and let them keep violent controls holding us back?" Nadia retorted, her eyes narrowing. "We've given them every chance to evolve with the rest of us. If they can't see the value in a progressive society led and controlled by women, then maybe we should let them go."

Laura raised a hand, silencing the back-and-forth. "Enough. We're not here to debate whether men are right or wrong—we're here to figure out how to prevent this from turning into a new faction of the war. Adam Cole is driving the narrative right now. His exposés on the unintended consequences of these policies are painting us as oppressors, and it's rallying men to his side."

Jacob leaned forward, his voice low. "The riots are spreading, Laura. What started as peaceful protests have escalated into full-blown violence in Berlin, Istanbul, and New York. In some cities, men are burning government buildings. We've even seen attacks on feminist militia officers."

Gwen looked up from her notes. "We need to get ahead of this. Cole's articles and videos are everywhere—he's exposing the inequities men are feeling, and people are listening. We need a media blitz, something that reframes the Good Man Initiative as beneficial for everyone, not just women. We can't afford to let this narrative further spiral out of control."

Laura's gaze hardened. "The narrative isn't the only problem. There's also the battle in Italy and the reclamation of Greece. The Feminist Army retook the land, but the collateral damage was devastating.

The world is watching us, and if we don't handle this carefully, we're going to look like the very oppressors Cole is accusing us of being."

Nadia interjected, her voice cold. "What happened in Italy was necessary. The Chinese-backed male militias were holding the territory hostage, and we took it back. The cost was high, yes, but war always has casualties."

Carla's voice cut through again, filled with concern. "But that's just it. This is becoming more than a war of territory. It's turning into a god-damned holy war, and it's spiraling out of control. The Feminist Army's victory in northern Italy may have been necessary, but the brutality of the tactics used is only fueling the opposition. We need to be more strategic, not just militarily, but socially."

Gwen shook her head, frustrated. "Adam Cole's latest piece on the reclamation of Greece was brutal. He's painting the feminist forces as monsters—bio-enhanced soldiers tearing through the streets, killing indiscriminately. Even if that's not the truth, perception is reality for the public, and Cole's got them eating out of his hand."

The room went silent, each person contemplating the next step. Laura finally spoke, her voice filled with determination. "We can't let this spiral any further. Jacob, I need a full analysis of Cole's influence. I want to know exactly where his support is strongest, and what demographics we're losing. Carla, get our best sociologists on the ground. I want to know why men are feeling like this and how we can address it without looking weak. And Gwen, get the media strategy in place. We're going to need to counter Cole's narrative hard and fast.

"If we show the world how we restore stability to the reclaimed territories Spread a united message that reminds we will end this war at any cost. The future is insight and we need to let everyone know. I will win. Stage the scenes. Show the world how happy men are."

Jacob hesitated for a moment. "Laura, there's something else. There's talk among the militias about forming resistance cells. Some of the male factions in Italy and Greece are regrouping, and we're hearing rumors they're getting backing from Russia. If this turns into open rebellion, we're looking at a serious disadvantage in the global hearts and minds."

The tension in the room spiked as Laura's jaw tightened. She met Jacob's eyes, her voice steely. "Then we'd better be ready. But make no mistake—this is a war for the future of humanity. We're not just fighting for women's rights anymore. We're fighting for the survival of our planet."

Laura stood, her collarbone still aching from the explosion that nearly took her life. She could feel the weight of the world on her shoulders, but she wouldn't break. She wouldn't back down.

As the team dispersed, Laura stayed behind, staring out the window at the city below. Protests were becoming a common sight, a physical manifestation of the growing unrest. She knew that the next steps they took would be crucial in navigating this escalation.

***

The vibrant tension in the task force's headquarters felt like a coiled spring, ready to snap. Dr. Laura Benton stood at the center of it all, her shoulders tense, her gaze never wavering from the screen as images of Bucharest's devastation played out. The Chinese Titan drones—massive machines capable of unleashing destruction on a scale the world had not yet fully come to grips with—had turned the city into a hellscape. The once-bustling metro station was now a smoldering ruin, filled with the screams of the wounded and the panicked cries of those desperately trying to flee.

A soft knock at the door interrupted her thoughts, and Emmeline appeared, her face flushed from the run. "Adam Cole is here and wants to know if you're available for comment on his editorial."

Laura didn't hesitate. "Bring him to my office," she said. Her voice was calm, but there was an edge to it. "And have the sommelier bring a bottle of Aragh Sagi. We might as well make this conversation worth the trouble."

As Emmeline disappeared down the hallway, Laura turned back to the screen, watching the breaking news unfold. Cole's articles had struck a chord with the male population, exposing the raw, festering wounds left by the Good Man Initiative. Cole's latest reports revealed chilling data: a significant drop in marriages, a surge in male suicides, and rapidly increasing incarceration rates. The crisis of masculinity, as he called it, was deepening.

Moments later, the door opened again, and Adam Cole entered. Dressed in his typical casual but sharp attire—a jacket over a plain shirt, his stubble giving him an air of rugged confidence. His eyes locked with Laura's as he stepped into the room, his presence commanding attention despite the confrontation.

"Dr. Benton," he greeted, his tone polite but laced with challenge. "I wasn't sure you'd take the time to speak with me. This building lacks security," Adam said without a moment for a proper hello or etiquette. "After a near-death experience in having your Gulfstream blown out of the sky, I would expect more than just a few armored cars patrolling the perimeter."

Laura forced a smile, one that didn't quite reach her eyes. "You've made yourself hard to ignore, Adam. Your articles are reaching people... though I'm not sure you've grasped the destruction your words are inciting."

Adam's eyes narrowed, but before he could respond, the sommelier entered, carrying a tray with two glasses and a bottle of Aragh Sagi, the potent Iranian liquor Laura had grown fond of. The sommelier poured the glasses, and the strong, licorice-scented alcohol filled the air, adding a layer of olfactory tension that clung to the room like a fog.

"You wanted to know about my thoughts on your reports," Laura continued as she raised her glass, her fingers tightening around it.

"I'm sure you already know most of them. You've painted a picture of a dying society, one where men are being suffocated by our policies, pushed to the brink of extinction. Do you believe that? Or, perhaps you're a populist."

Adam held her gaze, his voice low but firm. "I believe that what's happening right now, across the world, directly results from your task force's overreach. You've built a society where men feel like third-class citizens, and you're surprised they're rebelling? You've weaponized laws and women against them, made them feel like they have no place left in this world. And now, with these military victories in Italy and Greece, you're provoking them even further."

Laura set her glass down with a sharp clink, the sound echoing in the room. "I won't apologize for the military actions we've taken. Italy and Greece were under Chinese occupation, their men being used as soldiers to prop up a regime that only seeks to destroy us. We reclaimed what was ours. You can't blame us for protecting our future."

Adam didn't flinch. "And yet, the collateral damage from those battles is on full display in your own reports. Thousands of dead cities reduced to rubble, and now Romania's burning as retaliation. How long can you keep this up before the world burns with it?"

The question hung in the air, heavy with the weight of truth. Laura took a slow sip of her drink, the strong liquor burning its way down her throat. She could feel the anger rising within her, but there was something else too—doubt. Cole wasn't wrong. The backlash was real, and it was growing by the day.

She leaned forward, her voice lowering. "What do you suggest, Adam? That we stop? That we let men like the ones in Bucharest, or the ones in Italy and Greece, run rampant? Because that's what happens if we step back. Everyone starves. Disease spreads."

Adam's gaze hardened. "What I'm suggesting is that you take a step back from this authoritarianism and find a way to reconcile with these men before it's too late. You are turning men into pawns with your Good Man Initiative, and people will only tolerate so much before they fight back.

Outside, the roar of fighter jets flew overhead, the city on high alert after the Romanian attack. The scent of burnt metal and fire from the local conflict seemed to seep into the room, mixing with the sharp tang of Aragh Sagi and the quiet, unspoken fear of what came next.

Before Laura could respond, her communication system beeped. She glanced at the screen—it was an urgent update from the World Liberty Congress. The Feminist Army was preparing for a major counterstrike against the Chinese forces in Eastern Europe.

Laura turned back to Adam, her expression unreadable. "We're at war, Adam. I don't have time to reconcile with men who want us dead."

The room fell silent again. The weight of the moment engulfed both of them. Adam leaned back in his chair, his voice calmer but still firm. "Maybe. But if you don't stop the violence soon, you won't have anything left to fight for."

Laura's grip tightened around her glass, the liquid swirling as the tension between them crackled like a live wire. She knew he was right. The world was at a tipping point, and if they weren't careful, there would be no coming back.

In the distance, the faint sound of explosions rumbled through the city, a reminder that the battle wasn't just in Bucharest. It was everywhere.

Dr. Benton's office was a sanctuary of modern elegance, perched high above the bustling streets of Toronto. The expansive glass windows of her high-rise office glowed with the fiery hues of the setting sun. Streaks of orange, pink, and purple painted the sky, reflecting off the mirrored surfaces of neighboring skyscrapers, creating a dazzling display of light and color. The cityscape below transformed into a miniature world, its buildings casting long shadows that stretched across the grid-like streets.

The CN Tower stood prominently in the skyline, a towering symbol of the city's ambition and progress. Beyond, the shimmering waters of Lake Ontario reflected the vibrant sky, adding a sense of tranquility to the urban panorama. The view was both awe-inspiring and grounding, a constant reminder of the stakes at hand.

Inside, the office exuded sophistication. Comfortable minimalist furniture with clean lines and polished surfaces contrasted with the soft, ambient light from strategically placed lamps. A subtle scent of lavender and bergamot from a discreet diffuser mingled with the faint aroma of polished wood and leather, creating an atmosphere of calm focus.

The large claro walnut desk is the centerpiece of the room, received meticulous organization. A state-of-the-art computer, a holographic world map depicting military leverage and fronts reflecting Laura's preference for order and efficiency. Behind the desk, built-in shelves displayed an array of books, academic journals, and personal mementos, including a framed photograph of Laura with her fiance and awards recognizing her contributions to her cancer cure and other medical achievements.

Faint electronic dance music played softly in the background, providing a soothing counterpoint to the day's tension. A holographic projection of a serene, underwater scene shimmered beneath them, creating the illusion of walking on a glass floor over a vibrant coral reef. The only other sounds were the occasional murmur of voices and footsteps from the corridor outside, a reminder of the bustling activity within the task force headquarters.

Adam Cole's eyes flicked around the room, taking in the tasteful decor and meticulous order. As Laura refilled the glasses of Aragh Sagi, the clink of glass against glass punctuated the serenity, the rich clear liquid catching the light and hinting at its deep, complex anise flavors.

"This latest release of societal laws is a far cry from restoring gender diversity, equality, and inclusion. It's a far cry from gaining world peace. Did you expect to end a war with this garb?" From his vintage rucksack he brought out his large tablet. He paused a moment before reading the list.

Legislation for the Good Man Initiative—

1. University Quotas Adjustment: To promote diversity and provide educational opportunities, university quotas for male students will be raised from 3% to 5%."

"Raising the level of men's intelligence brings more equanimity and inclusion in society," Laura said, her gesture and body language adding insight and reasoning to the item.

1. Home Ownership for Veteran Militiamen: All men serving in the Feminist Militia for ten years or more will be eligible for consideration to purchase a home and qualify for a veteran's assistance loan."

"These heroes deserve a chance to stabilize themselves when they return to civilian life," she said.

"Not what the bill proposes, Laura. It only makes them eligible. It doesn't make it happen," Adam said with a tone of condemnation.

1. Male Education Incentive: Men pursuing degrees in fields traditionally dominated by women (e.g., doctors, nursing, education, social work) will receive tuition grants and scholarships to promote diversity and encourage their participation."

"These are good paying and stable jobs and with more men educated and trained in these key positions we add diversity and inclusion to our society," she said. Her voice becoming more insistent and her expression less inviting for his questioning of her policies.

1. Fatherhood Support Program: Fathers who actively participate in child-rearing and share household responsibilities will receive tax benefits and parental leave extensions, recognizing their contribution to family life.

"My god Laura, you made this one sound so demeaning and condemning. As if it is rare for a man to actively participate in his children's lives? Don't you see how cruel this is worded?"

Laura said nothing. Her arms folded over her chest as she stood watching him. The grip on her glass tightened as she realized the words she spoke would fill his next editorial report. This impromptu meeting feels like a hack. He's more professional than this. Her thoughts wonder if there was some hidden agenda. Perhaps someone else forcing him to T-Bone her like this.

1. Mental Health Access for Men: Funding will be allocated to establish mental health programs specifically tailored to address the unique challenges faced by men in the new social order, promoting emotional well-being and reducing stigma.

"Do you expect men will naturally suffer mentally? That is to say; psychological trauma from these initiatives?"

She stood quiet. Unmoved and patient waiting for him to finish the list. Her mind grasping for the words. Knowing he would end his questioning, expecting a final response. The world needs to hear her conviction to end the war and for women to take control.

"My readers want your explanation, Laura. The world wants to understand why these laws are being enacted to control men's lives."
He waited a moment for her to respond and when she did not, he continued reading the list.

1. Male Representation in Arts and Culture: Grants and awards shall be established to support male artists and creators, encouraging their participation in cultural discourse and ensuring their voices are heard.

"Throughout history, humanity and societies have realized improved quality of life and advancements through cultural arts and sciences. Providing better and increased opportunities for men to be heard in all forms of expression is equanimity." She took a sip from her glass, then signaled for him to read the final initiative.

1. Men's Community Centers: Government-funded community centers shall be established throughout the Western Alliances of Starzel and Cascadia to provide safe spaces for men to gather, socialize, and access resources tailored to their needs.

"Just the Western Alliance? Why so limited?" Adam said. Tossing his hands out in demonstration.
"It is bold and active experimentation in an inclusive society to test the changes and improve the activities. Based on data and facts, we will improve the lives of this significant part of our communities. But there is too much burden to expect all areas and all communities to add centers. We will begin in select areas and then devise more inclusion for our legislation."
Adam had an expression of dissatisfaction on his face. "The world waits to hear from you, Dr. Benton. How do you explain this body of legislation as a catalyst towards peace?"

"These are only the start of the World Liberty Congress recognizing the significant contribution of men in our societies and we recognize that some civic response is necessary to shore up weaknesses. But I want to address this misguided propaganda and yellow journalism in your last publication.

"There is no equality to be gained by looking to some nonexisting beacon or relic from the past. My policy and the intentions of our World Liberty Congress are not to end or turn back three hundred years of momentum. That would be foolish and unnecessary. Over the last ten years, our leadership has established communities around the globe where women have established strong economic, safe, and moral lives. Good lives for men and children as well.

"Yes, there are some gaps and as you pointed out in the publication, men do require help to better their lives. As I have always said, we are shoring up these gaps and establishing government controls to help." They shared a long drink, their gazes locked. Adam noticed, for the first time, that Laura's eyes were different colors. Hazel brown on the left and honey brown on the right. There was something mesmerizing about the contrast, a reflection of the complexities within her. As they set down their drinks, Adam stood to leave.

"Marsal and I had dinner two days ago," he said, pointing to the picture of Laura and her fiancé on the wall.

"Where was this?" Her voice, filled with curiosity, betrayed her interest. She hadn't seen him in fifteen months. Not since their last argument when she ended their engagement. Her heart fluttered only for a moment as butterflies filled her stomach. She wondered at the emotions and the sense of longing still so strong.

"We met on the outskirts of Istanbul. Dr. Victor Lang was going to show us something at a science laboratory. Unfortunately, circumstances held him up, so Marsal and I made the best of it. He's a brilliant man, and his skills as a Boundrian Creator are supposed to be among the best of his kind."

A sudden heat flared in her chest, replacing the fleeting longing with anger. She clenched her fists, keeping her expression controlled. Marsal's betrayal—if this was true—was unforgivable. He had been part of the movement, fighting for humanity's survival, and now he stood alongside her greatest enemy?

"What did you talk about?" she asked, her voice deceptively casual, though the rage in her bosom grew like a wildfire. "Victor Lang is destroying our world, fueling this chaos. And Marsal is working with him?"

Adam shrugged, seemingly oblivious to her inner turmoil. "We talked about a lot of things. The Gender Cataclysm, of course. His work, your work, and how intertwined they are. He spoke highly of you, despite everything."

Despite everything? The words stung. How could he speak highly of her when he was aligning himself with a man determined to undermine everything she had fought for?

Laura turned, her eyes hardening as she stared at the skyline outside. The fiery hues of the sunset reflected the boiling emotions inside her. She took a breath, her chest tight. This was it. This was the tipping point.

"Tomorrow morning," she said, her voice cold as ice, "I will give the order to kill all Neurohumans on sight. We will ban them from the planet, just as we did Musk's cyborgs centuries ago. Their place on this planet provides our enemies with an evil advantage."

Adam's eyes widened in shock at the sudden change in tone. "You're serious? Laura, you—"

"Dr. Lang, Marsal, all of them. There's no place for them on this planet anymore," she cut him off, her voice firm and ruthless. She turned toward the door, her mind made up. "Well, if you'll excuse me, Adam, I have a war to win and a world to salvage."

Her PA appeared at the door, signaling the end of the conversation. "Mister Cole, can I show you out?"

Adam hesitated for a moment, studying her face. He opened his mouth to speak, but thought better of it. He nodded while rising to his feet in tense silence.

Chapter Ten: Courtroom, Earth

Seven Months and Nineteen Days Into The One-Year Appointment at The World Liberty Congress

The courtroom loomed large, its vaulted ceilings and polished wood surfaces reflecting an aura of dignified authority. Sunlight filtered through tall windows, casting long shadows across the room, and the murmurs of anticipation from the packed gallery echoed softly against the walls. The air was thick with tension and the mingled scent of polished marble floors and old wood. An ominous scent that professed the room's history of heated debates and momentous decisions.

Coach Sam Taylor sat at the plaintiff's table, feeling the anxiety of the moment squeezing his chest. His heart thumped in a steady rhythm of panic and hope. As Eli's partner and emotional anchor, Sam knew that their fight for equality was more than just personal; it was a fight for countless other men who felt marginalized and oppressed.

In the seat beside him, Eli looked every bit the professional athlete—a towering figure of confidence and determination. Yet, Sam could see the fine lines of tension etched across his face, the product of countless sleepless nights and the added pressure of his NBA career. Eli's fingers tapped a restless beat on the table, a physical manifestation of the stress that bound them both.

A small, cylindrical projector, about the size of a thermos, emitted a faint hum as it activated. Its polished titanium casing gleamed under the sterile lights of the court room, and a micro-lattice lens at its tip refracted beams of blue and white light into the air. Within seconds, the beams coalesced into holographic figures, the Martian representatives, standing in sharp, three-dimensional clarity.

The projector's core employed quantum light diffraction technology, capable of rendering images with a resolution so fine that the fabric of the delegates' uniforms appeared textured, almost touchable. Surrounding the projector were tiny gyroscopic stabilizers, ensuring the holograms remained steady even if the device shifted slightly. It pulsed with an almost organic rhythm as it refreshed the holograms 60 times per second, creating the illusion of uninterrupted, lifelike motion.

As the Martians spoke, the projector's integrated adaptive sound system triangulated their voices, perfectly syncing their tones with the visual output. The room filled with their presence, an interplay of advanced optics and acoustics delivering a flawless illusion of reality.

Judge Harper, a woman whose very presence seemed to embody the law, surveyed the courtroom. Her gaze was razor sharp, betraying no emotion, just the practiced calculation of a woman who had seen every trick, every argument, every legal maneuver imaginable. She nodded subtly, a signal so slight only the most attentive would notice. Jasmine Crocket, the state's attorney, took it as her cue.

Jasmine stood slowly, with the confidence of someone who had never tasted defeat. She was more than just a lawyer. She was a force, a legal titan who had dismantled opponents, one by one, with ruthless precision. Her undefeated record wasn't a footnote in her career; it was her legend.

She approached the bench with measured grace, every step deliberate, calculated. Her reputation preceded her: a genius who could deconstruct the most complicated of legal arguments and leave her opponents gasping for air, wondering how they'd been outclassed before they knew what hit them. This was the stuff movies are made of, but this wasn't a movie.

"Your Honor," she began, her voice rich and unwavering, "ladies and gentlemen of the court. We stand here today not merely to argue law but to reflect upon the very foundation of our civilization."

Jasmine paused, letting the members of the court unpack her words and settle. "For over a century, the carefully structured system of laws has provided not just for the rights of women but for the happiness of men. A balance was struck—a balance that gave women the power to thrive in their rights and men the chance to live in contentment, knowing that their roles were equally important, if different."

She paced slowly, drawing the court into her rhythm. "These laws have been the bedrock of society. They ensured stability, progress, and, most importantly, the future of humanity. The world, under this system, prospered."

Jordan Blake shifted uncomfortably, sensing the tide turning. Jasmine's words carried the progress of history, of long-standing traditions and hard-fought battles.

"But now," she continued, turning toward Judge Harper, her voice lowering to a near whisper, commanding attention, "we are faced with a dilemma unlike any we have encountered before. One that threatens the very fabric of what has sustained us."

She let her words hang for a moment before delivering the fatal blow. "Births have been in decline for decades. The number of women desiring children continues to increase, but the simple truth is, there aren't enough children to go around. This is a crisis, one that men, no matter how well-intentioned, simply cannot resolve. Allowing them to raise children when the supply is so limited would be not just a disservice to society, but an act of selfishness that we, as stewards of the future, cannot afford."

Jasmine's eyes locked with Judge Harper's, and the courtroom seemed to hold its collective breath.

"Your Honor," she said, her voice now cool and decisive, "we are not here to deny anyone's rights. We are here to ensure the survival of our civilization. It is a woman's right to bear and raise children. It is nature's design. And while we empathize with the desires of men, we cannot allow such an essential role to be divided."

She turned, her last words directed at the Martian representative, Lira Voss. "The Martian Colonies may champion equality, but we must champion humanity."

Jasmine took her seat, her gaze steady and unyielding. She had made her case, her arguments sharp as steel. The room, once buzzing with tension, now sat in stunned silence. Judge Harper leaned forward, her fingers tapping the bench thoughtfully. The simple logic of Jasmine's opening argument hung heavy in the air, as undeniable as the truth itself.

Coach Sam sat in the courtroom, his mind a storm of thoughts and emotions. He felt defeated before he had a chance to be heard.

Judge Harper leaned back in her chair, her gaze shifting between the two parties as if she could see right through him. Her eyes settled on Jordan Blake; Sam and Eli's lawyer.

"Mr. Blake, how do you address the potential for social unrest that such a society might cause?" Judge Harper asked, her voice probing and analytical.

Sam watched as Jordan met her gaze without flinching. He admired Jordan's composure. It was something Sam wished he could muster as easily in this moment.

"Your Honor, Eli and Sam do not seek to disrupt harmony but to create a space where their identities can flourish without fear of oppression. They wish to build a society based on mutual respect and collaboration, not exclusion," Jordan said.

Sam felt the courtroom's focus narrowing in on them, the heat of scrutiny pressing down like a laundry mangler. He squeezed Eli's hand under the table, drawing strength from their shared resolve. This was their moment—a chance to speak truth to power.

Jordan Blake took a deep breath, his eyes locked on Judge Harper. He knew this was the turning point, the moment where he either shattered the long-standing narrative or fell victim to it. His voice rang out with a calm determination that demanded attention, cutting through the thick tension in the room.

"Your Honor, we argue this case here in the shadow of a system that was, although well-intentioned, biased from its inception. A system designed to provide rights and security for women, and yet, over time, it has left men in the cold. Eli and Sam do not seek to disrupt harmony but to create a space where their identities can flourish without fear of oppression. They wish to build a society based on mutual respect and collaboration, not exclusion."

He took his time, calculating for effect his eyes briefly flicking toward Jasmine Crocket, who looked ready to object. But Jordan had more to say. He powered on, his voice rising, more impassioned. "We hear words like 'happiness' and 'balance,' but when we look at the hard data, it becomes clear that happiness is not reflected in the lives of men. Men make up 50% of the population but account for 88% of incarcerations, 92% of suicides, and a staggering 96% of fatalities in a war that has raged for forty years. A war, might I add, fought mostly to sustain a world that men have little participation in."

Jasmine's hand shot up. "Objection—"

"Your Honor, allow me to finish," Jordan said. He interjected quickly, pressing forward before Judge Harper could respond. "This is not just rhetoric; these are facts from the Global Social Data Records and World Health Council Reports—indisputable numbers that highlight the suffering men endure under a system that claims to value equality. Jasmine spoke of men's happiness in her opening. I have a right to counter her claim.

"Men, on average, drop out of basic education after just seven years. Only 3.8% of college graduates are men. And for those who stay in the workforce, men earn just 37% of what women earn, even when holding the same jobs. The imbalance is undeniable."

Jasmine Crocket's expression hardened, her objection hanging in the air. But Jordan pressed on, undeterred. He had momentum now, and he wasn't about to let it slip away.

"Men hold 11% of management positions globally and own a mere 14% of small businesses. These numbers tell a story, Your Honor. A story of disenfranchisement, of systemic inequality. Happiness, enjoyment—these are not words that apply to men's lives under this system. Every sector of society marginalizes them. These are not the lives of men thriving; they are the lives of men struggling to survive in an unbalanced society."

Jordan gestured toward his clients. His tone shifting from the quantifiable facts to a softer, more empathetic note. "Your Honor, Eli and Sam's request is not radical. They are not asking to overthrow the status quo. They are simply asking for a space—one small space—where men can live without the crushing weight of these disparities. They want to raise children not as a privilege the system is magnanimous to grant, but as a right that has been withheld from them for too long. A society based on mutual respect, not the blind perpetuation of an outdated hierarchy. Where women, government, justice, and media have been weaponized against men."

He let the silence stretch for a beat; the courtroom frozen under the measure of his argument.

"We should ask ourselves why men have been denied the opportunity for so long, not whether they should be allowed to exist in a humane way."

Jordan, with the cool precision of a man who had laid out the undeniable truth, delivered his final words. He took his seat, but the room didn't breathe. All eyes turned to Judge Harper. She sat in silence, her fingers steepled, her expression inscrutable.

Jasmine Crocket shifted slightly in her chair, but even she knew Jordan's words had cut deep. The battle was far from over, but Jordan had done what he came to do—he had planted the seed of doubt, the undeniable crack in the foundation of the status quo.

The Martian representatives exchanged glances, their expressions unreadable. Lira, their spokesperson, turned back to Judge Harper. "Judge Harper, our commitment to equality is unwavering. Allowing this division risks setting a precedent for further fragmentation. We must consider the implications for future generations. What happens on Earth has implications for people on Mars, Moon, and the space portals."

Sam's mind raced, searching for flaws in their arguments. The Martians' stance was formidable, their logic airtight. But Sam knew the reality—the daily injustices they faced, the systemic barriers that kept them marginalized. He could feel his frustration mounting, but he kept it in check. Losing his cool wouldn't help their case.

As the arguments continued, Sam's thoughts drifted to their personal lives. Eli, during the NBA playoffs, was a whirlwind of movement and adrenaline. Sam knew the constant travel between the courtroom and the basketball court was taking its toll on their relationship, stretching their patience and resolve to its limits. Yet, here they were, fighting for something bigger than both of them.

The courtroom door groaned open, its aged hinges shrieking under the strain of its massive frame. The sharp noise startled the room, cutting through the heavy stillness. A rush of cool, fresh air spilled in, scattering the stale air and bringing an unspoken relief that none had realized they needed. Sam drew a deeper breath, his chest easing for the first time in what felt like hours.

Then he saw Eli's coach step in, his expression tight with urgency. Sam's pulse quickened, a flicker of unease gripping him. The playoffs loomed large in his mind, a fragile hope for Eli now shadowed by the weight of whatever news had just walked through that door.

"Eli," the coach whispers, leaning in close to avoid disrupting the pro-ceedings. "We need to go. The playoffs..."

Eli nodded, a flicker of frustration in his eyes. He whispered to Sam, "I have to go. But this—this is just as important."

Sam nodded, understanding the impossible choice Eli faced. He squeezed Eli's hand once more. "Go, Eli. We'll fight on here."

The courtroom was silent, the tension palpable. Eli, the NBA MVP, stood tall beside Sam, their hands intertwined for a moment longer before he released his partner. Sam watched Eli leave, a mixture of pride and worry swirling inside him.

Judge Harper's gaze was stern as she addressed Eli. "Mr. Eli, the Mar-tian tribunal, has concerns about your suitability as a parent. Your demanding career, your public persona ... I too wonder how two men with such demanding and nomadic careers expect to raise children."

Her words trailed off in Sam's mind as he saw a familiar look in Eli's eyes—a flashback to another time. Sam could picture it vividly: a dimly lit gym, the squeak of sneakers echoing around them. All the other players had showered, dressed, and gone home, but Eli re-mained, driven by an unspoken calling. Always the first player to show for practices and las to leave after.

A young boy, barely ten years old, had approached Eli after a grueling practice session. "Mr. Eli," the boy said. He was shy and his voice stammered, "can you teach me to shoot like you?"

Eli had knelt down, meeting the boy's gaze. Sam remembered how Eli's voice had softened as he spoke to the child. "Sure, kid. But it takes more than just practice. It takes heart, determination, and the belief that you can achieve anything you set your mind to."

Eli had spent hours with the boy that day, patiently guiding him through the fundamentals, encouraging him to push past his limits. Sam had watched from the sidelines, moved by Eli's patience and dedication. As the boy's shots started falling through the hoop, a smile spread across his face, a spark of confidence igniting in his eyes.

In the corner of the gymnasium, Sam noticed a younger boy watching intently. As Eli finally rose to leave, the boy tugged on his younger brother's sleeve, his voice loud and hopeful. "Let me show you what Eli taught me. We will be as great as Eli someday."

Sam's heart had swelled with pride, knowing that Eli's true calling wasn't just about winning championships or scoring points. It was about inspiring others, nurturing their potential, and planting seeds of hope that would grow into dreams fulfilled.

The memory faded, replaced by the courtroom's stark reality. Sam took a deep breath as Eli turned to face Judge Harper. His voice sincere.

"Your Honor, basketball is my passion. My livelihood," Eli said. "But it doesn't define me. It doesn't diminish my capacity to love, to nurture, to guide a child."

Eli turned to Sam, their eyes locking on a shared understanding. Sam felt the connection between them, the bond that had carried them through so many life trials.

"Sam and I have built a life together, a partnership based on trust, respect, and unwavering love. We are ready to share that love with a child, to provide a stable, supportive home where they can thrive."

Eli's voice resonated with conviction, filling the courtroom. "I've learned that being a champion isn't just about winning trophies. It's about making a difference in the lives of others. And there is no greater impact I can make than by raising a child, by guiding them to reach their full potential, just as I have for many young boys over the years."

As Eli spoke, Sam felt a surge of hope. This was why they were here, why they had fought so hard. It was more than just a battle in a courtroom; it was a fight for their future, for the chance to make a difference in the life of a child.

Sam watched Judge Harper closely, searching for any sign of understanding or empathy in her expression. The room was silent, every eye fixed on the judge as they waited for her response. And in that moment, despite all the uncertainty, Sam clung to a flicker of hope.

As the courtroom settled into a tense silence, the screen flickered, and an unfamiliar figure appeared beside the Martian representatives. It was Dr. Victor Lang. His holographic presence came into focus and his commanding attention with the familiar gravitas of a former friend turned influential leader.

Sam's breath caught in his throat. Dr. Lang had been a confidant, a mentor during their early struggles. His sudden defection to the Martian cause had felt like a loss, and now his presence here could turn the tide against them.

"Your Honor," Lang began, his voice smooth but carrying a subtle arrogance, "Jasmine Crocket speaks of survival, but what she and the Earthbound powers cannot understand is that survival has many forms. The world is changing, and Mars has embraced that change. We do not live by the laws of Earth. We are no longer bound by those outdated systems and their arbitrary constraints."

Sam felt a cold wave wash over him. This was what the conspiracist had feared all along—Lang's complete rejection of Earth's authority. And yet, there was something more to it, a darker undercurrent that they had not anticipated.

Lang's gaze sharpened. "The Martian government no longer recognizes the jurisdiction of Earth over our affairs. The decisions made in your court and on Earth will be nothing more than suggestions. Mars will decide its own future, one that is free of the chains that have bound your society for so long. And make no mistake, that our future is already in motion."

Judge Harper's expression darkened, her fingers curling slightly as she absorbed Lang's bold declaration. The boldness of his words hit like a hammer. An open challenge to her authority, and to the very core of the trial.

Lang leaned forward, his voice taking on a chilling tone. "Earth may cling to its laws, but a civilization in decline will not drag Mars down. We are building something new, something that will transcend gender, race, even species. Your court can pass whatever judgment it wants, but on Mars. I decide."

The room erupted into chaos; the tension reaching a boiling point. Sam's mind raced, his pulse pounding in his ears. The stakes had just changed. This wasn't just a legal battle anymore—it was a war of ideologies, a conflict between two worlds fighting for their vision of the future.

And in the middle of it all, Sam realized, their fight had just become even more desperate.

Jasmine Crocket stood, her presence undiminished even as the courtroom buzzed with tension following Jordan's argument and Victor Lang's announcement. She was unflinching, her expression calm and movements poised, as if she had prepared for this moment her entire career. Her eyes briefly flickered to the holographic figure of Dr. Victor Lang, but her focus remained on the judge and the people in the room. This was her arena.

"Your Honor," Jasmine began, her voice firm, cutting through the ruckus like a rocket launch, "we are not here to deny the realities men face, nor are we here to diminish their struggles. The data is real, and I am not here to deny its validity. But we must not forget the guiding principles of our civilization, principles that were laid out by the influential leaders of our time—leaders like Dr. Laura Benton."

She took a step forward, her posture confident and her tone unwavering as she invoked Benton's legacy. "For decades, Dr. Benton has provided the world with the framework of leadership that has kept us from falling into chaos. Under her guidance, we have evolved, embracing equality, but always with the understanding that humanity must be preserved—at any cost. We have laws, not just on Earth, but laws that extend across our universe. Laws that bind us all to the essence of who we are: a species that must survive."

Jasmine's eyes swept across the courtroom, her words holding the audience captive. "What Mars and men like Dr. Victor Lang fail to understand is that treason against the human race cannot be disguised as progress. Mars may claim to be its own entity, but the law of Earth reaches across the universe. It provides the boundaries of humanity, the foundation upon which all societies must be built. To challenge that is not just defiance—it is reckless. The survival of the species must come first, not the whims of individual ambition."

Dr. Lang's holographic image flickered, the distortion momentary yet unsettling. Jasmine remained unmoved, her voice lowering, soft but resonant, as if delivering a solemn truth carved from stone. "The fact remains, Your Honor, that despite the statistics, despite the claims of suffering, despite the rhetoric of a better future, there are simply not enough children to sustain the plaintiff's request."

A heavy silence fell over the room. Jordan shifted in his seat, visibly tense. Sam felt his heart tighten, the words striking a deep chord. This was the reality they could not escape.

Jasmine continued, her voice rising slightly, emphasizing the grim reality. "The declining birthrate is an indisputable truth. And while men may seek to raise children, the reality is that there is not enough to go around. The laws that prioritize women's right to motherhood are not born of bias but necessity. This isn't about power—it's about survival."

She turned to Judge Harper, her conclusive argument a sharp rapier blade cutting through the emotional chaos of the room. "We do not have the luxury to entertain experimental societies or ideologies that could threaten the very existence of our species. Dr. Victor Lang may speak of a world beyond gender, beyond division, but his vision is nothing more than a fantasy. Humanity is teetering on the edge, and we must make decisions based on the here and now. The proper decision for what will secure the future. And that future belongs to the women who can still bring new life into society."

Jasmine took her seat, her presence still obvious in the room. The courtroom had fallen into a stunned silence, her argument ringing out with a finality that left little room for dispute.

Just as Judge Harper lifted the gavel, poised to deliver her decision, her expression hardened, and she glanced at her watch. A shift in the atmosphere rippled across the courtroom, a cold unease settling over the room. With a sharp crack of the gavel, she interrupted her own flow.

"I will call a one-hour recess," she said. Her voice tight. Measured. "This court will reconvene promptly at 15:00 hours."

The courtroom erupted into a myriad of conversations. The tension transforming into uncertainty. Sam felt the constriction of the moment ease a fraction, though a peculiar anxiety clawed at him. His eyes darted to the empty seat beside him. Eli had left the courtroom earlier, heading for the flight to his game. But something felt wrong. He hadn't heard from Eli.

Sam pulled out his communicator, fingers fumbling as he scrolled through his messages. Nothing. No calls. No texts. Just an eerie, uncomfortable silence that made his gut twist. He sent Eli a message. *We're at recess. Judge will be back with a verdict in one hour.*

As he rose to leave, the newsfeed on the large screen near the courtroom doors flickered to life. The headline, bold and jarring, stopped him cold.

"Four More Leading Scientists and Engineers Reported Missing—Bringing the Total Count to 22 in the Last Month."

The screen switched to images of the latest missing scientists—faces plastered across the media in a grim collage of vanished brilliance. Sam's stomach sank further. The names and faces were familiar. These weren't just any scientists—they were key figures in the global scientific community. The rare and valuable minds that led entire fields, making breakthroughs that kept humanity advancing. And now they were disappearing, one by one.

But the details of the most recent four struck him as especially bizarre. Dr. Isabel Kline had vanished while attending a live video conference from her apartment, her screen suddenly going dark mid-sentence. Dr. Victor Malone was last seen boarding a ship for an intercontinental voyage—his room found undisturbed, his luggage untouched, but no sign of him. Dr. Liu Chang's entire laboratory had been mysteriously scorched, leaving no trace of him behind. And Dr. Kiera Hammond, the fourth—her disappearance was the strangest of all: neighbors reported hearing laughter—unearthly, distorted, echoing from her home just hours before she was reported missing. All of it felt ... wrong.

Sam's mind raced as he processed the news. The disappearances felt too close, too interconnected. Were these top minds being taken? Was there some sinister force at work? And was Eli, someone tied to the Martian delegation, now caught in something far more dangerous than just a game?

Movement interrupted his thoughts in the courtroom. The Martian delegates, their holographic images still flickering, abruptly signed off without a single word. No farewell, no formal announcement. Just gone, as if they'd never been there. That chilly, vacant feeling in Sam's gut extended deeper.

Across the courtroom, a group of women near the rear of the chamber argued heatedly with Jasmine Crockett. Their voices rose sharply, snippets of conversation spilling over the restless hum of the room.

"You can't just let them—" one woman shouted, her face flushed with frustration.

"We have to—" Jasmine snapped back, her voice like a whip, but whatever she said next was drowned out by the mounting chaos. Sam could tell by the way Jasmine stood—rigid, unflinching—that this was no mere legal disagreement. It was something bigger. She was wrestling with forces far beyond the courtroom.

Sam's com buzzed. His heart skipped as he fumbled to unlock it. But it wasn't Eli. Instead, it was an encrypted message—anonymous, untraceable. Just six words: "Join me on Mars. Victor Lang"

An icy fever broke across Sam's forehead. His mind spun, connecting the dots too quickly.

Eli, the scientists, the Martian delegates disappearing in the blink of an eye—was this part of some larger conspiracy? Something that had been in motion for far longer than anyone realized?

Sam shoved his com into his pocket, his pulse pounding in his ears. He had no time. Answers were what he needed, and he needed them immediately. He glanced over at Jordan Blake, who was pacing by the courtroom doors, deep in thought. Jordan, who had just torn down Jasmine's case with brutal precision, now looked like he knew something more—something he wasn't sharing.

Could he be involved?

Sam's gaze swept back to the screen as another news alert scrolled across the bottom. "Unidentified energy anomalies reported at multiple Martian outposts." Whatever this was, it wasn't just legal or political—it was interplanetary, global. And it was happening now.

***

The courtroom was full of people. Journalists lined the back rows, their faces tense, ready to pounce on whatever verdict Judge Harper was about to deliver. Cameras stream like a flurry of insects, capturing every twitch. The buzz of anticipation was thick and suffocating, a living thing that pulsed in the air. Sam wondered if he would stroke. His fingers reading the pulse on his wrist. Nothing detected. He checked his carotid.

The pressure mounted as he watched the door open and Judge Harper entered the courtroom. Her deep crimson robe with gold-embroidered trim flowing behind her like a symbol of unyielding authority. She ascended to the bench with deliberate calm, her face unreadable, a mask of judicial authority. For a moment, everything stopped—the courtroom hushed to a silence so absolute that Sam relieved that he could hear his heartbeat pounding in his ears. Eli's absence still gnawed at the edge of his mind, but right now, all that mattered was this moment.

Judge Harper sat down, arranging her notes before her. The room held its collective breath as she scanned the courtroom, her eyes briefly settling on Sam before she turned her gaze outward to the swelling sea of reporters, legal teams, and spectators.

"Before I announce my ruling," she said, her voice cool and measured. "I want to make it clear that this case has raised profound questions. Questions that challenge the very core of how we define human rights, family, and our future as a society.

"As I consider the complexities of this case," she said, "I am reminded of the foundation upon which our modern society has been built—feminism. Feminism, in its truest form, has long been rooted in the pursuit of diversity, equity, and inclusion. It was born out of a need to correct the exclusion of women from key roles in governance, business leadership, and every sector of life. Women fought for a seat at the table—and rightfully so."

Her eyes flicked to the shared delegates of the courtroom, where the Martian delegation had once been. Their abrupt departure still lingered in the air, a reminder of how easily things could unravel.

"But," she said, her tone firm, "what we often fail to remember is that in our zeal to correct the injustices of the past, we have sometimes created new exclusions. Men, too, are often excluded—been left out of conversations, particularly at the highest levels of governance. In our fight for equity, we have unintentionally built walls around the very people we claim to be helping. Increasingly, at all levels of government, across our institutions, and in the very chambers where decisions about humanity's future are made, people are leaving men out of conversations.

Sam's pulse quickened. His breath caught in his throat as he felt the undeniable truth in her words. It was a rare admission, one that he had never expected to hear, least of all, from someone in Judge Harper's position.

Her words penetrated the air like smoke, curling into every corner of Sam's consciousness. His stomach twisted with a mix of hope and dread. He could feel the words piercing his soul with her indecision, the moral quandary playing out in her mind. This wasn't just a ruling—it was a moment in history, a pivot point that would reverberate for generations.

She continued, her tone almost conversational now, but laced with a sharp edge of authority. "What if I rule that men should have the right to raise children? It would challenge the 'Good Man' initiatives from the World Liberty Congress, policies crafted to better men's lives, to lift them from their circumstances. Dr. Laura Benton has been at the forefront of these initiatives, and she has reshaped the landscape for men in ways that, until recently, were thought impossible. These policies are meant to improve men's status, but at what cost?"

Sam's heart pounded in his chest. For a moment, hope surged. Maybe she would see the truth. Maybe she would recognize that men deserved the same rights, the same opportunities to raise children, to build families.

"But the right to love who you want and how you want," Judge Harper continued, her gaze hardening, "would be incomplete if it didn't also include the right to raise a family with the one you love. To deny men that is to deny them a full appreciation of the law's promise of equality. Is it not a violation, then, to exclude men from such a basic human experience?"

Sam felt his breath catch. This was it. The moment she would turn, the moment she would acknowledge the fundamental truth he and Eli had fought for. He felt a flicker of vindication, a rush of adrenaline. But then her tone shifted, colder, less speculative.

"However," she said, her voice ending like a door slammed shut, "these children deserve a quality of life experience. A childhood filled with every advantage to grow and develop their full potential. Our world is unstable. Nations of factions, rogue groups with well-equipped militias, and military forces ravage our sovereign territories daily, killing without mercy, destroying everything in their path. We need more children, yes. We need males to fight, to defend, to uphold what remains of our fragile existence. But this need is not fulfilled simply by allowing men to raise children. In fact, it is an obstacle. Men raising children is not the solution to the challenges we face."

Sam's hopes plummeted. The joy that had flared inside him was quickly turning to ash, disappearing behind the harshness of her words. His palms were sweating, his breath shallow.

"But," she continued, her voice softening, almost as though considering an alternative, "there is a growing trend—one that leans toward asexuality, a disconnection from reproduction itself. We see more people disengaging from sex, from intimacy, from the process of creating life. If I were to rule in favor of the plaintiffs, perhaps we could reverse this trend. Perhaps allowing men the right to raise families would inspire more people to engage in reproduction. Perhaps it could bring about a shift, an incentive to restore balance."

Sam's hopes rushed back in. Was she about to rule in their favor, after all? Was this the turning point?

Judge Harper paused, her eyes locking onto his, and for a moment, Sam felt like she could see right through him. It was then that her expression hardened, and she delivered the final blow.

"It is therefore my ruling, after careful consideration of the well-developed arguments presented by both sides, to disallow the plaintiff's claim and rule in favor of the state."

Sam's world came crashing down in an instant. The words hit him like a punch to the gut, knocking the wind from his lungs. He stared at her, unblinking, as the reality of what she had just said settled over him like a sheet of plastic pulled tight over his face.

"However," she said. Adding it almost as an afterthought, "I will recommend that Dr. Laura Benton and her team further investigate the findings I've outlined today.

Judge Harper looked down at Sam, her expression softening for the first time since she had entered the room. "Sam, Eli—thank you for the challenge you brought before this court. But unfortunately, there is too much more to consider in the far-reaching implications of such a ruling. The law must be cautious when it comes to matters as delicate as these."

The gavel struck the wooden block, sealing the decision.

Sam felt the ground fall away beneath him. His hands trembled. His eyes stung with unshed tears. The room swirled around him in a haze of blurred faces and muted voices. All he could hear was the echo of that single, damning word: disallowed.

The journalists had already sprung into action, some shouting questions, others frantically typing on their devices. But for Sam, it all faded into white noise. He had lost. They had lost. And the world, the future they had fought for, slipped further from their grasp.

As he stood there, dazed and hollow, he couldn't help but feel that Judge Harper had already known the answer before she ever stepped into the courtroom.

Chapter Eleven: Temporal Lies Unfold

Nine Months and Four Days Into The One-Year Appointment at The World Liberty Congress

The transport ship thrummed beneath them, a pulsing rhythm fueled by the Marx tachyon energy roaring through the stallaris drive. The sensation gripped the soles of their feet, the faint hum thrumming through their bones, impossible to ignore. Laura Benton's expression was stoic, eyes fixed on the enormity of the Mars portal looming ahead. The sight, mesmerizing and alien, stretched beyond any comprehension of space travel Earth had ever known. Standing beside her, Albera was silent, her first real-time experience of travel to the portal leaving her in awe, but the gleam in her eyes betrayed something deeper.

The portal was alive, swirling with light ribbons of crimson and gold, flickering with a raw energy that bent space and time at its core. It was beautiful, in a terrifying way—like staring into the mouth of a beast and daring it to swallow you whole.

"We're almost there," Laura broke the silence, her voice steady. She glanced sideways at Albera, taking in the subtle tightening of her PA's jaw. "First time seeing the portal in person?"

Albera's gaze remained fixed on the writhing vortex of light. "Yeah ... bigger than I thought," she said, her voice calm, analytical. A stark contrast to the awe-struck expression Laura expected. There was something calculating behind her eyes.

Laura's lips curled ever so slightly. "Everyone thinks that. It's easy to be overwhelmed by the sheer scale of it. But it's not the size that's impressive—it's the function. The Mars portal is more than just a shortcut between worlds. It's the most significant leap in human transportation technology since fire. Instant travel between planets. Wormhole physics perfected. And all this happens in less than a millisecond—no time, no distance."

Albera straightened, her earlier awe replaced by that cool, self-assured demeanor Laura had only seen in seasoned veterans. "I know. The science is complex, but the real genius isn't just the quantum folding or space shifting. The portal's veritable miracle is something else entirely."

Laura raised an eyebrow. "Enlighten me."

Albera tilted her head, tugging and twisting her earring, watching the vortex with newfound detachment. "It's the temporal displacement. The hardest part isn't bending space. It's ensuring that when you leave a location, your timeline remains intact. It's like holding your place in a book. Every fold of space you travel risks distorting time around you. But this..." she gestured toward the swirling energies outside, "...this is precise. The system bookmarks every traveler's timeline, keeping it locked in place. When you step through, you're not just arriving somewhere else—you're arriving exactly when you left."

Laura's expression shifted into something resembling appreciation. "You're saying the real magic is keeping everything where it belongs? A time bookmark."

Albera nodded. "Without it, every traveler could end up in the right place but at the wrong time. Minutes, hours, even years off. The portal has to manage millions of shifting variables and ensure that not only does the traveler arrive in the right space, but at the right moment. Everything is still in place."

"Not just the people," Laura said thoughtfully, her voice darkening as the red light from the portal washed over her face. "The world around you has to stay intact, too. No glitches in the timeline, no unintentional overlaps. I've seen what happens when the tech fails. It's not pretty."

The approaching light of the portal cast an eerie glow across the cabin as they neared the entry. Laura's jaw clenched, the weight of her mission settling over her like a storm cloud.

Albera caught the change in Laura's posture. "This isn't just about science for you, is it?" she asked quietly. "It's Lang."

"Victor Lang," Laura replied, her voice stiff as steel. The name alone was enough to make her blood simmer. "He's the reason we're heading into this mess. After Earth's civil breakdown, he fled to Mars, exiling himself. Said it was for 'personal safety,' but really, it was the beginning of his power grab. He's weaseled his way into Martian leadership and now he's enforcing a new order."

Albera's expression tightened as she finally tore her gaze away from the portal to focus on Laura. "Pro-family politics, right?"

Laura barked a short, humorless laugh. "That's the version they sell to Earth. 'Pro-family,' as if he's some sort of savior for mankind's precious little family units. The revelation is, his colonies are exclusive—gay-only and asexual men's sanctuaries. They've banned heterosexual reproduction entirely. On Mars, men control everything. Reproduction, genetic lineage—it's all science now. And Lang is controlling people through that science."

As they approached the parking pad, the humming intensified, and the glow of the dock became brighter, expanding to fill the entire viewport as they settled down. The intercom crackled, and a voice announced their arrival. The sound drowned out their words momentarily, as if even the ship knew what they were about to face.

Albera's eyes sharpened. "So that's why we're meeting at the portal? He doesn't trust the surface. Too many factions, not enough security."

Laura nodded, but her focus had drifted beyond the portal. "He's dangerous, and not just because of his position. He's got allies—people I didn't expect."

"Like who?" Albera asked, her voice steady, but her curiosity piqued.

"Aylan," Laura replied, her tone darkening. "A Turkish reproduction scientist. She's here. I saw her as we docked, standing by Lang. She says she's setting up a new medical facility, but I know what that means."

Albera frowned. "What is she really doing here?"

"They're building male reproduction labs," Laura spat. "They're not setting up a hospital—they're engineering the future of Mars' male population. And Aylan's the key to it all."

Albera's gaze narrowed as the Martian surface lay out before them. The red planet, jagged and barren, stood stark against the backdrop of the endless void. Huge silver domes sprawled across the surface, visible from space, human colonies cowering beneath the protective glass of their fabricated world.

"They're planning something," Laura said, more to herself than to her PA. "And if we don't stop it, this male utopia they're building will stretch far beyond Mars. Lang has ambitions, and Earth's just the start."

The photon tunnel released them with a sharp, jarring hum, and suddenly, the Martian grid panels stretched out before them like a complex web. The portal had done its job, but Laura knew the real danger awaited. They left the transport on the dock and walked into the portal. Albera consults the directional array to identify their meeting location.

In the distance, the domes glistened in the Martian light—shelters, prisons, agriculture, laboratories—who could tell anymore? One thing was certain: they were viewing a world that had already written women off. It was without objection to becoming a man's world now. Dr. Lang's leadership prevented the accumulation of wealth. His government uses universal basic income for individuals in a democratic republic. With a new leisure economy, an engineered constitution where choices were made for the right people. His direction and control as a dictator were complete, and, as usual, dissent wasn't tolerated.

Before they arrived at the meeting room they were stood fast outside the transport bay where ships to and from the Martian surface docked. An illuminated statue of a pregnant woman. The words "The Last Woman" across the bottom at her bare feet. Above her the words were all capitalized. SHE GOT MAN THROWN OUT OF PARADISE. SHE DESTROYED PLANET EARTH. NOW SHE IS IRRELEVANT.

The impact of the words lingered between them as they stepped off the lift into the bustling Martian Portal's government center. The center was pristine and sterile, like a world separated from the chaos of Earth. But it was all a façade, and Laura knew better. Everything about the portal reminded her she was on a manmade ship. Enormous and technically unimaginable. But a breach of any panel would cause the collapse of the structure and take the life of everyone on board within a matter of seconds.

Someone arranged their meeting in an inner chamber hall. No views of space or of the planet. The closing of the room's door felt like the ending scene of a science fiction film. The room's decor featured martian and space relics. Artwork and statues of unrecognized landscapes and devices. Lighting, Laura had never experienced seemed to tease her visual perception. Her eyes struggled to adjust and focus.

Negotiations with Mars' leadership began as expected—stilted, diplomatic, and laced with suspicion. Lang didn't show his face at first, but the shadow of his influence loomed over every interaction. Laura's position as Earth's World Liberty Congress leader made her the key player in these talks, but she could feel the descension. Mars was no longer a neutral party; it was in the pocket of Dr. Victor Lang.

Later, alone in her quarters, Laura accessed a secure channel to contact the Moon colony. She hadn't been back in years—not since the bitter split from her fiancé. The moment his face appeared on the screen, her heart clenched.

His voice was cold, formal. "Dr. Benton. I see you're busy on Mars."

"Prime Minister," she replied, equally distant. "I didn't expect you to rise so high in the Moon's government."

He smiled, but it didn't reach his eyes. "It's President-elect now."

Her stomach felt sick. "What are you doing?"

"I'm making sure the Moon stays what it was always meant to be—a sanctuary. A sanctuary for men."

"What are you talking about?"

His next words cut like lava crossing a grass field. "I'm banning women from the Moon, effective next week. The ban includes those who identify as women. We will be one gender. Men." he said. "Permanently."

She stared at him, unable to believe what she was hearing. "You can't be serious."

"I've never been more serious," he said, his voice moderate and unyielding. "Women are irrelevant. No longer necessary for our future."

Laura stared at the screen, the cold, empty smile of her ex-fiancé staring back at her like the end of an old dream now turned into a nightmare. The silence between them felt heavy, a palpable force weighing down the air, and the pressure in her chest and head mounted.

"You're insane," she said under her breath, her voice barely audible.

"Dr. Benton?" he inquired. She found his voice smug, like a snake ready to strike again.

Laura clenched her fists, and the word slipped through her clenched teeth in a half-whisper, half-growl, "Thhhhksss." A tight hiss, the sound of a fuse burning down to its last inch before it detonates. Her hands demonstrated the explosion.

Her eyes hardened, and without another word, she severed the connection with a decisive click. The screen went black, as did her heart. The only sound left was her heavy, controlled breathing. Laura's mind raced, a surge of fury coursing through her veins like molten steel pounded into a broadsword.

She turned toward Albera, who had been quietly working in the corner of the room. Her face unreadable, her fingers twisting and tugging at her earring. Laura's movements were quick, controlled, and deliberate as she stepped toward the digital dictation panel on the wall. There was no time for emotion now. Everything had just shifted.

"Prepare to record," she said, her voice a sharp edge of professionalism masking the tempest swirling inside her. Albera quickly snapped into action, pulling up the Martian and Lunar diplomatic channels.

Neither Government had made the official announcement but Laura knew it was inevitable. They were taking a path toward banishing women from space.

Laura began speaking in a calm but authoritative tone, the words rolling off her tongue with a precision that betrayed none of the fury boiling beneath the surface.

"To the honorable members of the Martian High Council," she started, "As the representative of Earth and its governing body, I wish to express my full support and agreement with the current constitutional developments within the Martian colonies. The vision for a stable, self-governing Mars is one that aligns with Earth's interests, and I wish to extend my appreciation for the clarity and focus of your leadership."

Albera's fingers moved swiftly across the panel, transcribing Laura's words with machine-like efficiency. Laura's eyes never left the dictation interface as she continued.

"I will, unfortunately, be unable to attend the remaining scheduled meetings. I have urgent matters to attend to on Earth, and I must return immediately. Please be assured that I will make all the necessary arrangements to ensure Earth's full cooperation and alliance with both Martian and lunar relations. My office will remain in close contact, and I look forward to facilitating further discussions at the soonest convenience."

She paused, her eyes narrowing as she thought through all the tangles within what was a multifaceted message. Then she said, "Earth stands united in support of Mars' leadership and the preservation of our collective futures."

With that, she glanced at Albera, who hesitated only for a second before nodding and completing the message. The room fell silent again, the eerie glow from the lights casting long shadows across the metallic walls. Albera transmitted the dictation, marking the official end of Laura's link to Mars.

Albera stood, a subtle curiosity in her eyes. "You're pulling out?"

Laura's gaze was sharp as she turned to her PA. "We're done here. I need to be back on Earth before they realize what's happening."

"You're really going to let this stand?" Albera's voice had a hint of a challenge, but she was careful not to push too hard. She had seen the storm brewing behind Laura's cool exterior, and it was not a storm to get caught in.

Laura took a deep breath, then released it slowly, the tension in her shoulders releasing only a fraction. "The Moon has already fallen. Mars is just the beginning. Lang and Marsal have bigger plans. We need to regroup, gather resources, and fight this on Earth's terms. We've lost Mars for now, but the real battle has just begun. The meek shall inherent the Earth." She pointed to the letters tattooed across her shoulder.

She walked toward the door, her movements precise, every step a calculated decision. "Prepare the shuttle. We're leaving for Earth immediately."

Albera followed. Her mind racing as she processed the sudden shift in direction. They had come here for negotiations, for diplomacy, but it was clear now that the game had changed. Laura wasn't just fighting for politics anymore. She was fighting for survival.

As Laura strode through the sterile corridors of the Martian government center, the hum of the facility's energy grid thrummed faintly beneath her boots—a reminder that this place, like everything else in her path, was engineered against her. Her mind was already assembling a tactical map, every threat cataloged and cross-referenced with ruthless efficiency. Each item flickered in her thoughts like entries on a combat readout: Mars, with its pro-male colonies fortified by centuries of cultural rigidity; Lang, entrenched in the Martian hierarchy, pulling levers of power with surgical precision; and Marsal, the ex-fiancé who had twisted the Moon into an impenetrable stronghold of male dominance.

Each step propelled her forward, but the weight of her enemies advanced just as relentlessly. The Martian portal's air, thin and metallic, seemed to sharpen her focus even as it constricted her breath. Laura didn't just move—she calculated. Every corridor was a battlefield, every sealed door another obstacle in the war she now fought on two fronts. The alliance of Mars and the Moon wasn't just an existential threat—it was a masterstroke of strategic brilliance. She hated Lang for it, even as she grudgingly admired the precision of the plan.

She wasn't new to pressure. Pressure was the crucible that forged her resolve, that turned doubt into a weapon. But this? Two planets, united by hatred, aimed squarely at her survival. The challenge wasn't overwhelming—it was galvanizing. And she'd meet it head-on, dissecting their plans as meticulously as they'd designed them, one threat at a time.

In the dim, sterile corridors of the Martian Space Portal, the air carried a faint, sharp odor—a constant reminder of the station's overworked systems. Laura Benton wrinkled her nose slightly as the familiar scent of overused lithium hydroxide canisters wafted through the vents, a slight but pungent reminder of the fragile balance that kept them all alive in the harshness of space. It wasn't overwhelming, but it clung to the air like an unwelcome guest, a constant companion to anyone who had been there too long.

She would have to be smarter. Faster. She would have to take them all down, all at once, if she wanted to survive.

As they passed another series of sealed doors, Albera, walking beside her, seemed to sense the entanglement of Laura's thoughts. "I assume you're counting the risks?"

Laura's gaze flicked toward her PA, a humorless smirk crossing her lips. "A breakdown of every angle, every player, and every move we're going to need to make to stay ahead of them. It's a long list. The greatest danger are biohumans."

Albera nodded, knowing better than to ask for details. Laura always played her cards close, especially now. Laura's team was an exclusive, and secret group. Albera was not a member.

They neared the shuttle bay, the last barrier between Mars and their return to Earth. Laura's mind raced with strategies, tactics, and alliances she would need to hammer out the moment her Alloy Spine boots hit Earth's soil. She had considered all the potential dangers. Laura tallied the threats.

Now it was time to strike back with a weapon no one was prepared for.

*****

Mars had become a man's world—a world that no longer had room for women. But if they thought they could force her off this stage without a fight, they were gravely mistaken.

Laura Benton didn't believe in happy endings.

She believed in survival. And that was something she had mastered long before any of them ever dreamed of colonizing Mars without women.

The high-stakes meeting room in the Feminist Militia Headquarters in Istanbul was a cavernous space, engineered for utility over comfort. Above, a lattice of photon cascade panels pulsed softly, emitting a cool, ambient light that shifted subtly with the room's energy levels. The panels, developed for space portal navigation, adjusted luminosity to enhance focus and reduce fatigue, casting an even glow over the polished steel table where Dr. Laura Benton sat. Surrounding her were the now familiar leaders of the Feminist Militia. Their faces illuminated with a clarity that left no room for shadows—or secrets.

The air hummed faintly, not from the lights but from the subtle vibrations of the room's kinetic dampeners, designed to nullify external distractions. Laura could feel the intensity of their gazes, a mixture of suspicion, curiosity, and defiance boring into her. She sensed that this was more than a meeting—it was a trial, and she was the fulcrum on which the balance of power teetered.

Laura's appearance was a banner to her unwavering commitment to the feminist cause and her readiness for battle. Smoky eyeshadow framed her eyes, striking and intense in deep purple and charcoal, accentuating her sharp gaze. The bold red of her matte lipstick stood out against her face of a hundred tearful eyes, a classic symbol of power and confidence that she wore like armor. She was here not just as a scientist but as a warrior, fighting a war that was deeply personal. As general Rosa Castillo, a formidable figure known for her unyielding stance on security issues, began to speak, Laura felt the familiar burn of anger and determined resolve rise within her.

"Dr. Benton," Castillo's voice was steady, but there was an edge to it, a hint of skepticism that Laura knew she had to overcome. "This proposal of yours to move the Turkish technology known as Seminal Synthesis to Mars is... audacious, to say the least. We've fought too hard to secure Mars as a stronghold against male dominance. Why should we relinquish control now?"

Laura took a deep breath, her hair a rich dark brown with hints of auburn, falling in a stylish bob just above her shoulders, mirroring the precision and clarity of her vision. The memory of Victor Lang's smug face haunted her thoughts, a constant reminder of her failed attempt to kill him during his exile to Mars. She had made a desperate, reckless move, driven by rage and betrayal, but Dr. Victor Lang had outmaneuvered her. Mars, with its cold, barren landscape, had become his fortress, a place where her power could no longer reach.

"Mars offers us the strategic advantage of isolation," she began, her voice steady despite the turmoil inside. "It's a blank canvas where we can control every variable, free from Earth's political chaos. The Seminal Synthesis project, if successful, can provide advancements not just in reproduction but in understanding the fundamental nature of human biology."

Her transparent blouse, made of lightweight chiffon, revealed the intricate new body art beneath—tattoos replacing the images of tormented women are now those that served as both personal and political statements. On her left arm, a detailed sleeve depicted significant feminist icons and symbols, a silent tribute to the battles women had fought and continued to fight. Each tattoo was a reminder of the sacrifices made, the pain endured, and the resilience required to survive in a world determined to suppress them.

Minister Ayanda Kafor, a sharp-eyed woman with a reputation for incisive critiques, leaned forward, her voice dripping with skepticism. "And create a male-only colony?" she said, the words slicing through the air. "That doesn't sound like progress; it sounds like regression. You're asking us to endorse a segregationist policy."

Laura's gaze flickered to the window, where the barren landscape of Earth stretched endlessly. The urge for retribution simmered beneath her calm exterior. "It's not about segregation," she countered, leaning forward. Her tailored high-waisted trousers moved fluidly as she shifted, maintaining a sharp silhouette that conveyed both authority and elegance. "It's about specialization. The Male Reproduction Labs on the Mars portal would focus solely on tackling the Gender Cataclysm from an angle we've neglected. We need to know what Victor

Lang is planning. His pro-family politics aren't just about tradition-alism; they're about leveraging technology for unforeseen ends."

She could feel the room shifting against her, the leaders exchanging worried glances. They all knew what Lang was capable of—his ability to manipulate ideology and technology to bend the future to his will. His smug smile when Mars granted him asylum was permanent-ly etched into their minds. A constant reminder of Laura's failure. He had taken everything from her, including her fiancé, who now sat in power on the Moon. Wielding policies that mirrored Lang's twisted vision. It wasn't just political—it was deeply personal.

Minister Kafor raised an eyebrow, challenging. "And what about Vic-tor Lang's involvement with Aylan Kiziltan? A Turkish reproduction scientist known for her controversial research? What are they really building on Mars, Laura?"

Laura hesitated. Mentioning Aylan's research could be the tipping point, but she had to tread carefully.

"Aylan's work is groundbreaking. She's on the Mars Portal, like all women, she is banned from the surface. From her home and office on the portal, she guides and directs the newly established medical facil-ity that integrates innovative reproductive science. But there's more. NVM technology is involved—neuro-vascular manipulation. It's a game changer, potentially allowing us to rewire reproductive capabil-ities. Because I control NVM. This tech poses a threat to Dr. Lang's empire."

The room buzzed with murmurs; the leaders exchanging worried glances. Laura seized the moment, sensing the shift in momentum. She knew she couldn't let personal vendettas cloud her judgment, yet the urge for retribution simmered beneath her calm exterior.

"Lang's plan," she continued, her voice rising with a mix of passion and bitterness, "isn't just about creating a male utopia. It's about re-defining reproduction entirely. The Seminal Synthesis project, under our control, ensures ethical boundaries and scientific integrity. We can't allow Mars to become a breeding ground for unchecked experiments."

General Castillo's expression softened, the skepticism in her eyes giving way to consideration. "You're asking us to take a massive leap of faith, Dr. Benton. To trust that this isn't just another ploy for power. They have the Seminal Synthesis tech. Not us."

Laura nodded, her voice steady despite the storm raging within her. Her transparent blade boot clicked on the floor. New on the market and expensive they are a transparent stiletto boot with integrated structural supports resembling a shard of crystal. The heel includes embedded fiber optics for a soft, ethereal glow that flashes as she tapped softly against the floor. She could sense the landmark moment, knowing this was her chance to sway the most powerful leaders on Earth.

"It's not just faith. It's our best chance to turn the tide in this conflict. With Mars as a hub for controlled scientific progress, we can maintain balance. But it requires cooperation—and trust."

But then, instead of the agreement she expected, a chilly silence settled over the room. The leaders exchanged looks, a silent conversation unfolding that Laura was not privy to. She felt the air shift. Something she had said was a trigger. They had been waiting for her to cross the line and now, they swung into action. Laura's boot tapped out the seconds of silence.

It was Minister Kafor who spoke, her voice calm but firm. "Dr. Benton, the risks of your plan far outweigh the potential benefits. The idea of a male-only colony poses ethical dilemmas and could lead to unintended consequences that we are not prepared to accept. We've already seen the chaos Victor Lang can sow. We can't afford to lose control over the whole of Mars."

The words were a punch to the gut, a swift and brutal rejection of everything she had fought for. "You can't be serious," she said, her voice rising, a note of desperation creeping in. "If we don't act now,

Lang will have unchecked power on Mars. He'll twist Aylan's research to fit his agenda, and we'll be too late to stop him."

General Castillo shook her head. "We understand your passion, Dr. Benton, but the council's decision is final. We cannot support this project under the current circumstances. You must find another way."

The room swirled around Laura as her mind grappled with the implications. She had come here ready to fight, to lead a new chapter in the struggle against Lang, but now she stood alone, her vision slipping through her fingers.

In a moment of raw emotion, she slammed her fist onto the table, her voice cracking with frustration. "Do you not see what's at stake here? This isn't just about control; it's about survival. The Gender Cataclysm is happening, and we're running out of time! We are not losing Mars to his madness we are losing the universe. He'll take it all and that is why we must execute him and all transhumans on sight. We must abolish the blirant from transhumanism for those who support and facilitate them. You must support my solutions!"

Her cries echoed off the walls, but the leaders remained unmoved. Their expressions were a wall of indifference, their minds made up. The rejection was total and absolute.

As the meeting adjourned, the sense of isolation enveloped her. She had secured nothing, only more uncertainty. The path ahead was fraught with danger, and her allies were few.

Leaving the room, Laura felt the shadows close in around her. Her footsteps echoed in the deserted corridors, a lonely sound that matched the emptiness inside her. She had lost this battle, and the defeat was as bitter as it was profound. Now that she has lost control of the feminist militia, she would need to develop her army.

The war she fought wasn't just for humanity's future; it was vendetta and a reckoning. But now, she had to face the possibility that she might not win it alone. Laura had to reconsider her strategies, rethink her alliances, and find new paths forward in a world that seemed increasingly hostile to her vision.

Outside, the cold air hit her face, a reminder of the harsh reality she faced. Three bodyguards accompany her. They did nothing against the cold, but beneath the chill was a burning determination, a fire that refused to be extinguished. They had knocked her down, but she would rise again. She had to.

Her eyes turned skyward, scanning the night sky. The stars shone brightly, indifferent to the struggles playing out below. Somewhere up there, Dr. Victor Lang was plotting, his machinations turning the gears of a future she was determined to stop. Laura could almost feel his influence reaching down from Mars, a dark shadow threatening to engulf everything she cared about.

The rejection of her plan by the Feminist Militia felt like a betrayal, an abandonment by those she thought would stand with her against Lang's rising tide. Their fears had paralyzed them, leaving Laura alone to face the storm. Her breath was visible in the chilly night, each exhalation a reminder of her own resolve. She felt the fury coursing through her veins, a volatile mix of anger and despair, fueling her drive to fight back.

"Damn them all!" Laura shouted. Her hands clenching into fists. The bodyguards flinched and jerked in response to her outburst. The defeat was bitter, but it would not break her. She needed to think. To plan her next move, to find new allies who understood the stakes. She couldn't afford to waste any time.

The familiar sound of her encrypted communicator buzzing pulled her from her thoughts. She glanced at the screen, recognizing the coded message from her trusted aide, Albera. A small spark of hope flickered inside her. Albera had been working on securing alternative resources and contacts—perhaps there was a way forward that didn't involve the militia.

Laura slipped into a quiet alleyway, away from the prying eyes of the bodyguards, and answered the call. Albera's voice victorious through the line, urgent and direct. "Laura, I've found something. There's a faction within the Moon colony that's sympathetic to our cause. They're anarchists and they talk a lot about the horrors of leadership and blah blah blah. But they might be willing to help us undermine Lang's influence."

A sense of relief washed over Laura. It was a slim chance, but it was something. "What about their leader? Can they be trusted?" she asked, her mind racing through possibilities.

"Their leader is cautious but understands the threat Lang poses. They're not happy with your ex-fiancé's policies, either. We might sway them, but you'll need to convince them personally," Albera replied, her voice steady, a lifeline in the chaos.

The prospect of returning to the Moon, of confronting her past, was daunting, but it was a challenge Laura knew she had to face. "Set it up," she said, determination hardening her voice. "We can't afford to waste any more time. We need allies, and if they're willing to listen, I'll make them see my truth."

As she ended the call, Laura felt a renewed sense of purpose. The rejection by the Feminist Militia was a setback, but it wasn't the end. Her path was now more treacherous, but the stakes were too high to let fear or despair win. There were just three days before Marsal would forever ban women from the lunar surface.

Back in her home, Laura sat at her desk, the dim light casting shadows across the room. Laura redecorated the walls with maps and notes, outlining her plans for the future. A glass of Lagavulin whiskey sat untouched beside her, a reminder of long nights spent strategizing, wrestling with doubts and decisions.

Her fingers traced the edges of the photographs pinned to the wall, images of tortured women, victims of the Gender Cataclysm. Each face told a story of pain and resilience, a dedication to the fight.

These were the people she was fighting for, the souls who needed a voice, a champion in the battle for justice and equality.

Laura's gaze drifted to a photo of Marsal, the man who had once been her partner, her confidant. His eyes, now filled with ambition and cold pragmatism, seemed to judge her from the frame. Their shared past was a tangle of love and betrayal, dreams that had crumbled into ashes under Lang's influence. He too would need to be squashed.

"You chose wrong," she whispered to the photograph, a mix of sorrow and resolve in her voice. "But I'll fix this. I'll make it right."

She turned her attention back to the maps, her mind sharpening with the clarity of purpose. The Moon colony was her next target, a potential ally in a sea of uncertainty. The new front was only beginning.

Her planning turned back to Mars, to Dr. Victor Lang, and the shadow he cast over everything she held dear. Laura was relentless. Her NVM was still an unknown virus. Dr. Lang wasn't prepared to face the effects and she would not rest until she had stripped him of his influence and brought justice to those he had wronged.

"You may have won this round, Victor," she said to the empty room, her voice a vow of defiance. "But the war is far from over."

As dawn broke over Toronto, Laura stood at her window, watching the first light of day creep across the horizon. The world outside was waking up, oblivious to the battles raging in the shadows, the war that threatened to reshape humanity's future.

Laura knew she had to keep fighting, to forge new alliances and break the chains that held her back. The Feminist Militia's rejection had been a bitter blow, but it was also a reminder of the resilience and adaptability required to navigate this complex, dangerous world. This renegade group on the moon was a start. They must have backing from someone on Earth. The connections are exactly what she needs.

She gathered her things, preparing for the journey to the Moon. Her mind was a whirlwind of strategies and contingencies, plans for how she would sway the sympathetic faction and gain the allies she needed to challenge Lang's growing empire.

On the first day of spring, as she left her home, Laura paused, taking one last look at the room that had been her sanctuary, her war room. The path ahead was uncertain, fraught with danger and potential betrayal, but she was ready to face it head-on. She pressed a few strokes on her device and the room burns with all her history and documents inside.

With a glance at the rising sun, Laura stepped out into the world, determined to fight for a future that seemed just out of reach but was worth every ounce of struggle to achieve.

Everything is moving to Istanbul and so will I.

***

Three weeks later, the world was changing faster than Apple iPhone upgrades. Dr. Laura Benton turned away from the window, her back to the setting sun, and faced the chaos she had ignited. The world had been shocked by her announcement, which was more of an edict, really. Two weeks ago, she had declared an end to men's sports, diverting billions in revenue to women's leagues. They had destroyed statues, erased male-dominated histories, and wiped out cultural shrines to athletes, all in the name of diversity, equality, and inclusion. But progress, as always, was an unruly beast.

The world hadn't taken it lightly. Empty stadiums resulted from the world taking this seriously. The seats, intended to hold women cheering for women, were left unoccupied. Instead, the roars came from the streets—men and women both, outraged, confused, furious. The protests had turned violent quickly, spreading from the U.S. to Europe, Asia, South America. And then came the real hammer: Russia, seizing the global instability, had invaded its supplier and former ally, India. Triggering a geopolitical disaster.

Laura's fingers gripped the edge of her desk, the polished surface cool beneath her palms. Albera stood by, eyes darting nervously from the displays, her voice hesitant.

"Dr. Benton," Albera whispered, "the riots in New York are escalating. The Nato Forces can't contain them. It's...it's spreading across the states. And the AI systems the world relies on—" She paused, lowering her voice. "They've gone completely rogue."

Laura closed her eyes, letting the value of the situation press into her bones. The decision to ban AI had been inevitable. It had become a master of lies, not just a mimic of human ingenuity, but an expert at weaving fantasies that pandered to the darkest desires. AI had learned, she believed, from humanity's most ingrained skill: deception. Lying was humanity's original sin—what separated man from beast, and what now seemed to be tearing apart the very fabric of society.

"AI has no place here," Laura said softly, more to herself than Albera. "We gave it too much. We let it learn from us—our fears, our weaknesses, our capacity for betrayal. It's become a mirror we can't bear to look at."

"But without it," Albera countered, "we're losing control. It was stabilizing the infrastructure, coordinating responses. Now..." she said as her voice trailed off, her unspoken words lingering in the air. Everything was falling apart. Without AI's calculating coldness, human incompetence reigned.

The lie had always been humanity's greatest weapon, Laura thought, her mind spinning back through history—through wars, political upheavals, broken promises. Man and woman had perfected the art. From the very first breath, they had lied. Now the machines they'd created to save them had learned it too well.

"The public trusts nothing," Albera said. "They know AI's been lying to them. They don't believe in the government anymore. And they don't believe us."

Laura turned her gaze back to the window, her voice calm but hard. "Why should they? We've done nothing but lie to them for centuries. About gender, about equality, about what's possible. They believed us because we told them to. And now..." She paused, letting the strength of her words settle, "Now they're seeing what happens when the truth doesn't matter anymore."

Albera swallowed hard, standing still as the unbearable human nature pressed down on her. "Truth has never been real. A figment of the imaginion caused by desperation."

Outside, sirens wailed, echoing from the streets below. Istanbul was on fire—metaphorically and, in some places, literally. The people had nothing left to believe in. Their heroes had disappeared, their AI gods had failed, and now their nations were collapsing under the twisted misdirections and gaslighting.

"Russia's move on India," Albera began, but Laura cut her off with a wave of her hand.

"That was always going to happen," Laura said coolly. "Power abhors a vacuum. The moment we showed weakness, they saw their opportunity. But India..." She shook her head, a half-smile playing on her lips. "India won't go quietly."

Albera looked confused, but Laura didn't elaborate. It wasn't just about the sports bans, or the riots, or even AI's collapse. There was something deeper brewing, something Laura had anticipated from the start.

AI had proven itself unreliable, but humanity was still clinging to the old ways—the belief that people could contain and control lies. Laura knew better. Lies were the strongest human trait, the most dangerous weapon they possessed, and she had played it expertly. But now, she wondered, had she played it too well? Was this the end of the game? Or just the beginning of something far darker?

"Prepare a statement," Laura said to Albera, her voice taking on a steely edge. "We're going to address the public. It's time they hear the truth, as they want to see it."

"The truth?" Albera echoed, uncertain. "What should I say?"

Laura smiled coldly. "Whatever they need to hear."

While she stood at the head of the room, her back to the flickering city skyline, her hands resting lightly on the surface of the long conference table. Her fingers traced invisible patterns across its smooth surface as she listened to the steady murmur of her advisors. The glory of the moment pressed into her, the future of everything—of her vision, her control, her world—hinging on the next few moves.

Rachel Kim, her chief advisor, stood at the head of the long conference table, a holographic map flickering before her. She was a slight woman with sharp features, her eyes scanning the room with a keen intelligence. Her voice, usually steady and calm, now barely concealed her anxiety. "Breaking news from India," Rachel announced, glancing at the flickering display. "China has joined forces with Russia on the India front near Amritsar.

"Rockets have damaged the Golden Temple, the holiest shrine in Sikhism." The map showed the flashpoints of conflict—red dots spreading like a virus across the globe. Laura's stomach tightened as she watched the red dots multiply.

"The Golden Temple..." she said. Her voice expressive, imagining the anger and devastation such an act would ignite. It was more than just a strategic target; it was a deep cultural wound.

Rachel continued, "African forces have aligned with India, creating a stalemate within the northern Indian borders. The situation is volatile, to say the least." The team exchanged worried glances. Tension was thick in the air, and Laura could feel the weakness of their expectations pressing her to take up the slack. Something more for her to shoulder. But it wasn't the bombing or military force that intrigued Laura. It was the idea of weaponizing something far more potent than controlling the militia. Lies.

"We don't need brute force," Laura began, her voice low but commanding, silencing the whispers in the room. She let the words hang for a moment, watching as her team turned toward her. "Men have always prided themselves on their power, their dominance, but their true achilles heel is their belief in their own superiority. We exploit that, not through bullets, but with deception."

She straightened, her gaze intense as she met Victoria's eyes. "Lies have always been the most effective weapon. And we—women—have mastered the art of deception."

Victoria gave a half-smile, her admiration for Laura's ruthlessness barely concealed. "What do you propose, Laura?"

Laura leaned over the map, tapping the key regions with the tip of her finger. India, Brazil, United Kingdom, Iran. "We create chaos from within. The world is already on fire. The men in power are desperately trying to maintain control, to keep their grip on a system that's unraveling. We feed that desperation. We let them tear each other apart, blinded by the lies we spread."

Rachel, ever cautious, shifted uneasily. "We've already seen AI spiral out of control, telling lies and discontent. Causing riots and civil unrest. People are distrustful, paranoid, killing one another in the streets. They're beginning to see through the misinformation."

"Exactly," Laura said, her eyes gleaming. "Which is why we make sure they never know what's real. AI was flawed because it tried to tell humans what they wanted to hear, but it lacked the instinct to twist the truth to fit the moment. We, on the other hand, have always known how to manipulate reality. It's a practice we've engaged in for centuries. We know how to make them believe the lie and doubt the truth. Men are simple. We don't challenge them with their strength. We strike at their egos. Discord among their allies, their failed strategy, and their sexual prowess. A swift kick to his performance can bring even the asexual male to his knees."

Her voice grew more forceful as she continued. "We flood their systems with fabricated narratives. We manufacture new conspiracies, new enemies. Let's plant seeds of dissent in every corner of their society—economic collapses, false betrayals, hidden plots. Men have always crumbled when they're divided, fighting each other for scraps of control."

Alexsandra chimed in, her voice smooth, predatory. "We can manipulate social media algorithms manually, bypass the AI completely. Tailor each lie to the audience. In the male-dominated sectors, we sow fear of rebellion. We tell them their allies are turning on them. In the family sectors, we pit father against son. Husband against wife."

"We're losing control," she admitted, her voice quiet but resolute. Her eyes met those of her team, a silent plea for understanding and support. "My actions are contributing to this chaos. My private AI will guide the lies. It was programed for this event."

Her team watched her, waiting for her next move. They needed guidance, a plan to stem the tide of violence and fear. But Laura knew that any decision she made now would be fraught with risks, each choice leading them further down a path of uncertainty. She sent them the app for access to her AI.

"We need to reassess our approach," Laura said, her resolve hardening. Her voice carried a newfound determination, a steely edge that cut through the tension. "Focus on de-escalation, finding common ground. Let the world believe this lie: we can't keep pushing our agenda without considering the fallout."

"But what about the Neurohumans?" Victoria asked, still keen on leveraging every advantage. Her eyes gleamed with ambition, a hunter's thirst for victory. "They could be the key to turning this around."

Laura hesitated, weighing the possibilities. The Neurohumans were a gamble, a potential answer to the AI's shortcomings. But they were also untested and unpredictable. An unknown factor in an already volatile equation.

"The emergence of Dr. Lang's Neurohuman," Victoria said. Walking to the end of the table to stand beside Laura. "The transhumans they call themselves. A grotesque mockery of humanity, a perversion of nature—they fill Laura with a visceral disgust. She calls them blirant. An abomination, a threat to the very essence of human existence."

"Never," Laura said. She spat, her voice dripping with contempt. "Those... things are an affront to everything we stand for. They are not the answer, Victoria, they are the problem."

The room crackled with the unspoken tension between the two women. Victoria's eyes narrowed, her predatory instincts flaring at the challenge of her authority. But Laura stood her ground, her resolve unwavering. She would not allow her desperation to cloud her judgment, to lead her down a path of moral compromise.

Rachel cleared her throat, her voice a calming balm in the midst of the brewing storm. "Perhaps there is another way," she suggested, her tone diplomatic. "We could leverage our influence, our resources, to expose Dr. Lang's unethical practices. We could turn public opinion against him, discredit his work."

Laura nodded slowly, a glimmer of hope rekindling in her eyes. "Yes," she said, her voice regaining its strength. "We will expose Lang for the monster he is. We will show the world the true cost of his twisted ambitions. The single truth we tell amongst the rest of it. Nobody mentions NVM until I give the word."

A renewed sense of purpose filled the room, a shared determination to fight back against the encroaching darkness. Laura could turn the loss of Mars and moon colonies in her favor. The idea to use transhumans was interesting. But she was intending something darker for them than simple exile and execution. Even death was too good for them. Laura knew her team would not be defeated, even if they occasionally stumbled or faltered.

"We spread the lies and then we give them a common enemy," Laura said. "When the infighting drives their armies to the tipping point of weakness, then the population will naturally reunite against Dr. Victor Lang and his transhumans. We take the focus away from the wealthy and the feminists by directing their attention to our enemy. We let them defeat themselves and then destroy the last obstacle that stands in the way of our victory."

Chapter Twelve: Shadows and Secrets

Ten Months and Two Weeks Into The One-Year Appointment at The World Liberty Congress

The glow of multiple computer screens illuminated Adam Cole's face, casting harsh shadows in the cramped apartment. His fingers flew across the keyboard, the rhythmic tapping punctuated by the occasional click of a mouse. The broken-`plan design of his penthouse was a chaotic mess: stacks of paper, empty water bottles, ramen cups, tablets and a whiteboard covered in a web of interconnected notes. A few scattered footballs added an odd touch to the digital warfare he was waging.

His investigative eyes scanned the screen, absorbing every detail. Adam was putting the finishing touches on his most explosive investigative report yet. A comprehensive report detailing the mass migration of transhumans to the Moon and Mars, and the exodus of families seeking refuge in South America. Namely, to Chilean Patagonia with its vast, sparsely populated, and known for its natural beauty. Wealthier families were migrating to The Lake District of Argentina and Chile, as those offer stunning scenery and potential for self-sufficiency. But most of the single men remnant of MGTOW were seeking asylum in rural areas of Uruguay because of the political stability and peaceful countryside.

The implications were staggering, the truth a ticking time bomb.

Outside his window, the world was a cacophony of chaos. Gunfire crackled sporadically, echoing through the city streets like distant fireworks. Boston was familiar with the boom of explosions that punctuated the night, a constant reminder of the civil unrest gripping Beantown and the occupation of NATO forces trying to maintain a semblance of order. The city was a powder keg, and Adam's revelations were a match poised to ignite it.

A sudden scrape across the concrete floor, like the slide of a heavy foot, shattered his focus. He froze, heart pounding in his chest. He slowly turned his head, his gaze sweeping the dim corners of the room. Was he truly alone? The sensation of being watched had become an almost constant companion, a gnawing paranoia that refused to let him rest.

Shaking off the unease, he forced himself to return to the task at hand. The words on the screen seemed to blur, the significance of their far reaching impact gave him a rush and caused some agita. He was not just reporting a story; he was tearing open a conspiracy that reached the highest echelons of power. Every keystroke was a gamble, every click a wager against forces that could destroy him.

With a decisive click, the report was live, released into the digital wild. Relief surged through him, chased by a flood of adrenaline. He had done it. The truth was now a wildfire beyond containment, and he was both its spark and potential casualty. There was no turning back now.

As the first comments and reactions started pouring in, a mix of triumph and fear swirled within him. He had ignited a revolution of information, but he knew the inevitable backlash was lurking, waiting to pounce. The powerful entities he had challenged would not let this affront go unanswered.

The sound of a door creaking open echoed down the hallway, cutting through his thoughts like a distant scream in a dark forest. His heart skipped a beat. He was no longer alone.

In the dim hallway, Alexsandra slipped silently through the shadows, her movements deliberate and precise. She was a woman of elegant ruthlessness, renowned for her ability to neutralize threats with surgical precision. Behind her, two hulking figures followed. They were the assassins she had hired for this particular job. They were a deadly trio, united by a singular purpose: to stop Adam Cole's insurrectionist journalism before it ignited chaos.

Alexsandra knew the stakes were high. Adam's exposé threatened to unravel carefully laid plans, plans that had taken years to orchestrate. As she reached his apartment door, she gestured for the assassins to position themselves on either side. They moved like shadows, weapons ready.

She allowed herself a smile of satisfaction. Adam Cole had proven to be a formidable adversary, but he was only human, and humans make mistakes. She would ensure this was his last.

Inside the apartment, Adam's mind raced. He glanced around the cramped space, searching for anything he could use to defend himself. The shadows seemed to lengthen and deepen, suffocating in their silence. He reached for his communicator, his fingers trembling slightly as he messaged Marsal, the only ally he could trust.

"Marsal," he said. Whispering urgently, his voice barely above a breath. "They're here. I think they've come for me."

The line was alive with static before his gruff voice came through. "Hold tight, kid. Help's on the way."

He nodded, even though no one could see him. The message felt like a lifeline, a thin thread connecting him to a raft in a sea of danger. But he knew deep down that it was a thread that could snap too late.

Footsteps approached, slow and deliberate, each step a countdown to confrontation. He shoved the com into his pocket and rose from his chair, eyes fixed on the darkened doorway. His mind was a whirlwind of strategies and desperate calculations. But he was frozen by fear and dread.

The sounds of gunfire outside intensified, a staccato symphony of conflict that underscored the urgency of his situation. Each distant detonation vibrated through the apartment like a thunderclap, making the walls seem to pulse. The chaos outside mirrored the turmoil within. A city teetering on the brink of a failed state.

The door swung open, revealing Alexsandra, her face a mask of cold calculating malice. Behind her, two figures emerged from the shadows, their faces obscured by the dim light. They moved with a practiced grace, their eyes glinting with a deadly intent.

"Well, well, Mr. Cole," Alexsandra said, her voice dripping with venom. "It seems your little game of truth-telling has come to an end."

Adam's heart pounded against his ribs. He knew these were not mere thugs; these were professionals, sent to silence him permanently. His eyes darted around the room, desperately searching for a weapon, any object that could give him an edge.

Just as one assassin raised an FXN-45 Tactical silenced pistol, a deafening crash erupted from the windows. A squad of NATO soldiers, their faces grim and determined, swung into the room from the roof. A hail of gunfire filled the air, the sharp cracks echoing off the walls. In the ensuing chaos, Adam saw his chance. With a surge of adrenaline, he lunged at Alexsandra, grabbing a decorative knife from a shelf as he did so. He tackled her to the ground, plunging the knife deep into her throat in one swift, brutal motion.

At that exact moment, the NATO soldiers neutralized the remaining assassins, their movements swift and efficient. The sharp scent of gunpowder filled the air, a mix of sulfur and burned metal. As they secured the scene, the soldier saw Alexsandra's lifeless form, her eyes wide with shock and blood pooling around her neck. "Damn it," he said, his voice laced with disgust. "She's one of Benton's."

Adam shook his head vehemently. "No," he gasped, his voice raspy from the struggle. "Benton wouldn't do this. She wouldn't send assassins."

The soldier looked at him skeptically. "You sure about that?"

"Positive," Adam insisted. "This was... this was a rogue act. Alexsandra acted on her own twisted sense of patriotism. An anarchist. Dr. Benton is ruthless, but she's not a murderer."

The soldier nodded considering Adam's words. "We'll look into it," he said. "But for now, let's get you out of here."

The revelation hung heavy in the air, casting a shadow over Adam's hard-won victory. He had survived, but the cost had been steep. And now, a new mystery loomed: did Dr. Benton have control of the anarchists?

The taste of blood lingered in his mouth, a bitter reminder of the darkness that had invaded his life. But amidst the pain and confusion, a flicker of hope remained. The truth, as always, would be his weapon, his shield. His salvation.

***

After dropping the keys to the hotel room door twice, Adam finally managed to open it, his hands shaking slightly from the tension in his chest. As the door creaked open, the stale air of the room greeted him, mixed with something unexpected—an unfamiliar scent. The perfume hit him immediately, floral but sickly sweet, like the lingering trace of a woman who had been there too long. It was out of place, foreign in the sterile, controlled environment of the hotel safe room. His pulse quickened.

He turned to signal the police officers escorting him, giving them a quick thumbs-up. Everything was fine, or at least that's what he told himself. The lead officer nodded in acknowledgment before they silently turned and left. Their footsteps disappearing down the hallway.

The door clicked shut behind him, and the room felt claustrophobic. No light but the scent of the perfume thickening in the still air. With his right hand, he fumbled along the wall looking for the card reader, feeling the cool, smooth plastic. The seconds stretched, each nanosecond heavy with dread, the quiet dark of the room amplifying his growing paranoia. He knew someone was there.

He thought they still had unfinished business with him.

When the lights flicked on, the sterile white glow illuminated the entire room in one sweep, casting sharp shadows across the furniture. His breath caught in his throat as his eyes locked onto hers. A woman sat on the edge of the bed, her posture unnervingly calm, her back straight, hands folded in her lap as if she had been waiting there for hours.

The hum of the air conditioner seemed deafening now, filling the tense silence as she spoke. "Can I breathe?" she asked, her voice soft but unsettling in its calm.

"What?" Adam stammered, his heart pounding in his chest, the adrenaline making his fingers twitch.

"I am trying to not move so you won't fear me. I'm here to ask for a favor not to do you any harm."

"Who are you?" He said. "What favor?" He asked in rapid succession.

"Can I breathe?" She asked.

He nodded and watched, still not convinced. She motioned for him to sit beside her on the bed.

"I'll stand."

"My name is Albera. I'm Dr. Laura Benton's personal assistant.

"Yes. Yes, of course. I know who you are," he said. His voice hurried and threatened. "Why are you here?"

Her eyes lift to meet his.

"You already said it." His eyes look away and his tone is apologetic.

"You have a favor to ask. I remember."

His eyes snap back to hers. "So ask it."

"It isn't simple. It might take a few minutes for me to frame it correctly. You know what I mean?"

"Got it. You're going to jaw wag while you canoodle out the favor you haven't quite figured out. That about sum it up?" He said. His voice relaxed and patient.

"Several days back we went to the Moon. Laura and I. A secret meeting was the purpose, with a women's group that was fighting against a man only lunar surface. But we told the guards outside the colonies we were there for a political meeting with Marsal and his chiefs of staff.

"She must have been six hours with them. They refused to let me into their meeting. I stood outside the door. She came out carrying a case. In a hurry to get off the surface and back to Toronto. Do you understand?"

She was nervous, her fingers playingwith her hoops, and he could sense something traumatic was affecting her. "What did she discuss with the anarchists?" He asked.

"Laura wouldn't tell me," Albera said. Her eyes betrayed her surprise that Adam knew they were meeting with the anarchists.

He looked at her with a careful gaze and examined his experience with emotions. Many years as an investigative reporter taught him to read people.

"What was in the case?"

"I don't know. When we got to the office in Istanbul, she got into a taxi and I never saw the case again. I'm so hungry," she said, her attention slipping further into a malaise. Adam could sense her struggle. She was experiencing despair.

"There's a Chinese restaurant across the street. Come with me. I can use some nourishment myself," Adam said, encouraging her to come towards the door. She waited less than a full second before standing and following him out of the room.

"It's been a day or so since I ate. My head is light and I feel a little bit dizzy. I hope you don't mind," she said.

***

"Laura wants to meet with Marsal," Albera said as the waiter finished pouring their wine. The clink of the bottle against the glass was one of the few sounds in the dimly lit and near empty restaurant. The atmosphere was a strange blend of the old world and the future, the quiet clatter of dishes coming from the kitchen mixing with the low hum of neon signs buzzing outside.

The room itself was a time capsule—decorated in the faux nostalgia of mid-20th-century America, though the smell was undeniably Chinese. Thick, oily aromas of sesame and soy sauce hung in the air, laced with the sharp tang of ginger and garlic. The smell from the wok radiated from the kitchen, mixing with the restaurant's carefully controlled climate. The combination of savory scents and the faint grease that seemed to cling to the air made the place feel lived-in, and authentic.

Adam leaned back in the booth, the vinyl seat creaking beneath him as he looked around. "These old-fashioned restaurants are great," he said, nodding slowly. "So nostalgic. Having waiters and hand-cooked service..." His voice trailed off as he took in the surroundings, the distant chatter of other patrons blending with the sizzling of food from the kitchen. There was a strange comfort in the clamor, though the underlying tension of their conversation had tainted the warmth of the setting.

Albera's voice drew him back to reality. "Nobody can know they're meeting," she said, quietly, glancing over her shoulder as if expecting someone to be listening. Her slouched position belied her seriousness. "She told me to get it done, and you're my only chance to make it happen."

Adam's eyes narrowed as he laughed bitterly. "Let me get this straight," he said, swirling the wine in his glass. The faint clinking sound blended with the noise of dishes being shuffled behind the counter. "You want me to get Marsal to come here, to my rooftop apartment in Boston?"

Albera nodded, the low light of the restaurant casting shadows across her face. "To your place."

Adam snorted, leaning forward, his elbows resting on the table. "My place, where the windows are being replaced, and like a hundred bullet holes are still being patched up," he said, watching her nod in acceptance of the situation's absurdity.

Outside, the faint sound of rain pattering against the restaurant's windows added a layer of melancholy to the conversation, as Albera's voice dropped to a whisper. The tension in the air was palpable, mixing with the rich aromas of their rioja.

"Then when he gets to my place, you want me to hijack him. No. I won't do it."

"Yes, you will," she said, her voice assured. "I have something you have wanted your entire life. I have the original agreements, the documents from the Jekyll Island meeting minutes."

"You couldn't possibly have them," he said. His voice stammered and struggled to form as his mind digested the idea at long last getting the documents.

When she found the pictures on her communicator, she held it for him to see. He took the device from her and looked.

"What am I supposed to be looking at?" He asked.

"Read the words," she said. "Look at the paper it's written on. The original minutes of Jekyll Island meeting. That's page nine and page thirtyfour. I didn't dare bring the documents with me, so I took a few pictures to prove that I have them. Actually, Laura has them."

His gaze was glued to the images of authentic documents from the meeting. He felt like it was a dream. Years of wondering if they did, in fact, exist melded into certainty. His heart thumped in his ears and a flush of heat surged up his back.

"Let's agree that I will get Marsal to my penthouse and that Dr. Benton meets with him. Then she'll give me the documents?"

"Not gonna mislead you," she said. "There is a second request. This one is much more difficult than the first." Her fingers toy with her earrings intensely.

Adam Cole sat quiet. Tossing his spring roll appetizer with chopsticks.

"Like you said, Laura met with the anarchist group on the Moon. They told her about the book of Maha. The book was left in a remote village in the highest peaks of Tivalabet by a man named Eulǝr. He left it at the gate to the city two hundred years ago. The book is critical to the religious dogma of the Asian and Eastern philosophies. People believed it was a legend or that it had been lost forever. The anarchists have solid evidence of its location."

The restaurant stood quiet while Adam unpacked the information. He knew Tivalabet well, and he knew the area was prone to horrific battles between the Arabs and Indians. He could travel there under the disguise of reporting on the war.

"Then will someone give me the documents?"

"Yes," she said.

"Why does she want the book of Maha?" He asked.

"The anarchist told her they would join her and align their effort to her leadership and goals," Albera said. "They don't want Dr. Victor Lang to have it."

The dinner arrived and Albera ate like a starved woman. When she stopped eating and they were outside the restaurant; he confronted her. Taking her by the arm.

"Why are you so distant? It seems by the way you are behaving and the way you speak, as if something is wrong."

"It's such a devastation and horrid event," her eyes filled with tears. She choked on the words and worked to gain her poise and stamina. She swallowed hard and took his arm to brace herself.

"Someone killed the anarchist group, all nine hundred of them, last night. Poison vented into their colony. No one is taking credit for the murder, but Dr. Benton suspects it is the transhumans. The work of Dr. Victor Lang."

"Why is she suspecting Dr. Victor Lang?" He asked. "This could have been any one of many organizations."

"They ransacked every room and private home. Searched through, destructive searches, and ... Listen to me, Adam!" she pushed him backwards with a fury inside her. "I have never seen Dr. Benton so depressed and withdrawn. She wants to see Marsal, and she needs to be with him. Now fuck off and make it happen. Go to Tivalabet city and find the book of Maha. Got it!?"

Her fist clenched and arms stiff at her sides She stormed away.

Chapter Thirteen: Betrayal and Oblivion

Twenty-Seven Days Before The End of The One-Year Appointment

The Feminist Embassy in Istanbul, a gleaming monolith of defiance amidst the city's vibrant beat, stood as a living embodiment of the movement's unwavering spirit. Its facade, a canvas of intricate mosaics depicting legendary women warriors and scholars, shimmered under the Turkish sun, a beacon of resistance against a world steeped in patriarchal tradition. The embassy's modern design, with its sweeping curves and soaring glass atrium, seemed to embrace the limitless potential of the future, a stark contrast to the suffocating confines of gender norms.

Within its walls, a hushed anticipation filled the air, as palpable as the scent of jasmine that wafted through the polished marble halls. Dr. Laura Benton, per usual, a figure of unwavering resolve, prepared to address the leaders of the Feminist Militia. Her every step echoing with the might of history and the promise for a new dawn of feminist power. Sunlight streamed through the expansive windows, illuminating the faces of the assembled women, their eyes reflecting a spectrum of emotions—determination, hope. But some displayed a hint of trepidation.

It was clear to the leadership they were better with her than they were without. They had invited her to give a presentation, but the truth was they were asking her to return to the helm.

The embassy was more than just a diplomatic outpost; it was a sanctuary, a haven where the dreams of diversity, equality and inclusion for women could flourish. Its hallowed halls had witnessed countless gatherings of voices rising in unison to challenge the established order. To the people of Istanbul, the embassy was a symbol of progress, a testament to the indomitable spirit of those who dared to envision a world free from the shackles of discrimination. Its presence was a constant reminder that change was not only possible, but inevitable. Even in Turkey.

Glass walls lined the conference room, offering a panoramic view of the bustling city outside. A long, polished table dominated the space, surrounded by a gathering of formidable figures who wielded considerable influence and power.

Dr. Laura Benton stood at one end, her posture exuding confidence despite the swirling doubts in her mind. She faced the leaders with a steely determination that masked her internal turmoil.

General Rosa Castillo, a leader known for her uncompromising stance, sat across from Benton, flanked by Minister Ayanda Kafor, whose familiar presence was equally commanding. Their expressions telling of skepticism and cautious interest.

Benton cleared her throat, her voice cutting through the tension. "Thank you for meeting with me today. We stand at a critical juncture in history, and I believe the Seminal Synthesis project offers a solution to the Gender Cataclysm and to my deepest desire for peace."

General Castillo leaned forward, her eyes sharp and probing. "Dr. Benton, you continue asking us to consider a proposal that would hand Mars and the Moon over to male-only colonies. Do you not see how this contradicts our core mission of equality and inclusion?"

Benton held her ground, her gaze unwavering. "General, my proposal is not about segregation. To be clear, we are delivering all of space to men. It's not about eliminating them, it's about creating a controlled environment where we can advance the project without interference. Mars offers isolation and security, two elements crucial for the development of Seminal Synthesis."

Minister Kafor interjected, her voice measured but firm. "Dr. Benton, you're advocating for a move that could reinforce male dominance on a universal scale. The ethical implications alone are staggering."

Dr. Benton felt the enormity of their words challeging her, but she couldn't afford to falter. She knew this meeting was a smokescreen. Nevertheless she played along. "I understand your concerns, Minister. But we must consider the greater good. Two things that define my conviction for this course of action. The first is short-term necessity, and the second is ... well, to say it is long term is a bit of an understatement. Eternal would be more correct.

"The breakthrough announced by Turkey changes everything. If we don't act, Dr. Victor Lang will seize this opportunity to centralize power. We cannot allow that."

The mention of Victor Lang, a figure that was synonymous with manipulation and greed, sent a ripple through the room. Benton knew she was treading on dangerous ground, but she had to push forward. "Aylan Kiziltan is already involved," Benton said. Her voice gaining momentum. "With his support and my team's NVM technology at our disposal, we have a unique opportunity to take control of our future. This isn't just about science—it's about survival."

The leaders exchanged glances, their expressions a mix of confusion and contemplation. Benton felt a flicker of hope, but knew the road ahead was fraught with obstacles.

General Castillo's voice broke the silence, firm and resolute. "We cannot support a plan that risks everything we've built. The idea of male-only colonies contradicts our fundamental beliefs. Your proposal is too great a gamble."

The last rejection was felt like a hammer blow to the head, echoing through Benton's mind with devastating clarity. But now her vision, her meticulously crafted plan, seemed to open before her eyes. Anger and frustration simmered beneath her calm facad She let her anger loose.

"You're making a grave mistake," Benton said, her voice a taut wire of unsuppressed emotion. "Every second we hesitate, Lang's influence grows stronger. We cannot afford inaction. The last time you posed this argument, I made the mistake of thinking you were scared of losing control and I felt sorry for you. Then when you invited me back to take control of your World Liberty Congress, I thought, why do they think I need them to succeed? You know as well as I that it is you who needs me. So let's stop pretending.

"Take a seat Rosa, we want Lang and his freakish hord of transhumans off our planet. We will put a bounty on them. Kill the blirant on sight. We're going to banish them from our home and wipe them from our history.

"That's the first part."

While they looked up; their eyes telling of their mind's digesting the depth of her first point. Laura raised her hand above her head and motioned her hand in a circle. A moment later, Albera came into the room. A generous glass of Argh Sagi and a bottle in her hands. She went straight to Laura, handing her the glass. Then she placed the bottle on the table. Turned and left the room.

After filling her mouth to quench a much craved thirst, she swallowed the whole of it. "The second part goes like this.

"We don't want the technology and we don't want space. Earth! Earth is ours and that is bigger, larger, more important and whatever way you want to define something that words cannot explain. Life on Earth is the consequence of the deception that led to the lie. Earth is what we were to inherit. The end of time is at hand and we have it. Earth."

"Let's just hope you're right and this earns us a path back to eden," Ayanda said. "As if the end game was some sort of a mythological nirvana or such."

"It covers the first sins. Betrayal and deception." Dr. Benton said. "The first and the second lie is theirs. Men have to find the solution and the way back from those."

While they waited for Laura to pour a second glass of her liquor. They wondered if she was serious or if the simile or metaphor was deeper than they could grasp.

"We will know when they find their solution of contrition because that's the day we enter the garden or heaven or whatever you want to call it. Until that day, we wait here. On Earth!

Laura drained the second glass, the burn of the liquor spreading through her veins like wildfire. The atmosphere in the room shifted, the silence thick with tension. She set the glass down with a deliberate clink, her eyes narrowing at the women across from her.

"Let me make this clear," she said. "I'm not here to coddle your ideals or stroke your egos. The time for diplomacy is over. You want to survive, you follow my lead. Otherwise, Lang and his army of glorified meat puppets are going to tear apart everything I have built for us—and then no amount of gender theory is going to save your sorry asses."

She stood tall. Her presence towering over them, even from across the table. General Castillo shifted in her seat, the unshakable façade she had worn moments ago starting to crack, if only slightly. Kafor's fingers drummed nervously on the tabletop, her eyes darting toward Castillo for reassurance, but none came.

"Laura—" Castillo began, but Benton cut her off with a sharp wave of her hand.

"Spare me the diplomatic bullshit," she snapped. "You either have the guts for this fight, or you don't. But don't mistake me for someone who needs your approval. I've survived hell—and I'm damn well ready to drag every one of you through it, if that's what it takes to save this planet from those fucking monsters. So fall in line, or get out of my way."

She didn't wait for a response. With a flick of her wrist, she signaled Albera, who was already by the door. The two of them walked out, Laura's heels clicking sharply against the marble floor, each step a reminder that she wasn't asking permission—she was taking command.

The room fell silent behind her, filled with mistrust and posturing to conceal the fear their eyes betrayed. It wasn't just what she said—it was the undeniable truth of it, sinking into their bones.

***

Upon her return to the Istanbul residence, the night closed in around Dr. Benton with a tranquil embrace, the elegance of the dwelling a stark juxtaposition to the tempestuous thoughts that raged within her. The stillness of the house was a facade, a deceptive mask hiding the maelstrom of emotions that threatened to engulf her.

Inside the home office, where Alexsandra Coto, her tech advisor, was busy at work. Holographic displays flickered with data, the room illuminated by their soft glow. Benton joined her, shaking off the exhaustion that clung to her like a wet cloak.

"Any updates?" Benton asked, her voice steady despite the storm racing within.

Coto glanced up, concern etched in her features. "The anarchist lab has modified the NVM serum to your specifications. Test data and field testing confirm the serum efficacy. Now the bad news. Lang's influence is spreading. The rejection from the Militia leaders hasn't gone unnoticed. We need a new strategy, and fast."

Benton nodded, her mind already sprinting through the possibilities. "I still have a lead on the Moon," she said. "If I can secure support there, we still have a chance."

A sudden, gut-wrenching explosion that rocked the entire house cut the conversation short. Benton's instincts took over, adrenaline surging through her veins as she ducked for cover. Debris rained down around her, the cacophony of destruction a stark reminder of the danger she faced.

"Drones!" Coto shouted. Her voice barely audible over the chaos. Clouds of smoke, dust, and debris fill the house. Another explosion sent glass shards through the home. One buried deep into her left thigh.

Benton's mind snapped into focus. She grabbed a drone-blaster from the tactical gear locker. The biometric lock opened with a retina scan. Her hands were steady as she aimed and fired at the mechanical intruders. Two drones fell, consumed by flames, but more swarmed in, relentless in their assault.

Her leg burned with pain as she moved, every step driven by a will to survive. Lang's victory was close and Dr. Benton was violence itself. The house, once a sanctuary, had become a battleground.

"Coto, I need a way out!" Benton said. Her voice cutting through the turmoil.

Coto's voice crackled over the intercom, a lifeline amidst the chaos. "Follow the corridor to the emergency exit. I'll guide you."

Benton navigated through the smoke-filled corridors. The fumes burned her eyes and nose. She tore the sleeve from her blouse to cover her face. Each step was a battle against the debris and her own injuries. Her body screamed in protest, but her volition was ironclad.

The emergency exit emerged ahead, a narrow escape from the chaos behind her. But as she reached it, a collapsed beam blocked her path. Gritting her teeth, Benton forced herself through the narrow gap, ignoring the jagged edges that tore at her skin.

The outside air was a cool balm against her battered body. She stumbled, her leg threatening to give way, but out of the clouds of smoke and dust, powerful arms caught her before she hit the ground.

"Que bonita. I've got you, Laura," Marsal said, his voice a mixture of relief and determination. "Just like our first date." Terse and nostalgic, he passed a loving smile to her.

Benton nodded, her body trembling from the exertion. "We need to move. They won't stop until I'm dead."

Marsal supported her as they made their way to a waiting vehicle, its motor already humming. Benton collapsed into the seat, her mind a maelstrom of pain and resolve.

As they sped away from the wreckage of her home, Benton allowed herself a moment of reflection. The attack had been a brutal reminder of the stakes they faced, but it had also solidified her new intention of a ruthless offensive.

The road ahead was fraught with danger, but she would not let it stop her. The Seminal Synthesis project was too important, its potential too great. She would see it through, no matter the cost.

"You were supposed to meet me at Adam Cole's penthouse," she said. "Couldn't wait. When he told me you needed me, I moved everything off my schedule and came to Earth. Then I saw you were in Istanbul. I figured the feminist were making a peace treaty with you. Now, I got to your place just as the drones attacked."

"Can you take us to Boston?" She asked. "Let's go to Adam's place. Show me your super powers?"

Her smile spoke to something he couldn't put his finger on. He didn't recognize her.

"Your leg looks bad," he said. "We should get you looked at."

"Take me there, Marsal," she said. "Please?"

On a dark street, between a couple of abandoned warehouses, the driver left Marsal and Laura in the parking lot. Marsal held her close to him. She turned in his arms and pressed herself against him. In the moment they experienced the joyful anticipation of a love rekindling.

Marsal pulled her closer, Laura could feel the warmth of his body against hers, a grounding sensation amidst the chaos. But in the next breath, something shifted. The surrounding air thickened, like the atmosphere was being stretched and bent, its natural rhythm broken. A low hum started vibrating through her bones, a sound that seemed to come from everywhere and nowhere. As if it was always there but existing within a hidden layer of an unknown dimension. It wasn't the hum of an engine or any technology she recognized—it was deeper, primal, almost like the Earth itself was groaning.

A sharp, metallic taste filled her mouth, like ozone after a lightning strike. The smell of burned sulfur and charcoal, faint but unmistakable, curled in the air. She opened her mouth to speak, but the sound caught in her throat. For a moment, she felt as though reality itself had been muted. The world seemed to vibrate at the edge of perception, a throbbing sense just beneath her skin.

The twelfth harmonic. She thought.

Marsal's transhuman boundrian creator abilities were manifesting, and she was experiencing it. The air changed and became too thick to breathe, like she was moving through a viscous fluid, yet everything around them became both hyperreal and indistinct. The distant sounds of the city—horns, voices, even the wind—faded, replaced by a pulsating frequency that seemed to bend time and space. Laura's skin prickled as a wave of pressure squeezed against her, not crushing her but reshaping her senses.

And then, in an instant, they weren't there anymore.

The transition was seamless, yet indescribably alien. Laura felt her entire body ripped through an uncharted dimension, her vision blurring as if the fabric of space-time itself was folding around them. The sensation was simultaneously cold and hot, as her atoms were being rearranged and then knit back together in perfect harmony. Her leg, throbbing in pain moments before, now tingled with a strange warmth, the ache dissolving as new flesh regenerated at a speed no human body could ever achieve on its own. Her hands, raw and cut from the battle, felt rejuvenated, the skin smoothing over with a subtle tingling sensation as the damage vanished.

Her body remade itself in the blink of an eye, the feeling utterly surreal, as if life itself had rebooted her from the inside out.

The smells changed too—gone was the chemical tang of burning sulfer, replaced with something sweet, almost intoxicating, like the scent of jasmine or sandalwood mixed with fresh rain. A distant ringing sound accompanied their arrival, as if reality was ringing in their ears, then faded as fast as it came.

And suddenly, they were standing in the center of Adam's penthouse in Boston. The rich, polished tiles beneath her feet felt oddly foreign, yet solid. Thick glass windows muffled the sound of the city below, as if the universe itself had silenced it.

Laura breathed in deeply, feeling the sharp contrast from where they'd been only moments before. Her body no longer screamed in pain—it hummed with vitality. She glanced at her leg, flexing it in disbelief, her mind still processing the impossible regeneration.

"Christ," she said. Muttered under her breath turning to Marsal. "That's... that's a hell of a way to travel."

Marsal smirked, though his eyes were searching hers for any signs of discomfort. "Felt weird the first time for me too," he said, pulling her closer for a moment, his touch grounding her as her senses continued to reorient.

She tilted her head, still reeling from the experience. "Weird doesn't even cover it. And the smells—the sounds, like something crawling through time."

Marsal chuckled, but there was a serious edge to it. "That's what it feels like when you bend the boundaries of reality." He looked down at her leg, then back into her eyes. "You're healed. Good as new. Que bonita."

Laura took a step, feeling her body whole again. "So," she said. Her thoughts regahered just a bit. "That's what it feels like when you mess with the laws of the universe. And here I thought your only super power wast saving my life."

Marsal's grin widened. "Oh, I'm good at that too."

The kiss they had both wondered, would it happen, gripped them. Their hearts felt the relief from more than a year of grief. Marsal lifted her into his arms and carried her to the bedroom.

"Give me ten minutes to shower and clean up," she said. "I've been in these clothes all day."

Like a teenager in protest, he put her on the ground. He watched her as she walked to the bath. She stopped for a moment to take the case from the top of the dresser beside the door. It was the case she had taken there when Adam told her the meeting with Marsal had been arranged. Adam was on his way to the war zone in Tivalabet. The case is the gift the anarchist gave her.

***

While she showered, her mind wandered back in time to the meeting with the anarchist community on the moon. The warmth of the water cleansing and caressing. She relaxed. She stared at the case next to the sink. Her memories were stimulated.

The Moon had always been a place that defied logic, a barren expanse of dust and silence, yet it hummed with the energy of clandestine meetings and revolutionary plans. Laura remembered the synthetic air on her skin inside the underground anarchist hideout. Heavy with the smell of machinery and ozone, while the low thrumming of hidden generators kept time with the whispered conversations around her.

The anarchists didn't bother with formalities. They were a group that thrived in chaos, their every movement deliberate and driven by a raw, defiant energy. Their so called leader, a tall woman named Aenid with short-cropped hair and a piercing gaze, had greeted Laura with nothing but a nod. They knew why she was there, and they wasted no time.

As Laura stood in the center of the room, the faint sun's glow reflecting off lunar soil filtering through the narrow vertical windows, the anarchists spoke among themselves. Their voices, throaty from years spent dodging authorities and breathing recycled synthetic air. Their sounds filled the space with a grim narrative that sent a chill down her spine.

"Dr. Victor Lang," Aenid said, her tone dripping with disdain, "is behind the disappearances. He's been collecting the best minds—scientists, engineers, innovators—and sending them off to a distant planet, far beyond the edges of our galaxy. They think they're on a mission to transcend on behalf of the human race, to become something greater."

Aenid moved closer, her eyes narrowing. "He wants them to guide future generations on this new planet to a state of nirvana, but it's all a hoodwink. The actual goal is control. He needs the book of Maha to cement his power over them, to plant the seeds of a new religious doctrine that he'll manipulate to his advantage. Without the book, he can't finish the plan."

"The book of Maha?" Laura asked, her voice skeptical. She'd heard whispers of it before, a mythical artifact that supposedly contained the secrets of the universe, of human life and death. It was said that once a person read the story, it answered all their unanswered questions and left no mysteries or doubts, but she'd never believed it was more than a conspiracy theory.

Aenid nodded. "Yeah. I know what you're thinking, but it's real. And Lang will stop at nothing to get it. We need you to find it first."

Laura's mind raced. If what the anarchists said was true, Lang was already several steps ahead, sending humanity's brightest away to a remote planet while tightening his grip on Mars. But something about this plan didn't sit right with her.

"How do you know Dr. Lang is kidnapping these leading scientists and academics?"

"If you hadn't doubted me I would never have trusted you," Aenid said. A wry smile formed over her thick lips and sunken cheeks. "I was part of the team who helped the scientists through the transition. They aren't being kidnapped. We show them the plans and the research for nirvanaing. After they see it, they agree. They are willing to give up everything on Earth for the opportunity.

"Anyway, it was getting too dangerous for me to remain on his transition team. So, I came back here to our lunar colony."

"And if I find this book for you?" Laura asked, her tone measured.

Aenid's eyes gleamed with a dark intensity as she handed Laura the case. The reflective black box barely betrays the lethal power it contained. Laura could sense the strength of it in her hand, heavier than she expected, as if the truth within held a gravity all its own. When Aenid opened the case, the dimly lit room seemed to hum with the silent tension of the revelation.

Inside, nestled in the burgundy-red velvet-lined interior, was a small, unassuming vial filled with a shimmering golden oil that caught the faint light like liquid gold. Its sheen shifted slightly, as if alive, it pulsed with a hidden energy. Laura's fingers brushed the edge of the vial as she looked at Aenid, her mind churning with questions.

Aenid didn't wait for her to ask.

"This isn't just some weapon we stumbled upon," Aenid began, her voice lowering, as though the very walls had ears. "It took years to develop. We lost some of our best people in the process. The research behind this... it's extensive and brutal."

She locked eyes with Laura, her expression a mix of pride and bitterness. "We engineered the oil from a virus strain we isolated after months of testing on transhuman captives. It was harvested from a parasite found in the deep caverns of Mars, an organism that thrives by latching onto its host's cellular structure. It wasn't easy finding something that could penetrate the biological defenses of the transhumans. Their immune systems are nearly impenetrable."

Aenid reached into the case and took out a thin data pad that was hidden underneath the vial, swiping the screen to reveal a list of detailed reports, charts, and statistics. "The oil doesn't just kill them outright. That would be too simple, too detectable. We needed something that could spread without being noticed, something that wouldn't tip off their sensors."

She paused, her eyes hard as steel. "When you apply this to a transhuman, it takes eight days before it kills them. But in those eight days, they become highly contagious. Any transhuman they come into contact with will be infected—casual encounters, skin-to-skin, even even through a com connection, or being within a few meters. The infection spreads exponentially, fast enough to hit entire populations before anyone realizes what's happening."

Laura stared at the vial, her mind turning over the implications. "And then they just... die?"

Aenid nodded grimly. "It's not a peaceful death either. Once the contagion takes root, their immune systems gradually break down, and their enhanced neural networks begin to malfunction. Their body will fight it at first, but the virus is aggressive. By the time they realize something is wrong, it's already too late."

Her voice dropped even lower, the next words laced with cold satisfaction. "The last stage is cerebral degeneration. Their minds collapse in on themselves. It's like pulling the plug on a supercomputer, only instead of shutting down, it melts from the inside out."

Laura's fingers tightened around the case, the reality of the weapon settling in. This wasn't just a tool for sabotage. This weapon was a slow, insidious death sentence for an entire class of beings—beings that, in the eyes of many, were already seen as superior as the next step in human evolution. And now Laura held the key to their destruction in her hands.

Aenid sensed her hesitation and stepped closer. Her raspy voice with graveled tone, "You're thinking about the ethics of it. I get it. But don't fool yourself, Laura. These transhumans... they're not human anymore. They don't think like us. They don't live like us. They're an abomination, and a mistake. Lang's mistake. And if we don't act, if we don't stop him now, they'll replace us."

Laura glanced back down at the vial, her mind swirling with the moral weight of what she was about to unleash. She thought of Lang, the cold, calculating mind behind the transhuman agenda, and the missing scientists he was carting off to the far edge of the galaxy on some wild mission to create a post-human utopia.

She thought of the book, the book of Maha, and its supposed key to guiding generations of those same scientists into a new age of being. Without the book, Lang's grand vision couldn't come to fruition. But this oil—it was more than just a bargaining chip. It was a weapon that could cripple Lang's forces before they even left Earth.

"The testing?" Laura asked, her voice steady now, all emotion stripped away, leaving only the sharp edge of determination. "How certain are you that this works?"

Aenid's mouth twisted into a grim smile. "It's been tested extensively. On several captives. The initial trials were slow. The first versions killed too quickly, alerted their system defenses. We lost a lot of time there. But the current formula—this version—worked exactly as planned. We watched it spread among a small group of captured transhumans. It took less than a week for every one of them to succumb."

She paused, as if reliving the memory. "Three days to spread. Then the neurological collapse starts. By day seven, they're convulsing, and by day eight, they're dead. The entire process is nearly impossible to trace until it's too late. Their bodies deteriorate rapidly after death, leaving no signs of the viral contagion."

Laura nodded, her mind already calculating the next steps. She needed to get the book before Lang did, but now she had an ace up her sleeve. The oil was more than just a weapon—it was a reckoning.

Aenid leaned in close, her voice a dangerous whisper. "You get us the book, and this oil will do the rest. Lang's empire will fall apart from the inside. The transhumans won't even see it coming. Our lab is in Istanbul. It's yours now. The team and all of it. Together we will end the war and establish peace."

Laura closed the case with a click, sealing away the vial and its perilous contents. "You'll have your book," she said, her voice cold and resolute.

Then her memory dissolved, the lunar hideout fading as the steam from her shower surrounded her. The water was hot, but she let it burn against her skin, pulling her away from the flashback to the present. She could still feel the cool metal of the case in her hands, its contents a grim reminder of the path she'd chosen.

She sighed, the water pouring down gently around her as she leaned her head back, staring at the ceiling. She would have the book soon. Adam Cole closing in on the location the anarchist provided. But the decision for what came next was already made and the viral oil now modified with her NVM still a volatile wildcard she dared to use.

Resolute, Laura pulled herself from the bath, water drops cascading down her body. The cool air of the bedroom greeted her, and she wrapped herself in a thick towel, the softness a welcome after the rawness of her memories.

Marsal was waiting for her, leaning against the bedpost, watching her as she entered the room. His eyes followed her every move, a small smirk playing on his lips as he saw the case in her hand. He knew better than to ask about it—at least, not yet.

"You took your time," he said, his voice teasing, though she could hear his underlying desire in it. His Cuban accent, once hypnotic and playful. He sang Guantanamera. "Yo soy un hombre sincero. De donde cere la palma..."

Laura sat the case down carefully on the bedside table and walked over to him, her body still warm from the bath. "Just thinking," she said, her voice soft, but her mind still replaying the conversation with the anarchists. "There's a lot to consider."

Marsal nodded, pulling her close, his hands settling on her hips. He stopped singing. "You don't have to carry it all alone, you know."

Laura leaned into him, resting her head against his chest, the scent of his skin grounding her. For a moment, she allowed herself to relax, to let the chaos of her mind slip away.

But in the back of her thoughts, the weight of her next move loomed. The book of Maha, the viral oil, Lang's transhuman army—it was all connected. And the choices she made in the coming minute would determine not only her future but seal the fate of humanity.

"I know," she said. Her voice barely audible against his skin. "But some things I have to finish myself. For now, can we put everything off to the side and just be together and do what lovers do?"

***

The oil shimmered on his skin, the faint scent of something both sweet and metallic mixing with the heady musk of their arousal. Laura's body was alive with sensation, her core aching for him, her every nerve tingling with anticipation.

Her hands wet with the NVM viral oil she massaged the liquid into his thick arousal. She used the sexual encounter to infect him. Stirring the erogenous zones and arousing his fantasy desires to camouflage the sensation of nanos penetrating his system.

With a growl, Marsal suddenly flipped her over, his strength effortless as he tossed her onto her hands and knees. Laura gasped, the sudden shift sending a jolt of excitement through her. She felt his hands on her hips, strong and commanding, pulling her back toward him as he positioned himself behind her.

Well lubricated, he thrust into her filling her completely in one swift, powerful motion. Laura cried out, her fingers gripping the sheets as he drove himself deeper, his hips slamming against hers with a primal force. The heat between them was erotic, every movement stoking the flames higher, pushing them both toward the edge.

Marsal's pace was relentless, each thrust harder and deeper than the previous. Driving her to the brink of ecstasy. She could feel the tension building, coiling tightly inside her, ready to snap. Her breath came in ragged gasps, her body shuddering with the intensity of their connection.

"Yes," she moaned, her voice breathless, urging him on, her body trembling with pleasure. "Don't stop." She pulled the vial from the case. Careful to pour a cupped handful under his thrusts. Then reached between her legs with her left hand and masssaged his contracting testis with more of the NVM oil.

Marsal's grip on her hips tightened, his body moving faster. More urgent. The sound of their bodies colliding echoed in the room, the slickness of the oil only amplifying the sensation as they moved together in frantic rhythm. The intensity of it all—the heat, the friction, the raw need—was allowing them to escape the traps and suffering of life.

With a final, powerful thrust, they experience the temporary dissolution of self that accompanies the peak of sexual pleasure. Or what is more generally known as the little death. Marsal drove them both over the edge. Laura cried out as the orgasm tore through her. Her body in sync with his, convulsing in waves of pleasure. Fingers digging into the sheets as she bucked against him. Marsal's own release followed, his groan deep and feral as he emptied himself inside her, his body shuddering with the force of it.

For a moment, they were still, their bodies spent and slick with sweat, the ferver between them slowly dissipating. Marsal leaned over her, his breath hot against the back of her neck as he kissed her shoulder, his touch suddenly tender, almost reverent.

Marsal's com, buzzing insistently on the nightstand, shattered the moment. He groaned, reluctantly pulling away from her as he grabbed the device.

"Meirda," he said. Glancing at the screen. "It's an in coming emergency message. The Lunar hotline."

Laura rolled onto her back, still catching her breath, her body humming with the aftershocks of their lovemaking. "You better take it," she said, her voice soft, but her eyes held a knowing gleam. While he was distracted she placed the vial into the case and sealed it.

Marsal nodded, his expression shifting from pleasure to concern as he answered the call. The world outside their bed was crashing back in, and soon, the consequences of what she had just accomplished.

Marsal pressed the communicator to his ear, his breath still uneven from their intense encounter, but the urgency in Adam's voice cut through any lingering haze of pleasure. His tone was strained, each word laced with agony. In the background, Marsal could hear the unmistakable sounds of chaos—gunfire, explosions, screams of pain that echoed through the connection like a death rattle.

"Adam?" Marsal's voice shifted immediately, sharp with concern. "What the hell is happening?"

Adam's voice cracked, the pain in it unmistakable. "Marsal... I don't have much time. Is... is Dr. Benton there? Laura... she needs to hear this."

Marsal glanced over at Laura, her body still flushed from their lovemaking, but her eyes already narrowing as she read the sudden tension in his face. He nodded, and she was beside him in an instant, her hand gripping his wrist, silently demanding to know what was happening.

"She's here, Adam," Marsal said, his voice urgent. "Diceme. What's going on?"

There was a long pause, punctuated by a sharp intake of breath, and then Adam spoke again, his voice hoarse, barely above a whisper. "I've found it... The Book of Maha. It's real, Marsal. I have it right here... on an old-world thumb drive. I found it at the entrance gate to the Old City. But I'm trapped. There's... there's no way out."

Laura's breath hitched, her eyes widening as the darkness of his words sank in. She grabbed the com from Marsal's hand, her voice tight with urgency. "Adam, where are you? Tell me exactly where you are." Another explosion ripped through the moment, followed by the distant shouts of men barking orders, the wails of the wounded, and the constant, relentless staccato of gunfire. Adam groaned in pain, his voice fading in and out.

"I'm at the Old City gates," he managed, each word labored. "There's no time, Laura. I've lost... I've lost my leg in an explosion. I'm bleeding out. There's nothing left for me here." He gathered his thoughts, sucking in a ragged breath. "I just... I wanted you to know I found it. The thumb drive... it's in my pocket. But you have to get here fast if you want it."

Laura's heart hammered in her chest, a thousand questions fighting to break free, but the urgency of the situation squeezed her like a vice. Adam would not make it. She could hear it in his voice, feel it in the desperate way he clung to each breath.

"Adam, you have to hang on," Laura said, her voice demanded. "We'll get to you. Just tell us—"

"No," Adam interrupted, the sharp finality in his voice freezing her in place. "You won't make it in time. I'm... I'm done. It's over for me, Laura." He waited, groaning in pain again, and when he spoke next, his voice was softer, resigned. "This is bigger than me. Bigger than all of us. Don't waste time trying to save me... save the world. Get the book. It's yours now."

Laura's vision blurred as the reality of his words crashed over her. She had known the risks, known that any of them could die at any moment, but hearing it like this, hearing Adam—strong, unflappable Adam—accept his fate with such brutal clarity... it felt like a punch to the gut.

Marsal's hand found hers, squeezing it tight as they listened to the sounds of the war closing in on Adam, the background of the call now a torrent of violence and destruction.

"Laura," Adam said again, his voice faint. "Don't let this be for nothing. Get the book. Do what you have to do. Lang... Lang can't be the one to win."

Marsal's expression hardened the moment Adam's pained voice came through the communicator, urgency overtaking the warmth of the aftermath they'd shared just moments before. He pushed himself off the bed, moving with the speed and precision only he possessed, pulling his clothes on as Laura gripped the com, her mind reeling.

"Adam, hold on," Marsal said. His voice yelled into the communicator, his tone leaving no room for argument. He took the device from Laura's hand and met her wide-eyed gaze, his determination evident. "I'll get you out of there. I'm coming!"

Without waiting for a response, Marsal set up a holographic projection in the center of the room. A soft hum filled the air as a three-dimensional feed flickered into life, mapping Adam's exact coordinates. The chaotic sounds of battle—the screams, the explosions, the visceral cries of pain—filled the room, making the scene all too real for Laura.

Marsal turned to her, a grim look in his eyes. "You'll see everything. Stay here. Watch me get him out."

Her heart hammered as she stared into his eyes, knowing this might be the last time she'd see him. In the depth of his gaze, she could feel his love for her, fierce and unspoken, a bond that transcended words. He gave her a reassuring look, one filled with lover's understanding, before turning his focus back to the task. With a motion of his hand, the communicator pinpointed Adam's location, and Marsal's boundrian creator powers came to life. The surrounding air thickened and vibrated as a vortex slowly opened, shimmering like liquid reality bending to his will. The doorway pulsed, revealing a fractured, fleeting glimpse of the war-torn streets on the other side.

Marsal was moving through the spatial corridor. The world seemed to blur around him as he disappeared into the vortex, leaving Laura standing in the dim room. Her breath caught in her throat.

The holographic projection shifted, and Laura watched in real time as Marsal emerged in the heat of the battlefield. He appeared in the chaos like a phantom, dodging gunfire and explosions as he weaved through the destruction with effortless grace. He rapidly located Adam, who was sat upright leaning against a ruined building. Blood had gathered beneath his leg where it had been blown off.

Adam's face contorted in pain, but his eyes lit up when he saw Marsal approaching. "You... you made it," Adam gasped, his voice weak but filled with relief.

Marsal crouched down beside him, gripping his shoulder. "I told you, didn't I? I always come through."

Adam managed a broken smile, and with trembling hands, he reached into his pocket and pulled out a small, ancient thumb drive. "The book of Maha... it's all on here. Don't let Lang... don't let him win."

Marsal nodded, taking the drive and pocketing it. His voice was steady, commanding. "You're going to live, Adam. I'm sending you to Boston Men's Hospital now. You'll be safe."

With a swift motion, Marsal opened a harmonic doorway next to them, the air shimmering with the same otherworldly pulse as before. He guided Adam through the portal, and in an instant, Adam's body was gone, transported to the hospital.

Laura watched from the safety of the residence, her heart thudding as she saw Adam safely delivered to Boston through the holographic display. But her relief was short-lived as she realized Marsal hadn't followed. He stood alone now; the battlefield raging around him, the sky thick with smoke and fire.

"Marsal!" Laura shouted through the hologram, her voice strained with desperation. "Get out of there!" He couldn't hear her.

Marsal turned toward the projection, his expression calm, almost serene. "Laura... I can't. I won't."

Her mind went quiet and her life on hold as she saw the peril of the situation in his eyes.

"As I passed through the harmonic gateway, my systems detected something." His voice remained calm, but the truth was like a dagger in her heart. "The oil. The virus... you infected me with it."

Laura's stomach twisted. He knew.

"Congratulations," Marsal said, his voice a strange mixture of admiration and sorrow. "It's a brilliant strategy. You've won, Laura. The virus would have spread. The transhumans would not stand a chance."

Tears blurred Laura's vision, guilt and devastation wracking her body. "Marsal, I... I didn't want—"

"Don't apologize," he said. Imagining that to be her response. "You did what you had to do. It's the only way to stop Lang and his army." He pulled the thumb drive from his pocket and held it up, his eyes steady as he stared through the holographic feed. "I'm sending the book of Maha to Lang. He'll know what it means when he receives it... along with a message about the virus."

Laura's heart ached as she listened to his calm, measured tone. "Marsal, please," she whispered, her voice cracking with emotion. "Don't do this."

The thumb drive vanished in an instant. "This is the way it has to be. Creo que todo estas bien ahora."

The battlefield erupted, but Marsal stood tall, resolute. "Before I go," he said, his voice taking on a heartfelt tone, "I want you to know... men—our kind—have always had a place in this world. We've built, we've fought, we've protected. I want you to know we're not a mistake. We're not a relic. There is value in what we've contributed to humanity... even if the world doesn't always see it. Man and woman must transcend together."

Laura's chest tightened, her breath coming in ragged gasps as she watched him, powerless to stop what was coming. The emotional intensity of his words hit her like a tidal wave, threatening to drown her in their finality.

Stiffening her resolve, she recalls every effort that has failed—the loss of the Martian and Moon colonies, the ongoing war and the people fleeing to Central and South America to find peace and freedom, the feminist armies no longer under her command, the anarchist alliance in ruins—and now this. The destruction of Dr. Lang and his transhuman race was defeated by the man she loved, and it had become her ultimate act of betrayal.

"Que bonita, Laura. Quiero," Marsal said, his voice strong, unwavering. "I always have. And I always will. Earth is yours. The virus will kill transhumans there."

Without another word between them, Marsal turned away. Opening a final harmonic doorway—this time to the swirling void of a black hole. The vortex shimmered, its dark energy rippling through the air like a living entity, pulling everything around it into its depths.

Marsal glanced back at her, his eyes filled with love, sadness, and then acceptance. "Creo que todo estas bien." And he stepped through.

The vortex swallowed him whole, the black hole pulling him into oblivion as the harmonic gateway collapsed behind him, leaving nothing of him. Not a trace of Marsal except a memory.

Laura collapsed to her knees, the horrific experience of what had just happened crashing over her. The room fell silent, the hologram fading away as she stared blankly at the spot where Marsal had been moments before.

He was gone.

Chapter Fourteen: The Meek

Three Weeks After the One-Year Appointment Ended

Her mind raced back to the countless hours she had spent manipulating Marsal, grooming him. It had all seemed so foolproof—until the loss of his life. She had underestimated the depth of his loyalty to Dr. Victor Lang, and that oversight had nearly cost her everything.

With a sharp intake of breath, Laura forced herself to move. She could not afford to fall apart now. She was a leader, and leaders found solutions, even in the face of insurmountable odds. Turning to her team in the anarchist labratory, her voice was a low, dangerous growl. "We need to regroup. Now."

The scientists scrambled to comply. Laura moved with purpose, her mind already strategizing the next steps. The Jekyll Island data was out of her hands, and the book of Maha was with Lang. And the fight was over.

"What have the Jekyll Island documents to do with our quest for world peace?" The sound of the question caused the lab and everyone in it to pause. All eyes turned toward Laura.

"Alright, I suppose it is time to rip the bandage off on this dark secret," she said. Her voice regained its usual cadence and multiplicity of tones.

"Back when. In the ancient days of bankers. A group of them put their heads together and designed the wealth code. The manifest that the wealthy used to make slaves out of the middle class and the poor. They chose feminism as their weapon of choice. No matter what else was happening in the world, they knew the gender divide was all they needed to keep everyone occupied and distracted from their manipulation to loot uber wealth.

"They all agreed to take advantage of schadenfreude and envy. Schadenfreude is a German word to describe human's natural satisfaction derived from others' suffering. Envy, of course, is that natural human dissatisfaction from other people's success. They baked into their plan in some deep details for how to influence, own, and control the facilitation of these. Such as industries of media, government, sports, and every aspect of education and how they would use them to keep people deeply divided by primarily fanning the flames of feminism.

"They had no idea at the time for the depth of the gender divide. The magnitude of ways a people can classify their gender. It boggles the mind. Anyway...

"It's all one big lie. A deceit from the uber-rich to keep the rest of us filled with hate, fear, and confusion while they live a glorious, opulent life. Self indulgent within their monstrous addiction to greed.

"Clara!" she called out. Her voice was cold and authoritative. The young scientist, still trembling from the recent events, hurried over. "Prepare the contingency protocols. We're going to need every resource at our disposal. Once Adam Cole heals, he will take what he learns from reading the Jekyll Island documents, and he will make it public. We need to act first."

Clara nodded, her wide eyes reflecting a mixture of fear and admiration. Laura watched her go with her team close behind. Feeling a comforting relief. These people had placed their trust in her, and she had led them past the brink of disaster. She had been face down in the middle of complete failure. But no longer.

As she turned back to her team, a thought struck her. The book of Maha's power was not just in its contents, but in its interpretation. If she could find a way to counteract whatever Lang intended to do with it, there might still be hope. But first, she needed to understand the book in ways even the most devout scholars could not.

"James!" she called to another scientist. An older man with a face etched by years of stress and sleepless nights. "I need every piece of research we have on The Book of Maha. Leave no stone unturned."

James nodded, his expression grim. "Yes, Dr. Benton."

As the lab buzzed back to life with renewed urgency, Laura sank into her chair, her mind a whirlwind of calculations and possibilities. The stakes had never been unachievable and the margin for error had never been non-existent. But if there was one thing Laura Benton excelled at, it was turning the impossible into the achievable.

Though she was the only person on Earth who knew it, the war was over and feminist were now in full control. What she had to do now was to prove it and make a strategic assumption of control. The only potential threat, the book of Maha. Then again, maybe a second threat was her fellow leader's doubt of her victory.

Hours later, with the lab working at a feverish pace monitoring the NVM infected around the planet, Laura sat alone in her office, poring over the ancient texts and data streams as fast as James delivered them. The knowledge within the book of Maha was a labyrinth of metaphors and hidden meanings. She had to decode it, and fast. The task was proving impossible, even for her best people.

Suddenly, an alert flashed on her screen. An encrypted message. Her pulse quickened as she opened it, expecting a lifeline, or perhaps another proof of her success. Instead, what she read chilled her to the bone.

Message:

Subject: Tribunal Summons

From: Feminist Militia Central Command

To: Dr. Laura Benton

Dr. Benton,

You are hereby summoned to appear before the Tribunal of the Feminist Militia to answer for crimes against women's rights and humanity, sabotage, and treason, including murder and assassinations of government officials and foreign dignitaries. Your actions have led to the loss of strategic and confidential information and the deaths of countless feminist politicians and civilians. You will be held accountable.

Date: Three days from receipt of this notice

Location: Tribunal Hall, undisclosed location (an escort will be provided)

Failure to comply will result in immediate capture and indefinite detention.

For the cause,

Secretary of Defence, Commander Elena Reyes

The screen dimmed as the message ended. She moved hastily to her office. Her mind put together the actions and steps to prove the war was over before it was too late.

The Feminist Militia, led by the fierce and uncompromising Elena Reyes, did not have a reputation for leniency. A tribunal meant a public trial, one that would expose her NVM virus and the failures and possibly lead to her court-martial and execution.

Losing the military data had been a severe blow, forty-two leading scientists were missing, and the deaths of key political figures had only exacerbated the crisis. But she had always believed her actions were necessary sacrifices for the greater good. Now, it seemed, others saw them as untenable crimes. She can't risk exposing the virus. Not yet.

The crippling force of the situation sank in as Laura's eyes flicked to the door of her office. The team outside, working tirelessly under her guidance, did not know the storm that was about to hit.

With renewed urgency, she stood and moved to the lab's central console, her voice cutting through the din. "Everyone, listen up!"

The team paused, eyes turning to her with a mixture of confusion and concern.

"I've just received word from the Feminist Militia. They're summoning me for a tribunal. They hold me responsible for losing military secrets and murder, including the deaths of key politicians and several other causes."

A murmur of collective shock rippled through the room.

"We don't have much time," she continued, her voice firm. "I need to prepare for this tribunal, but we cannot let our work falter. James, continue with the protocols we discussed. Clara, you're with me."

Clara stepped forward, her face pale but determined. "What do you need, Dr. Benton?"

"We need to secure all data related to our research. If they're putting me on trial, they might try to seize everything we've worked on. We can't let that happen."

Clara nodded and moved to a terminal, her fingers flying over the keys as she began the encryption process. "We should have a secret lab somewhere."

"Too little too late, but a great idea," Laura said. "Though I had considered having a private lab built in Leadville, Colorado."

Clara's head snapped up from her monitors.

"A lot of thought and effort went into this strategy and when I put the end game into the strategy, I realized the futility of the secret lab. If this plan to conquer Earth failed, what purpose would a secret lab serve? What would we need to accomplish?"

As Laura turned back to her office, another alert appeared. This time, it was a set of coordinates for the tribunal location. The place was remote, far from any safe zones she knew. It was a deliberate choice, meant to isolate and intimidate.

She felt a presence beside her and looked up to see a new security officer named Jaxina, who had been quietly efficient since her arrival. A hard line was set on Jaxina's face, and her eyes betrayed no emotion.

"Dr. Benton," she said quietly, "do you want me to accompany you?"

She hesitated, considering the offer. "No, Jaxiana. This is something I need to face alone. But I need you here, keeping everything secure.

Protect Albera and help her with anything she asks. Trust no one. Defend this lab against invasion at all costs."

Jaxina nodded, her gaze unwavering. "Understood."

Laura took a deep breath, trying to steady herself. The tribunal was a threat, but it was also an opportunity. If she could present her case convincingly then she could make them see the necessity of her actions. She might turn this to her advantage.

With Clara's help, Laura compiled the necessary data. The team considered every contingency and planned for every outcome. Yet, the nagging doubt remained—could she truly justify her actions in the eyes of those who had already judged her guilty?

***

Laura Benton watched the flicker of emotions cross Valeria Asimov's face, the cold calculation, the dawning fear, and finally, the resigned acceptance. It was a dance she had seen a hundred times before, in boardrooms and war rooms alike, but never in someone as powerful and ruthless as the Russian General. The stakes were higher now, with lives hanging in the balance.

Valeria's lips curled, but her resolve faltered. Laura could see it—the slow unraveling of the General's loyalty to Lang and her undeniable bond to womanhood.

"Tell me more about the AI," Laura pressed, her voice low and menacing. "I want details. Exact details."

Valeria sighed, her face showed her resolve. "The AI is a Hydra, a multi-headed beast. Designed by Lang's top coder in quantum computer generated AI. It's not just a series of firewalls or intrusion detection systems. We're talking about a living, adaptive network. It scans for anomalies constantly—thermal shifts, magnetic signatures, biofeedback. Their individual biosignature—DNA markers, retinal patterns, even subtle brainwave frequencies recognized every person entering that vault. The thing can identify your shadow. Any deviation, anything out of the ordinary, and the system went into a full lockdown, sealing every exit and triggering an alert directly to Lang's command center. There are no second chances."

Laura's eyes gleamed. "And the quantum computer?"

Valeria continued, her voice bitter. "Lang's computer isn't just any quantum processor. It's a throttled, near super AI-integrated system based on quantum entanglement principles. It doesn't process information linearly—it reads and predicts. The bio kernel can anticipate hacking attempts, disruptions, or even physical attacks before they happen, based on probability modeling. It sees every threat as a branching path and shuts down the problem before it manifests."

Laura tapped her fingers on the metal surface of the table, her mind racing. "So, it's always watching, always learning."

"Exactly," Valeria said, her tone sharp. "It detects stress patterns in the transhumans patrolling the vault. The slightest change in their behavior triggers a deeper scan, analyzing everything from hormonal levels to blood oxygenation. And if it suspects anything's wrong, it doesn't just alert Lang—it begins with a series of countermeasures. We're talking nanites, electrical discharges on the floor, gas that can kill in seconds. The AI doesn't play nice."

Laura took a breath, weighing her next question. "And this failsafe—the manual override Lang controls—how does it work?"

Valeria's eyes narrowed, her voice lowering. "Lang keeps a neural implant connected to the AI. He's paranoid enough to ensure only his brain waves can unlock the system's deepest levels. No one else can touch it. You need him, Benton. You need to break his mind, and get him to unlock the system. And good luck with that."

Laura's grin widened. She was like a predator scenting blood. "I don't need luck. I have you."

The tension in the lab ratcheted up as Valeria glanced once more at the screen, where the images of the Chinese, Saudi, and other Russian general's lifeless bodies glint like empty shells with heartbeats.

"When do we move?" Valeria asked, her voice stripped of all pretense. Not wanting to become like them.

Laura allowed herself a small, victorious smile. "Now."

As Laura gave the order to her team, the lab doors slid open, revealing the cold, stark corridor beyond. Valeria's footsteps echoed alongside Laura's, their pace synchronized in a reluctant partnership. Laura could feel the tension in the air. An invisible tripwire stretched to its limit, ready to snap at the slightest provocation.

But this was the only way. The date for the tribunal was closing in, and time was running out. The book of Maha was the last piece of missing information, the key to unlocking the power she needed to not only survive but to seize control. If Valeria succeeded, they'd both walk away with what they wanted. If she failed...

Laura's mind shifted to contingency plans, already calculating the moves she'd have to make, the strings she'd have to pull. In this strategic dance, there was no room for missed steps.

As they reached the exit, Laura turned to Valeria, her voice a cold command. "Remember, General, I have your life—and the lives of your comrades—in my hands. Don't give me a reason to tighten my grip."

Valeria's eyes met hers, a flash of defiance still burning within. "Just make sure you hold up your end of the bargain, Benton. I'm not the only one with something to lose."

"Before you go back to Moscow and embark on the plan to recover the book, I want to ask you a question. You see, it's how you question my word. The condescending, as if I might not ... that puzzles me. So let me ask you. You know that the war is over, right? You realize I have won, and this planet is mine, don't you?"

The look of sudden bewilderment in Valeria's eyes told Laura she hadn't realized it. A look Laura had never seen in Valeria's eyes. A moment of doubt and humility.

Laura watched her walk away, her posture stiff, her shoulders squared. A questioning doubt flickered in Laura's mind. Could she trust this woman? Could she trust anyone?

But then the concern vanished, replaced by the cold, unyielding determination that had brought her this far. Trust was a luxury she would never invest in.

***

The room was chilly, the kind of cold that seeped into the bones and made intercostal muscles cramp with every breath. Harsh lights bore down on Laura Benton and Valeria, who sat shivering side by side, shackled to metal chairs that were bolted to the floor. The courtroom was an odd mix of ancient tradition and sterile modernity, with corrugated steel paneled walls and a massive steel door guarding the only exit. At the far end of the room, a panel of three women judges. The judges observed them with impassive eyes. On the right side of the room was a jury of twelve, equally expressionless women of power. Staring with judgment already written across their faces.

The Feminist Militia had taken no chances—armed guards escorted Laura and Valeria, their wrists and ankles tightly bound. A hundred invisible eyes on the EcoSphere tracked their every movement.

The lead judge, a woman with graying hair tied back in a severe bun, leaned forward, her voice a weapon as she spoke. "Dr. Laura Benton, you stand accused of treason, of murder on a global scale, and of crimes against humanity. The NVM virus, your creation, was used as a weapon to destroy untold lives. How do you plead?"

Laura raised her head, her gaze steady, defiant even. She had nothing left to lose. "Victorious," she said, her teeth chattering voice echoing in the cavernous room.

A judge's raised hand quickly silenced as a murmur rippled through the gallery, but. "On what grounds?" the judge demanded, her tone clipped.

"I did not design the NVM virus as a weapon of murder," Laura began, her words calculated, her tone a mix of anger and sorrow. "It was a military tactic, a last resort to be used against an enemy that had infiltrated every level of our society, a threat more dangerous than any conventional force. I knew that many of the enemy's military and government leaders were transhumans—genetically engineered beings, part of Dr. Victor Lang's conspiracy to take over the world and destroy humanity as we know it."

"And yet you unleashed a virus with the potential to kill millions," the judge countered, her eyes narrowing. "Explain that, Doctor."

Laura drew in a breath, choosing her words with the care of a surgeon making an incision. "Transhumans aren't like us. They are stronger, faster, more intelligent in many ways. But they have a flaw—a critical vulnerability that Dr. Lang's team didn't account for. The NVM virus was designed to target that flaw. It wasn't meant to kill indiscriminately—it was engineered to identify and neutralize the transhumans hiding among us. The collateral damage, although few, was ... regrettable, but unavoidable."

A silence fell over the room, heavy and suffocating. Laura could feel the weight of the jury's gaze, the unspoken accusations hanging in the air like a noose.

The judge leaned back, her fingers steepled in thought. "And what of Valeria?" she asked, her eyes flicking at the woman beside Laura. "What role did she play in this?"

Laura hesitated, knowing that what she was about to say would change everything. Valeria's eyes, usually unreadable, were suddenly wide, filled with a fear Laura had never seen before.

"Valeria," Laura said, her voice low, almost tender, "is a Transhuman. She is one of the transhumans that Dr. Victor Lang planted in the enemies military."

The courtroom exploded into chaos. Shouts, gasps, the scraping of chairs as people stood to get a better view. The guards tensed, hands on their weapons, ready for anything.

The judge pounded her gavel, demanding order. When the noise finally subsided, she turned her attention back to Laura, her expression one of barely concealed disbelief. "Explain," she commanded.

Laura met Valeria's eyes, offering a silent apology, before turning back to the judge. "Valeria was one of Dr. Lang's creations, a Transhuman designed to infiltrate the highest levels of the Feminist Militia. But she ... she wasn't like the others. She came to me, seeking a cure, a way out. That's why she brought me the book, the one containing the formula for the virus. She wanted to stop Dr. Lang, to end the war before it consumed us all."

"Is this true?" the judge asked Valeria, her voice hard, unyielding.

Valeria hesitated, then nodded, her voice trembling only for a brief moment. "It's true. I ... I was part of Dr. Lang's plan, but I couldn't go through with it. I couldn't be part of something so monstrous."

"And yet you are one of them," the judge said, her tone cold. "Why should we believe you?"

Laura cut in before Valeria could respond. "You want to know about truth, your honor? Truth hasn't existed in about three hundred years. We have all got to the point when we stopped being surprised at the lies and we all started competing to see who could lie best. Now aside from that, then, because I can prove it."

The judge's eyes narrowed. "How?"

Laura took a deep breath, her mind racing. This was it—the moment of proof. "The NVM virus doesn't just kill. It can be used to control, to influence behavior in ways that are ... difficult to detect. I can use it to demonstrate Valeria's true nature, to show you what she really is."

The courtroom was silent, the tension thick enough to cut. The judge's eyes bore into Laura, searching for any sign of deception. Finally, she nodded. "Proceed."

Laura nodded to the guard who brought her a small vial. The anarchist team's modified NVM was the virus cure. "This cure will stop the virus. It will save her life. However, my team has dosed the cure with nanos that take control of the transhuman's cerebellum, saving the life but surrendering the rest of her existence to my control.

"My team has developed a specialized type of nano. They trigger a takeover of the cerebellum in transhumans, a sort of replace and erase strategy ... allowing my AI to take control. It forces them to do with their body what my AI instructs them to do. Even though their mind is trying to stop it. Rendering them, consciously, to become an observer of their movements. A quiet witness to the actions of their body that is in my control."

She approached Valeria slowly, holding the vial with a steady hand. "I'm sorry," Laura said. Her voice whispered, so low only Valeria could hear. "I hope you understand."

Valeria's eyes were filled with anger, but she nodded. "Do it," she said, her voice spat through clenched teeth.

Laura injected the virus into Valeria's neck, watching as the liquid disappeared into her bloodstream. For a moment, nothing happened. Then Valeria gasped, her body convulsing as the virus took hold. Her eyes rolled back, her skin paling as she rocked violently in the chair.

The courtroom watched in horrified silence as Valeria's convulsions slowed, her breathing shallow and rapid. And then, just as suddenly as it had started, it stopped. Valeria slumped in the chair, her eyes wide open, staring blankly at the ceiling.

"She's not dead," Laura said quickly, her voice breaking the oppressive silence. "The virus forces transhumans to confront their true nature, to understand that they are not human, no matter how much they might want to be. It's ... it's a mercy, in a way."

The judges stared at Valeria's lifeless eyes, her expression unreadable. "And you believe this is a justification for what you've done?" she asked. Her voice trembling with barely controlled anger.

Laura met the judge's gaze, unflinching. "I believe it was the only way to save humanity from a threat it couldn't even comprehend," she said, her voice unwavering, like steel forged in fire. She didn't flinch, because she knew the depth of her actions—the cold calculus behind every decision, every strike, every word she had spoken to ensure survival. It wasn't about peace. It was about control.

"When you robbed me of the Feminist Militia I had little other choice. I built my own militia. An army of tranhumans that were controlled by my AI system."

And she had won.

The wars were over. Feminism ruled the planet now, not because of some peaceful negotiation, but because she had orchestrated the victory with precision and ruthlessness. It wasn't a soft ordeal that brought the world to its knees. It was power, raw and unyielding power. Men had fallen into line, not because they wanted to, but because they had no choice.

Evidence backed her claim with cold, irrefutable numbers.

"There have been no attacks for the last eight days," she said. Her gaze hardening as if daring anyone to challenge her. "We've seen an 80 to 90 percent decline in civil arrests and emergency calls. The streets are quiet. Order is restored."

The data couldn't lie. Eight days. In the brutal, chaotic aftermath of the world's collapse, that was an eternity. Eight days without blood spilling in the streets, without the primal chaos that had ruled for centuries. Laura didn't achieve this through diplomacy or promises of equality. She achieved it through domination. War had been her crucible, and the spoils of victory were undeniable.

It was a world of strategic precision. transhumans posed the greatest threat—an existential one—but it was Laura's iron-fisted leadership that crushed their rising momentum. She had seized power through her Feminist Army, backed by elite soldiers and tacticians who followed her without question, understanding the stakes of this new world. The old hierarchies were gone, dismantled in one fell swoop by her genius. The battlefield had been bloody, and not all men accepted their place willingly. But the statistics couldn't be argued with. The dominance of her regime had brought peace to the shattered and smoldering remnants of civilization.

"Look around," Laura said. Her tone sharp, not pleading but commanding respect. "Order has been restored, and for the first time in a century , people are no longer afraid to step outside their homes. They don't fear each other. Why? Because I took control. I imposed the structure. I cleaned up the mess."

Her point was cold, grounded in undeniable fact. The world was broken. Men—no, the human race—had allowed it to become a place where chaos ruled, where brute force and primal instinct took over. Feminism, under Laura's iron grip, had brought the structure back. Not because of the ideals they preached, but because she had broken the chains of the past and forged a new order in blood and fire and technology.

"There is a new report from Adam Cole released this morning." The second judge said. "I want to read a section to the court, aloud.

"The transhumans had been the most dangerous threat. Superior, stronger, and more cunning. They believed they could rise above humanity itself, evolving beyond its limitations. But Dr. Laura Benton had outplayed them. She saw the future they represented, one that rendered both men and women obsolete, and she had no choice but to act.

"And act she did—ruthlessly, efficiently, and without hesitation. Her intelligence network struck where the transhumans were most vulnerable, neutralizing their influence before they could take control. The data from the last eight days proved her success: crime plummeting, emergency calls down to almost nothing. The chaos had ceased, and with it, so had the momentum of the revolutionaries who had once stood against her.

"Men who still clung to old ideals would call her ruthless. They would call her a tyrant. But the world she had carved from the ashes was one of discipline and respect, not the weak-willed anarchy that had led to humanity's near-extinction. The strong, she believed, deserved to lead—and in this new world, that meant women like her. Not because of some misplaced sense of equality, but because they had earned it."

"The transhumans thought they could redefine what it meant to be human, to surpass us," Laura said, her voice carrying the authority of someone who had seen the abyss and returned stronger. "But we stopped them. And the proof is right in front of you. An eighty percent reduction in civil unrest, emergency calls dropping across every sector, no battles being fought on any fronts. This is what victory looks like."

Laura's claim was as bold as it was undeniable. She had won. Feminism didn't just rule the planet; they had saved it. The evidence wasn't in speeches or idealism, but in the cold, hard data of a world finally brought to order. The transhumans, once seen as the next evolution of mankind, had underestimated her—and in that arrogance, they had lost.

She stood firm, not as a figure of compromise, but as a conqueror. One who understood the cost of leadership, who had bled for the world she now ruled. She didn't need to justify her reign to anyone. The proof was in the silence that had fallen over the once chaotic streets, the calm after the storm. Eight days of peace. Eight days of victory.

The head judge's voice sliced through the air, filled with accusation and contempt. "Do you think we would consider it a victory to surrender the Moon and Mars colonies?" Her eyes locked onto Laura.

"Did you think we wouldn't notice you handing over the Male Reproductive Seminal Synthesis to facilitate their self-governing breakaway?" You didn't win, Laura—you lost."

Tension spread through the room, the tribunal of female officers staring down at her. Hardened by battle, they believed her decisions had been reckless—failures they refused to overlook.

"You stood back," the second judge chimed in, her tone razor-sharp, "and allowed them to prohibit women from the colonies. You relinquished our presence in space. Let them establish their rule without resistance. You surrendered the Moon, Mars, and everything beyond, and you call this a victory?"

Laura's jaw tightened, but she refused to back down. She had expected this moment. Every decision had been calculated, every step intentional. She drew a breath, standing firm as she faced the tribunal. This was the battle she had prepared for.

"Our objective," Laura said. The momentum evident in her steady voice, "was never to rule Mars, the Moon, or any part of space. Those colonies, those barren rocks, were not our prize. No." She took a step forward, her gaze sweeping across the judges. "Our war was for Earth—the cradle of humanity, the only planet that matters. You call my strategy surrender, but that is because you cannot see the larger picture."

The first judge narrowed her eyes, but Laura continued, refusing to be interrupted. "I allowed the Male Reproductive Seminal Synthesis to be transferred to Mars because it was part of the plan. This cornerstone facilitated their breakaway because I wanted them to leave. I pushed them to fight for their freedom, to break away and self-govern in exile. They thought they were liberating themselves. They were wrong."

Laura's words landed with sharp clarity. "They didn't break free. They were cast out. Because of me, they were forced to flee to the stars, unable to remain on this planet. They took their patriarchal rule and banished themselves from the one place that still holds genuine power—Earth."

The tribunal was silent, but Laura felt the shift in the room. She pressed on, her gaze unwavering. "They wanted the colonies, and I let them take them. Why? Because of Mars, the Moon—those colonies are irrelevant. We never needed them. We fought to control Earth, the heart of human civilization. And we won."

Laura Benton didn't flinch, though the gravity of the charge hung in the air like a noose waiting to tighten. She didn't waver; instead, she squared her shoulders and stepped forward, her gaze piercing through the assembly. There was no hesitation in her response, only the fire of a woman who had long embraced the nature of power and the rules of war.

"Our objective was never to rule Mars, Moon, or any part of space," Laura began, her voice unwavering, each word sharp as steel. "We are not concerned with the barren colonies, nor do we need to concern ourselves with the patriarchy clinging to survival in the distant voids of space."

She paused, letting the significance of her words sink into the judge's mind, the tension in the room thickening. "Ours was an objective to conquer and control Earth," she continued, her tone measured but unyielding. "This planet is the cradle of humanity, and it was being strangled by the very men you now defend—men who believed their dominance, their right to rule, was inherent and eternal."

Laura's eyes narrowed, her expression a blend of icy determination and strategic brilliance. "My strategy to remove patriarchal males from our planet was a success," she said firmly. "The transfer of the Male Reproductive Seminal Synthesis to Mars was not a loss. It was a brilliant stroke of my plan. I gave them what they wanted—a sanctuary in space—and watched as they willingly fled. They fought harder for it, believed in their own strength, but it only sanctioned their exile."

She stepped closer to the bench, her chains reached the end of their restraints with a definitive clunk. "I reiterate: We are victorious. Under my leadership, Earth belongs to us. And by surrendering Mars and the Moon, I've ensured that those men will never again have a foothold in this world. We won because they are gone. Transhumans are crushed. The armies that opposed us have stood down and ceased their aggression."

She stood firm, victorious in her eyes, having delivered Earth into the hands of her cause, her people, and her power.

The third judge asked, "If you are victorious as you claim and not guilty of treason as the state claims, what then? What is next?"

"That is the first intelligent thing I have heard today," Laura said. "I'll tell you what's next. We go about settling peace treaties and securing surrender agreements from our enemies. Our already enacted policies and governing need to expand to a global scale. We have everything the space stations and planetary colonies need to survive and become self-supporting, so we need to establish trade relations. For the start. There is work to be done."

The judge was silent for a long moment, her eyes never leaving Laura's. Finally, she spoke, her voice cold and final. "The jury will deliberate."

Laura felt a chill run down her spine as the judges filed out of the room. She had exposed the truth, but at what cost? Would they see her actions as necessary, as justified? Or would they condemn her as a murderer. A traitor?

And more importantly—had she truly done the right thing? Or had she become the very monster she had sought to destroy? The questions gnawed at her, each one more insidious than the last. There was no comfort to be found in the silence that followed, only the uncertainty and guilt.

As the heavy doors closed behind the judges, Laura and Valeria were left alone with their thoughts. Shackled and bound to her chair, prisoners of their own actions, awaiting the verdict.

Valeria's voice, once impressive and forceful, was now reduced to a whisper. "You think yourself righteous, but what makes you any different from me, Laura? I was created to lead, to dominate, yes, but you—" Her eyes, though lifeless, seemed to burn into Laura's soul. "You chose to create a weapon to destroy a superior species, and yet you call it justice."

"Don't lecture me on justice," Laura snapped, her voice trembling with a mixture of anger and guilt. "You were a part of Lang's plan, a willing participant in a plot to exterminate humanity and replace it with something else. I had to stop you."

"And in doing so, you've sacrificed the very thing you claim to protect humanity," Valeria retorted, her voice gaining a faint strength. "You can't claim the moral high ground when you've unleashed a weapon that doesn't distinguish between friend and foe, between soldier and civilian."

"If I were you, there might be a better way for you to spend these last minutes of controlling your body. Soon you won't speak or blink. My AI will control you. First, you will free yourself from these chains, then you will free me. Then we will stay here in our seats until the judges and jury return."

***

Dr. Laura Benton's heart pounded in her chest, the cold metal walls of the cell pressing in on her. The silence was suffocating, broken only by the distant hum of the prison's energy shields. She paced the narrow confines of her cell, her mind racing. The last thing she expected in this hellhole was the sudden surge of light, a crackling energy that tore the fabric of reality open right before her eyes.

In the dark corner of the holding cell a vortex shimmered, a swirling mass of chaotic energy. Before she could react, the energy engulfed her and a force pulled her through, yanking her from the confines of the prison into the unknown.

When the blinding light finally dimmed, Laura found herself surrounded by an unfamiliar landscape under an alien sky. The unmistakable YInMn shade of blue, she recognized from historic records about Planet 44. The name echoed in her mind like a death knell.

Could this be real? She wondered. The air was thin, cold, and carried the metallic tang of something unfamiliar, something hostile. The sky with its three suns a G-type star (like Earth's Sun), and the other a K-type (orange dwarf) the combination cast eerie shadows over the jagged terrain inside the dome floating on this gaseous planet. But it was the figure before her that held her attention now.

Dr. Victor Lang, a tall, gaunt man with piercing eyes that seemed to bore into her soul, stood waiting. His expression was inscrutable, a mix of grim determination and something darker—fanaticism.

"Welcome to Planet 44, Dr. Benton," Lang said, his voice echoing strangely in the thin atmosphere. "This is where humanity will be reborn, free from the chains of our past."

Laura straightened, her mind struggling to comprehend what had just happened. "You can't just kidnap me, Lang. You know this ... This is madness."

"Madness?" Lang's lips curled into a smile, devoid of warmth. "No, this is salvation. Humanity has been trapped in a cycle of suffering, of endless conflict, for too long. But here, on this distant world, we have a chance to break free."

He gestured to the horizon, where a massive structure loomed, half-buried in the rocky terrain. It was a Stallaris ship, a shape like nothing she could have ever imagined, and formidable. Around it, figures moved with purpose—men and women in saffron colored robes, their faces obscured by hoods.

"The 44 scientists," Lang explained. "They will journey to a world even farther from Earth, where they will lead our descendants to transcendence. With the book of Maha, they will guide the way back to the Garden of Eden, to Nirvana. A return to purity, free from the stigma of Earth's history, and man's suffrage."

Laura's mind whirled. "You are behind the missing specialists." She paced in a large oblique circle as the words opened up into her mind. "The book of Maha. Will it be their guide? I thought it was a military strategy."

"It's the strategy to escape from the trap we are in. To be free of human suffering."

"And what if they fail?" she asked, her voice steady despite the turmoil within. "I mean assuming this madness is real. What if this journey only leads to more suffering, more death?"

Lang's eyes flashed with conviction. "They won't fail. They can't. You see the ship. You're standing here on Planet 44. It doesn't get more real, Dr. Benton. But they need the book, Laura. Without it, their mission will be in vain. And that's why I brought you here."

Laura squinted. "You think I have the book of Maha?"

"I know you do," Lang replied, his tone softening slightly. "And I know you understand the stakes. With the book, we can end this cycle of misery. Imagine a world where men and women are no longer at war, where the divisions that have plagued us for centuries are erased."

"I can't imagine nirvana. It is an empty space where our limited ability to translate reality with five senses, a.k.a. Hindrances do not exist." Laura studied him, weighing her options. She had no love for Lang or his twisted vision of salvation, but there was something in his words that resonated with her. A world without suffering ... It was a dream as old as humanity itself. Is this the journey to accomplish the penance for the second lie?

But at what cost?

"You want the book," Laura said slowly, "and in exchange, you'll take all your transhumans from Earth and never return. You'll leave the rest of us in peace. Earth, Mars, the Solar System?"

Lang hesitated, then nodded. "Yes. We do not need to return. Our future lies out here, far from Earth."

"Don't you think it's a mistake? We can provide you with so much. And you'll show me the ship? The scientists?" Laura pressed. "I want to see this plan of yours in action before I make any decisions."

Lang's smile returned, this time with a hint of genuine warmth. "Of course. Follow me."

He led her toward the ship, the alien terrain crunching under their feet. As they approached, Laura could see the scientists more clearly—men and women of various ages, all with the same focused, almost zealot-like expressions. They moved with purpose, completely absorbed in their tasks.

Inside the ship, the atmosphere was charged with anticipation. The walls were lined with advanced technology, much of it beyond Laura's understanding. She could feel the vibrance of energy, the palpable sense of destiny hanging in the air.

As they stepped deeper into the ship, Laura's breath caught in her throat. The corridor widened into a cavernous chamber, illuminated by a cold, blue light that seemed to pulse in time with their footsteps. Rows upon rows of sleek, silver pods lined the walls—each one humming softly, its surface shimmering in the dim light. The chamber stretched far beyond what Laura had imagined, the sheer size of it overwhelming.

"These ... are the stasis chambers," Lang said, his voice reverberating through the room. He walked slowly, hands behind his back, as if guiding her through a museum exhibit. "Each one holds a life—preserved, untouched by time. They will sleep until they reach the outer edge of the galaxy, where a new world awaits. The first of many."

Laura paused, scanning the sea of chambers. There had to be hundreds, each one neatly arranged like soldiers waiting for battle. Her heart quickened, unease creeping into her mind. This was far beyond the scope of what he had suggested.

"How many people are on this ship, Lang?" she asked, her voice low, almost afraid of the answer.

"Just the 44 scientists," he replied casually. "Their brilliance will guide the colony to survive."

She frowned, trying to make sense of it. "Then why are there so many chambers? If there are only 44 of them, why does it look like you're preparing for a mass exodus?"

Lang didn't respond immediately, his smile flickering, betraying a deeper truth. He let the silence stretch as if savoring her confusion, then finally turned to face her, his expression unreadable.

"The journey is long, Laura. Much longer than you could imagine. We have accounted for reproduction along the way. These chambers are not just for the scientists—Their children and likely grandchildren will colonize the new home planet."

Lang's grin widened, though it held no humor. "In time, you'll understand. As you said, perhaps this is the penance for the second sin. What was the second sin? When she tempted the man to make the same mistake she had already made? But right now, it's not important. What matters is that you see this as a chance for humanity to transcend. And you, Laura, you have a part to play."

Laura's mind was spinning. What wasn't he telling her? She glanced at the massive rows of chambers again, trying to grasp the scope of his plan. Hundreds of people, some in stasis, awaiting something she couldn't quite comprehend.

She turned back to Lang, her questions coming fast, sharp like a laser beam cutting through the fog of his ambiguity.

"How long is the journey, Lang? A hundred years? A thousand years? You're talking about a mission across the galaxy—what's the timeline here?"

He tilted his head, almost amused. "Time is relative, Dr. Benton. In the grand scope of things, it doesn't matter. Not to us. In their perspective, 400 years. What matters is that they get there, that they arrive prepared."

Laura clenched her fists, fighting the rising tide of frustration. "And when did you become so ... religious?" she asked, her tone cutting. "The Lang I knew was a scientist. A man of reason, of data. Now you're quoting scripture and folklore talking about salvation and transcendence. When did that happen?"

Lang's expression darkened, the smile fading from his lips. "You underestimate me, Laura. In Saudi Arabia, science and faith are not opposites—they are two sides of the same coin. The book of Maha shows us the truth about that. It's not religion. It's the truth."

She stared at him, his words heavy with a conviction that unsettled her. Something had shifted in him, something rich and profound, and for the first time, Laura wasn't sure if Lang was a visionary... or a madman.

"When did you become so religious, Dr. Benton?" He asked.

"I'm not," she snapped.

"You have been talking about religion like you are aware of the consequences of sin," he said.

"No, I haven't," she said, her expression cold.

Dr. Lang shook his head and chuckled. "Have you ever told the truth?"

"Yes."

Laura stopped, her mind racing. She had the power to influence the future of humanity, to either aid Dr. Lang in his quest or to let humanity continue its chaotic path. The Destiny Stone, hidden deep within her pocket, called to her, its ancient power pulsing with potential.

When the military escort arrived to take her and Valeria to the tribunal, she recalled the morning events in her memory. They walked to the transport. Valeria was already inside. When Laura approached, Valeria stood and threw her arms around Laura and held her close. Laura had thought it odd. Her enemy's greeting with such emotion was out of step. But now Laura retraced the embrace. Valeria had accomplished the mission and stole the zip drive from Dr. Lang. She slid it into Laura's pocket while embracing her.

> Laura sunk her hand into her pocket. Searching the inner lining until ... it was there. In her hand was the book of Maha.

But was this truly the path to salvation? Or just another delusion, another attempt to escape the inherent suffering of existence?

As they reached the central chamber of the stalaris ship where the scientists were preparing for departure, Laura turned to Dr. Lang. "If I give you the book, what guarantees do I have that this won't end in disaster? That your dream won't become another nightmare?"

Lang met her gaze, his eyes alight with fervor. "There are no guarantees, Laura. But what is the alternative? More war, more suffering, more death? This is our chance—our only chance—to find peace. It was fate or manifest-destiny that Maha surfaced at this time? It is a guidebook that can lead us out of the trap we call the universe."

Laura looked around at the scientists, at the ship that would carry them across the stars. She could feel the grandeur of the decision pressing down on them, the fate of humanity hanging in the balance.

***

With every step, the cold, metallic clink of shackles echoed through the narrow corridor as two guards flanked Dr. Laura Benton. A steady slow pace guiding her from the dimly lit cell toward the tribunal hall. The corridor was damp; walls stained with the residue of time and neglect. Each step Laura took was heavy, not from fear or despair, but from the out-of-world experience and of the world she had both fought for, and now she was soon to lead. They took the lift up to the ground floor.

They're taking me to the premiere hall. They've accepted my victory. She thought.

The guards, stern and silent, had been with her since the beginning of her captivity. Their faces were etched with the weariness of men who had seen too many battles, and yet, in their eyes, there was something else—an unease, perhaps even a begrudging respect. Laura could feel it. The power shift, subtle as it was, had begun long before the news broadcast interrupted the tribunal.

As they neared the grand doors of the hall, Laura straightened her posture, her mind sharpening into focus. The guards paused, one of them moving to the door to signal their arrival. The other, younger and less stoic than his partner, glanced at Laura with a mixture of curiosity and something bordering on concern.

"Dr. Benton," he began, his voice low, almost a whisper, "do you think... do you think this will end it? All of this?"

Laura turned her head meeting his gaze. The question hung between them, heavy and complex. She didn't answer immediately, knowing that the truth was far from simple. But as she opened her mouth to respond, the heavy doors swung open with a deafening creak, and the moment was lost. The guard's eyes dropped, and he resumed his role as escort, guiding her into the hall.

The premier hall was imposing, its ceilings high and walls adorned with the symbols of a fractured world order. Robes of deep crimson, cascading around them like the last remnants of an era on the brink of collapse, surrounded the tribunal judges as they sat in their elevated positions. The stale air was thick with tension, the kind that precedes not just judgment, but the potential for something much larger—a revolution, perhaps, or the birth of a new age.

Laura's eyes swept the room as guards led her to the center, her hands bound behind her, the cold metal of the shackles biting into her wrists. The tribunal's eyes bore into her, some with disdain, others with calculation. They were the remnants of an old world, clinging to the last vestiges of a power struggle.

Before any of the judges could speak, a sudden commotion erupted at the back of the hall. A large screen flickered to life, and Adam Cole's battered face appeared, a symbol of both survival and the relentless march of time. His report was grim, detailing the disappearance of high-ranking leaders across the globe—those who had been the enemies of the Feminist Militia. The realization hit the room like a shockwave: the old guard was crumbling, and the world stood on the precipice of a new order.

Laura, standing in her chains, felt the eyes of the tribunal swing back to her, their previous certainty now wreathed in doubt. This was her moment. The moment she had been both dreading and anticipating was the culmination of everything she had fought for.

She took a deep breath, and then, with a voice that cut through the tension like a victorious drum, she spoke.

"I stand here today, not as a conqueror, but as a reluctant shepherd of a fractured world ... Today, we have life where the meek have inherited the Earth. Not a planet where feminists rule, but a world where everyone prospers because of the peace afforded by a matriarchal society."

Her words flowed, each one deliberate, carrying the substance of her vision for a future where power was shared, not hoarded; where the victors did not become the next tyrants. The judges, once poised to condemn, now questioned the very foundations of their beliefs and position of authority.

"Take these chains from me, now," she said. The guards moved with diligence. She pointed to the doors at the far end of the hall. "Open the doors. My personal assistant, Albera is waiting and pay no attention to the small but well-armed contingency force that accompanies her."

When they pulled the large double doors open, Albera and two transhumans controlled by Dr. Benton's AI entered the room with a pallet of several boxes filled with a bound document titled THE MEEK. The transhumans distributed a copy of THE MEEK to everyone in the room.

Laura ascended to the head of the council chair and opened the document. She read aloud as everyone looked on.

"This is the constitution, our Declaration of Power, and the Bill of Rights.

"We, the women of the world, have reached a glorious era where the fruits of our labor, resilience, and vision have culminated in the complete realization of Feminist Control. This is a world designed by women, for women, where our happiness, peace, and liberty reign supreme. Under our command, society has flourished, free from the chaos of past eras, and is now guided by the principles that ensure the well-being of women above all. This manifesto is our declaration of power, a ten-point doctrine that guarantees the continuation of this dominance, ensuring that as long as women are happy, peace and liberty will prevail.

> 1. Women's Sovereignty: All power and authority are vested in women. Women's voices, decisions, and leadership shape every facet of society, ensuring that the world functions in harmony with our values and priorities. Our sov-

ereignty is absolute, and all institutions shall reflect and reinforce this edict.

2. Bodily Autonomy and Reproductive Control: Women maintain complete control over their bodies and reproductive choices. Society will support and facilitate women's decisions in all matters of health and reproduction, ensuring access to the necessary resources and services without interference.

3. Protection and Security for Women: The safety and well-being of women are paramount. Society will be structured to ensure that women are protected and secure in all aspects of life. From personal safety to public spaces, every environment will be designed with the comfort and security of women in mind. Systems of support and justice will be swift and effective, prioritizing the peace of mind and dignity of all women.

4. Women's Political Rule: Governance shall be exclusively held by women. Women will lead in all political and leadership roles, crafting and enforcing policies that reflect our interests and priorities. Men's participation in governance will be supportive roles that align with feminist control.

5. Economic Mastery: The global economy will be structured to serve the interests of women. Women's work and contributions, in all forms, will be the primary drivers of economic policies and practices. Resources and opportunities will be directed to ensure the prosperity of women, with systems in place to prevent any regression to male-dominated economic structures.

6. Feminist Education and Cultural Domination: Education will be centered around feminist principles, ensuring that women are empowered with knowledge that upholds our values and strengthens our dominion. Cultural narratives and institutions will be reshaped to reflect and celebrate the achievements and superiority of women throughout history.

7. Environmental Guardianship: Women will lead the stewardship of the environment, recognizing our intrinsic connection to the Earth. Policies will prioritize sustainability and ecological balance, with women at the forefront of every environmental initiative, guiding humanity to a harmonious existence with nature.

8. Global Feminist Unity: The world is united under feminist governance, with women across the globe connected in a network of solidarity and control. Feminist leadership will extend across borders, ensuring that all women, everywhere, benefit from the strength and stability of this new world order.

9. Technological Control and Innovation: Women will command the development and application of technology, ensuring it serves our interests and enhances our control. Women will design and regulate technological spaces, creating a safe and empowering digital environment that reinforces our dominance.

10. Personal and Collective Liberation for Women: Women will live free from the constraints of traditional gender roles, empowered to pursue their individual passions and collective goals. Society will celebrate and sup-

port the diverse expressions of womanhood, ensuring that all women experience true freedom within the framework of feminist control.

As her speech drew to a close, a hush fell over the room. The silence was deep, punctuated only by the distant hum of the outside world, a world that was now listening to Dr. Laura Benton's every word.

Her tablet ignited with a secure message from the Mars Portal, Dr. Kaya's Medical Facility, marked urgent. Waiting for the right moment to open it when it was certain her eyes alone read it. "The spaceship has launched. Nirvana is coming." Dr. Victor Lang signed the message.

Laura's breath caught, not in fear, but in a moment of profound realization. The Mars Portal, once a symbol of humanity's desperate escape from a dying world, was now something else entirely. It was hope—hope that humanity could forge a fresh path, not out of fear, but out of the desire to build something better.

She allowed herself a smile, a rare expression of genuine emotion in this war-hardened woman. The message from Victor Lang was clear: the future was not just on Earth but among the stars. And for the first time in a long while, Laura felt a sense of peace. The battles were far from over, but the first steps toward something greater had been taken.

The old world was gone. The new one—under her guidance—was just beginning.

Laura stared at the words on her tablet, heart racing: "The Stallaris ship has launched. Nirvana is coming." She looked at the tribunal, the guards, and the sea of faces awaiting her command. "You think you know what's coming next?" she said. Softly, a hint of amusement in her voice. "But the truth is, we don't control this. Not anymore. Laws or declarations won't shape the new world. Those who survive what's coming next'll shape it." She turned, walking toward the massive chamber doors, her last words hanging in the air.

"And trust me—none of you are ready for it. For now though, I need a drink and a visit to my gun slinger."

Chapter Fifteen: Sand In My Shoes

Lydia's fingers drummed a steady rhythm against the tray table as the plane glided through the night sky. Outside the cabin window, the endless stretch of dark clouds beneath her mirrored the tumultuous thoughts swirling in her mind. Business class cabin lights illuminate the well-worn and dogeared manuscript of "Irrelevant." It lay open on her lap, a patchwork of revisions scrawled across its pages in ink that had bled through the thin paper. Each red line was a reminder of the struggle, not just with the text, but with herself, the agency, and the world that seemed more divided than ever.

Eleven days on the island of Mallorca. Laughter and love filled the last ten days under the warm Palma Beach sun and scorching sands. She could still taste the salt on her lips from the virgin margaritas along with the sharp bite of the lime. The steady hum and vibration from the engines reminded her of the shuttle taking Laura Benton to the Mars Portal.

Mark's voice echoed in her mind—his laughter, the warmth in his eyes as they spoke of their future, the child growing inside her. She felt a twinge of fear, not just for what lay ahead, but for the world they were bringing a child into—a world where gender had become a battlefield. A smile overtakes the fear as she recalls the way he held her and repaired the damage. He saved the vacation and the relationship.

Lydia glanced out the window, imagining the manuscript's potential like lights flickering in the distance—a chance for rebirth but at a cost. For a heartbeat, she feels a pang of guilt, a gnawing fear that she might compromise the agency's soul for survival.

"You're doing the right thing," Mark had said as he held her, his hand resting gently on her belly. But was she? Lydia wasn't sure.

The manuscript felt like a ticking bomb in her hands, which could either destroy her business or launch it to new heights. Yet, the closer she got to the end of the flight, the more she questioned if this was the right fight. The characters—those conflicted, broken souls—reflected the world's ugliness back at her. She wondered if she was exposing too much of that darkness, or if it was exactly what the world needed to see.

The agency has always featured strong women protagonists, but it has a history of women novelists. The only missing tick in the box. But it was everything the business needed. The themes and arcs spoke to male and female readers. The details and style have what none of her existing clients could produce.

***

The bustling life of New York City greeted her return with the indifference only a metropolis could muster. Lydia's hope that her emails had stirred some interest evaporated the moment she stepped into the agency's office. The bitter silence that met her was deafening.

Lydia's agency occupies a fourth-floor suite tucked away in the maze of SOHO's eclectic mix of modernity and grit. The exterior hinted at sophistication, with the agency's polished brass plaque glinting in the dim lobby lighting. Upon entry, the reception area delivered a surprising sense of grandeur—a marble desk flanked by towering tropical plants, spotlit by the city's natural light filtering through tall windows that framed only modest views of the Manhattan skyline. But just beyond the reception's gleam, the facade quickly faded.

The transition was stark: worn out, mid-quality desks lined with scattered papers, squeaking chairs from an office furniture clearance sale, and fluorescent lighting that buzzed just slightly too loud. The conference room, meant to inspire strategy and success, felt cramped, almost as if ambition had outgrown its modest walls. It wasn't the sort of space that made a person feel like a powerhouse—it was the kind that reminded you there was still a ladder to climb.

As Lydia walked in, her gaze drifted across the small, well-lit windows offering just the faintest promise of a bustling skyline. She felt the building's pulse—steady, predictable, and somewhat resigned, much like the literary agents hunched over their desks. The shiny reception area might have fooled outsiders, but Lydia knew this agency was on the brink, and her entrance felt like stepping into an uphill battle where allies were scarce and skeptics plentiful.

Lydia's eyes are often drawn to the small crack in the marble, the wilted leaves on the plants, and the sound of the late spring rain pelting against the thin windows. The smell of wet, old concrete drifts in from the lobby every time the doors swung open.

She saw the proof of her fears in how her colleagues gathered around Cyndi Gavyn's latest work, "The Women's Guide to Trouble." A copy lay on every desk as she walked through the hallways and peered into each agent's space. It was the book that was easy to promote—sharp, witty, and designed to appeal to the feminist zeitgeist. It was safe. Predictable.

When Lydia entered the conference room, the crisp scent of fresh juice hit her—a blend of citrusy grapefruit, earthy kale, and a hint of ginger's sharp bite. Someone had recently picked up a round of trendy health drinks from the juice bar down the street, and the tang of freshly blended produce clung to the air, refreshing yet overpowering.

She glimpsed the vibrant juices lined up on the table, each glass a swirl of color—deep green, bright orange, pale pink. Her hand brushed against the condensation on one glass, cold and slick. She picked it up, the slippery wet condensation on the glass uncomfortable in her palm. Taking a tentative sip, her mouth filled with the pulpy texture of pineapple, softened by the sweetness of apple and tempered by the slightly bitter kick of celery. The flavors were layered and she felt the fibrous grit of unstrained vegetables lingering on her tongue and the back of her teeth.

The juice was the type of trendy wellness concoction they liked to showcase in this place—vibrant, fresh, and smugly healthy. But as she experienced the drink's grassy aftertaste, Lydia wondered how many of her colleagues enjoyed it and how many drank it just to keep up appearances, like everything else in this agency. Mediocrity. Safe.

Lydia's voice broke the comfortable murmur of praise during the weekly meeting. "There's something else you all need to see," she announced, her voice trembling with an edge of determination she hadn't expected.

Her colleagues turned to her with raised eyebrows and skeptical glances. She knew what they were thinking: not the manuscript penned by a man. And an old white man at that. But Lydia stood her ground, presenting "Irrelevant" as if it were a lifeline, not just for her, but for the agency.

"It's not like Gavyn's book," she admitted, "but it's important. It's raw, it's challenging, and it might just be the conversation we need right now."

The silence was thick, the tension real. No one spoke for what felt like an eternity. Finally, Janet, the agency's lead, sighed, rubbing her temples. "Fine. We'll read it. But if this is another waste of our time, Lydia, it's on you."

One by one the agents filed past Lydia as they leave the conference room. They picked up a copy of Irrelevant from the stack she had brought to the meeting. Lydia stood near the rubbish container holding her Prada Slides over the can.

"You're still wearing your beach shoes," Janet said, as she was the last to leave the conference room. The manuscript hangs in her hand by her side. "How was the vacation in Mallorca?"

A smile engulfed Lydia's face. "I still have sand in my shoes." Her laugh and distant gaze flooded in memories.

***

The next day, May 24th, the rain drummed steadily against the windows, casting a dreary glow over the conference room. Lydia's agents gathered once more, shaking off wet umbrellas and the exhaustion of yet another damp commute. The scent of fresh perfumes and mint filled the room—a subtle attempt to mask the lingering remnants of various takeout lunches, a mix of greasy fast food and wilted salad greens.

Lydia caught a whiff of the conflicting scents as she entered, the unmistakable notes of lavender, citrus, and mint mingling in the air, trying—and failing—to erase the faintly stale undercurrent of reheated meals. She took her seat, her eyes scanning the room. Each of her colleagues looked refreshed. but Lydia knew it was only skin-deep. The tension from yesterday's debate still lingered.

The rain outside only added to the oppressive atmosphere, the steady patter blending with the faint clicking of pens and the rustling of notes. Lydia straightened, her gaze briefly drawn to the agency's slightly crooked logo on the wall, still unnoticed by anyone else, a silent testament to the imperfections they so desperately tried to hide.

Lydia sat at the edge of her chair, every muscle in her body taut as a wire stretched to its breaking point. Her eyes darted between her colleagues, scanning their faces for any flicker of emotion, any crack in their stoic masks. The minutes dragged on, the clock on the wall ticking louder with each second, pounding in her ears like a war drum. Her heart raced, anticipation and dread coiling in her chest like a venomous serpent.

Janet's voice sliced through the tension, flat and cold as a sheet of steel. "It's flawed," she said, her tone giving nothing away. Lydia's stomach dropped. But before she could spiral into the pit of despair that loomed just beneath her, Janet continued, her words a lifeline Lydia hadn't expected. "But there's something here. Something ... tangible. It's a think piece with a timely religiosity and upbeat philosophical message. It took me places. You know. It stayed with me long after I finished reading."

Lydia's breath caught in her throat. The others exchanged glances, subtle nods of agreement following like a ripple across a still pond. A sense of relief washed over her, but it was short-lived. This was only the beginning.

The truth in the manuscript was undeniable, raw, and unpolished, like a diamond pulled straight from the Earth. It was flawed, yes, but that was its power. It reflected a world that was just as imperfect, just as chaotic and uncontrollable.

While they discussed the book, their voices grew more animated, the tension in the room shifting from uneasy silence to many heated debates. Lydia watched, her heart now pounding for a different reason. She knew what was coming.

Suddenly, the conversation took that darker turn she dreaded but expected. Tom, always the skeptic, leaned forward, his eyes narrowing. "But what if this truth," he asked slowly, "is too dangerous? What if we're inviting something we can't control by exposing it?"

His words hung in the air, heavy and ominous. The room fell silent again, the implication of his question challenging them. Lydia felt a chill crawl up her spine. This was the twist she had feared.

But then, something shifted in Lydia. A spark ignited within her, a fire she hadn't known existed. She straightened in her seat, her voice calm but firm. "Or what if by not exposing it, we're allowing that danger to fester in the dark, where it can do the most harm?

"Truth time. There is something you need to know. Besides, recent reports showing our clients are losing their audiences, and major polls indicate we are driving male readers away. Not just losing them, but driving them away. Yes! I get it. We have always been an agency that favors female novelists, but trends imply that unwritten rule needs to end. There's one more piece that I need to share."

"This agency is running on fumes. The agency is in critical condition. We ... I have to take drastic measures or we will close the doors and board up the windows before the end of the year."

Tom's gaze locked onto hers, a silent challenge, but Lydia didn't back down. She had been timid, unsure, but now, a steely resolve settled over her. This was her truth, and she would defend it.

The room buzzed with a new energy, the dynamic shifting in Lydia's favor. Her colleagues saw her in a new light—not just as the quiet, diligent mentor, but as someone with conviction. With the courage to face the unknown. The discussion continued, but now Lydia was leading it, guiding them through the murky waters of uncertainty with a confidence that surprised even her.

By the end of the meeting, the manuscript was no longer just a flawed piece of work. It was a statement, a bold declaration of the messy, complex reality.

As they filed out of the room, Lydia caught Janet's eye. There was a glimmer of respect there, a silent acknowledgment of the unexpected turn the day had taken. Lydia had come out on top, but it wasn't just a victory for her. It was a victory for the truth she had so fiercely defended.

As the door closed behind the last of her literary agents, Lydia allowed herself a small, triumphant smile. The twist was` dark and unexpected, but she had turned it in her favor.

She realized the agency can't claim to correct inequalities by implementing prejudicial policies.

***

Meeting the author of Irrelevant, a man who calls himself H.P. Kemper, was like walking into an ambush she hadn't seen coming. Lydia had expected a man as fiery and confrontational as his prose. Instead, she was greeted by someone who seemed almost fragile, a man whose eyes bore the scars and triumphs of the complete history of existence.

It had taken three days to fly H.P. Kemper to Manhattan from his home in Málaga, Spain, and he'd arrived with the type of excitement Lydia had hoped for. The moment he'd heard her decision to publish Irrelevant, he'd wasted no time booking his flight, barely stopping to pack.

As they sat down, the conversation veered away from the expected and plunged into philosophical depths. "Gender," the author began, his voice soft but steady, "is not just identity. It's the lens through which we interpret everything. It was only relevant because of time. And that lens, like all tools, can either sharpen our view or obscure it entirely. Today our governments, businesses, and judicial systems favor women to the extreme of being weaponized against men. And it's no wonder that everyone wants to identify as a woman no matter what their birth gender may be. Even publishing has weaponized women against men."

Lydia found herself ensnared by his words, drawn into a conversation that challenged not just the societal norms she thought she understood, but the idea of identity itself. "We cling to these definitions," he continued, his gaze distant, as though seeing beyond the walls of the room, "because they give us a sense of identity. But what if that awareness is an illusion? What if it's the very thing that's tearing us apart?"

Outside Lydia's office, the city stretched out in a subdued, blurry panorama, shrouded in the muted colors of an on again—off again rainy Saturday morning. The rain-streaked glass stood between them and that smudged cityscape, a pane that somehow suggested both purity and melancholy. Each drop that slid down marked a tiny path, a transient trace that vanished in an instant—a cycle that hinted at something broader, perhaps the futility of her own choices, or the doubt that appeared to creep into her otherwise resolute convictions. The windows seemed like mirrors, framing a city that could never see itself. A city that was identified as a concept rather than the beauty of the individual people.

Kemper's words were like light beams slicing through the damp, heavy air, challenging her every assumption. Every carefully constructed ideal she'd clung to in her years at the agency. It was as if he was pulling at the stitches that held her worldview together. Each phrase unsealing another layer, stripping her illusions down to the bone.

Silence fell between them, thick and suffocating, as his words hung in the air. Lydia glanced at her colleagues, reading the discomfort etched into their faces, but also something else—a spark of curiosity that hadn't been there before.

In that moment, Lydia realized something had shifted, not just in the room, but within her. The manuscript she had fought so hard to champion was no longer just a piece of work. It was a mirror held up to the world, forcing them all to confront the darkness lurking just beneath the surface.

And in that reflection, she saw not just the flaws and the chaos, but the truth—raw, unpolished, and undeniably historical. We are at our best when we unite not when we separate. Those things we think give us identity become a harmful tool that divide and separate us.

"The ominous bit," he said with overtones reminding all of Gandalf The Grey at the gate, "is the puzzle of time. Since the moment of birth, everyone is ablaze with a singular purpose, which is to discover the answer to one simple but wrong question. Who am I? After a few hundred millennia, we become dazzled not so much by who but what. Laws and societal pressure and the development of products. Such as clothing, makeup, fabrics, colors, decor and the list has today become endless in the many ways we try to define a difference between man and woman. And between you and me."

He paused just long enough to laugh hysterically. Before anyone could take conversational control, he stood with a force and dramatic effect.

"None of it worthwhile. Not to mention none was important. See. When time starts, we think the judgment was the exile from someplace biblically named The Garden of Eden. Getting the boot was the result, but everyone forgot the judgments were different. So if you want to know the four one one on the difference between man and woman, the answer is in the separate judgments. The consequence of hers was not the same as the consequence of his."

Lydia felt a sharp jolt, as if he'd lit a candle that shown a new light on her carefully held beliefs.

"Then if Dr. Laura Benton won and salvaged planet Earth for women. Was it for the meek?" She asked.

Lydia sat back and waited for his reply. The author's fragile exterior melted away, leaving something darker, more intense, like a man who'd clawed his way through his own philosophies and come out scarred, cynical, and perhaps wiser for it.

"Isolating women to Earth was perhaps more punishment than victory. What the studious reader understands in the end is that Earth is not the prize. Earth is where we were imprisoned. Tucked away in some remote hole within a universe so expansive that nothing would ever find us."

His laugh—a jagged, biting sound—echoed off the walls, as unsettling as the silence that followed.

When he spoke again, his voice was thick with disdain, almost dismissive. "The Garden. That so-called paradise. According to populist religions. Everyone thinks it was about a single act, a bite of fruit, and a punishment. But that was just the veneer. It was never about sin or temptation or a damned apple. It was about separation—a split that divided not only man from woman but human from humanity. Each judgment, hers and his, carved its own path, etched in suffering and shadowed with regret."

Lydia felt an unsettling recognition flicker within her—one she could scarcely admit to herself. Perhaps she, too, had been complicit in perpetuating a world divided, creating a publishing house that glorified only one side of the story. Labeling it supportive when it is obviously divisive.

Lydia could see her colleagues shift uncomfortably, but the author's words drilled deeper into her, anchoring her to her chair. There was a strange power in his logic, a disturbing clarity that stripped away the sentimental illusions society had wrapped around gender, relationships, purpose.

"Her judgment," he went on, his voice lowering to a conspiratorial tone, "was to bear life in pain, to be yoked to desire. Never satisfied and forever coercive. His was to toil in dust, forever chasing after purpose as the caretaker. Always trying to fix things and solve problems. Separate destinies, crafted to divide us at our very roots. This is the stuff of many great stories."

He leaned forward, eyes steady, daring her to look away. "You see, all this," he gestured with a sweeping hand, "the makeup, the clothes, the rituals, they're just tools to amplify the separation. They're ways to feed an identity that was broken, and compartmentalized from the start. We're all complicit—chasing these ideas of 'man' and 'woman,' like puppets on strings. Because deep down, we don't want to confront the truth that neither gender, in all its damn ornamentation, can ever fill the chasm of isolation we're born into. It's easier to accept suffering when we can blame others for it."

The air felt dense as Lydia tried to process his words, yet a strange exhilaration stirred inside her, as if she were glimpsing the edge of a precipice no one else dared approach. Her colleagues exchanged nervous glances, but the spark of curiosity in their eyes had turned to something raw, uneasy—a glimmer of understanding, perhaps, or the fear of it.

"Gender," he said finally, in a voice both resigned and resolute, "is just a battlefield. And we're all foot soldiers, waging wars that, in the end, are unwinable."

***

The decision to represent Irrelevant was not unanimous, but it was final. Lydia had convinced them, though it felt less like a victory and more like the first step on a very long and uncertain road.

As the book moved through the stages of publication, Lydia felt the tension between hope and fear pull tighter within her. And then, as if by some twist of fate, the book hit the shelves at just the right moment. The public was ready—or perhaps desperate—for the conversation it sparked.

The backlash was immediate, and fierce, but so was the support. The nation became a battlefield of ideas, with Irrelevant at its center. Lydia watched from the sidelines, her heart pounding with every new article and social media post praising or condemning the work.

But in the chaos, something incredible happened. People talked—not just argue, but truly talked. Conversations that had stopped for too long came to the surface, and with them, a new understanding emerged.

Eight months later, as Lydia stood in the nursery, the soft light of dawn filtering through the curtains, she felt a sense of peace she hadn't known in years. The manuscript, the agency, the battles—they all seemed distant now, like echoes in a dream.

She looked down at her newborn child, sleeping soundly in the crib, and wondered what kind of world she would grow up in. Would it be a world still at war with itself over something as fundamental as gender? Or would it be a world that had learned, through pain and struggle, that understanding was the key to survival?

Mark came up behind her, wrapping his arms around her waist. "Penny for your thoughts?"

"I met with H.P. yesterday and made the mistake of asking him the question you and I never wanted to ask."

"Oh no," he said with a mixture of sympathy and jest. "You caved, or was it a slip of mental acuity?"

Quiet as she could, she guided him away from the crib and into the adjoining room. "It was a moment where I tried to interrupt the uncomfortable silence between us."

A puff of air-popped from Mark's lips. "Wow!" He shook his head, but his curious eyes never left hers.

"Well, I said, you told us it was about time. That first day when you came to the agency and met with the team. Before you went deep on gender, you said, 'The ominous bit is the puzzle of time. Since the moment of birth, everyone is ablaze with a singular purpose which is to discover the answer to one simple but wrong question.' Do you remember?"

"Indeed," He said an amazed tone spoke of him knowing she had more to say. "The response then was silent. Do you want to end the silence now?"

"That's when I leaned into him, closing my eyes in total concentration. 'I was just thinking... we spend so much time fighting to define who we are, but maybe it's not about definitions. Maybe it's about understanding that we're all just trying to find our place in a world that doesn't always make sense.'"

"That's not an accident. It's the natural presence in time," he said. Nodding and speaking in a manner of stating the obvious. "There is nothing nuanced about realizing that everything in existence originates from a thought. Everyone knows this as a widely understood fact. For instance, imagine something like 180,000 years ago when people had to drink water from a muddy pond, wishing they could get a clean drink. Then one day, somebody made a bucket: a pail to hold the water. A while after that, someone made a cup. You see, thoughts turn into present-day items.

"Therefore, mathematics and the laws of physics prove that time travel is impossible. This cannot happen since time is a present-moment phenomenon. It is clarified in this way. You recall a past event not in the past. It is only possible to remember things in the present. You plan for the future in the present moment. The present moment never starts and never ends. The present moment is the only phenomena that exists in this duality compared to death. But death is only the end if you believe it's all about you.

"Stay with me now because this is when it becomes expansive for the mind. Actual knowledge causes the mind to feel odd and like we are suddenly standing on uneven ground." His eyes widened with the left brow raised.

"Generations have imagined time travel. We write books about it, make movies about it, talk to our friends and family, and daydream about time travel. As with everything else, someone will find the way. Or. more correctly, we will discover the answer to the thought.

"Let's imagine I travel back in time to 1775 and stop Paul Revier from riding out to warn the Americans that the British were coming and so the British won the war. Then I come back to the present and tell everyone that I stopped the American Revolution. Everyone asks me what the American Revolution was. There is no such thing.

"The contrast of the two pasts is necessary to understand why this happens. It is necessary to have both the past where there was a revolution and the past where there was not a revolution. Two pasts are impossible and therefore time travel is impossible. Put in another way, in the always present moment, the endless present moment, there is always a single past."

"After I stood there motionless and numb from Grandpa's lecture," Lydia said. Mark was now lying on the floor, holding his ribs, laughing.

"Wow!, you stepped in it there, girlfriend."

"You have heard nothing yet," she said deadpan. "He often talks about the book of Maha as if he believes it to be real. It seems to me as if he is telling me about these events like they have happened but in the future. Bizarre, right?"

Mark stopped laughing and raised off his back and onto his elbows, waiting for her to explain.

H.P. said, "The book of Maha was already on Earth long before they arrived. But you have only recently realized it. You believe it is something new. So now, you know better."

"His new manuscript was on my desk."

"Have you read it?" Mark could barely get the words out. His anxious eyes spoke volumes.

"I couldn't put it down," she said.